Post C

Breaking Back

(Post Contact - Book 3)

Earth, ravaged by a killer virus, lies isolated beneath a deadly barrier of orbiting satellite and missile debris. High above, having fought off the alien attack, the surviving occupants of Base Primo must rally.

Rescuing Earth before everyone dies and mounting a counter strike against the aliens before they can return in even greater numbers are equally crucial goals. There is a moment when everything seems possible. Then, as the clock ticks down, the problems begin to bite. The shock of alien conflict rolls across the galaxy and power begins to shift on Earth, and the question still remains to be answered, can humanity stand.

At every turn the surviving humans learn more about themselves and the astral duties they have inherited.

In the depths of space, you can hide from your enemies, but you can never hide from yourself.

Books by D. C. Macey

THE POST CONTACT SERIES

Near future SF action thrillers

Post Contact: First Days
Published October 2022

Post Contact: Holding On
Published November 2022

Post Contact: Breaking Back
Published December 2023

THE TEMPLE SERIES

Contemporary archaeological thrillers

The Temple Legacy
Published August 2015

The Temple Scroll
Published August 2016

The Temple Covenant
Published April 2018

The Temple Deliverance
Published April 2019

Post Contact: Breaking Back

(Post Contact - Book 3)

Butcher & Cameron

D. C. MACEY

Published by Butcher & Cameron

ISBN-13: 978 1 7391948 2 6

Chapter 1

Leviathan O-3 in the Fold

Staring up at the viewscreen, Steph Simpson's thoughts wandered as she absently traced the lengthening light streaks that marked the passing stars. For the umpteenth time she broke into a spontaneous smile. The rescue mission to Osarus had gone perfectly. Jamie MacAulay and his crew were safe with her on board O-3, and now the Leviathan was powering through the Fold toward Base Primo. There, General Paul Dower was anxiously awaiting her return.

Chance had dictated that it was she and Jamie who had been the first to encounter Weeman and his people's technology. For the long-time friends, it seemed like a lifetime ago, but it was only something over a year since the little alien they all called Weeman had been shot down over Jamie's Hebridean estate. Together, she and Jamie had rescued and protected the visitor, who they soon understood was the last of his kind. From there, a bond of trust had formed, and eventually the two of them, together with General Dower, had been granted access to the secrets and knowledge that underpinned Weeman's Base Primo and its technology. There on the obscure and distant dwarf planet, in the strictest secrecy, and with Weeman's support, Primo had been repopulated by humans.

Then everything had gone wrong. Jamie and his crew had been lost, marooned in the furthest reaches of the Orion Arm while Earth had been plunged into war. Steph glanced down at the floor, hating what had happened next. Humanity's eternal flaws – a need for dominance and an unwillingness to trust others – had come to the fore. Earth descended into chaos. Missiles flew, satellites were destroyed, and the planet was enclosed in a suffocating blanket of blast wreckage that sealed the atmosphere, even as a deadly virus swept the globe.

Yes, she conceded to herself, Earth was still sealed off by a shroud of missile fragments. But they had managed to get the counter-virus down through its debris-filled atmosphere to the surface. There, it would have already begun to neutralise the contagion that had so ravaged humanity. At the surface, too, was her friend and fellow scientist Celine Gold. Steph was confident Celine could handle any problems that arose there, especially with the support of Brigadier Smith-Brown who had travelled with her. The British officer, always so straightforward, was a vital and trusted member of General Dower's leadership team.

And from the Perseus Arm had come the locusts. A terrifying race of predators hellbent on accessing the living larder that was Earth.

The monstrous locust-like invaders had eventually been stopped. Yes, there had been losses, many losses, but hard-fought victories against the swarm at both Base Secundo and Primo had been followed by the destruction of the fleeing locust cone. With the locusts gone, what few humans remained were safe from predation… for now at least. She shivered: they had won, but it had been close. Too close. But for individual bravery and sacrifice, and more luck than anyone might hope for, it could as easily have gone the other way.

Then the signal had arrived, and her spirits had leaped – against the odds, Jamie had survived.

In spite of the myriad of demands on Primo's scant resources, the general had let her undertake the rescue mission on condition that there were no delays. In, out and return to HQ on Primo – not a day to be wasted. She had complied with his instructions to the letter.

Her arrival with O-3 had brought relief to Jamie and his crew. Their great Leviathan starship had been downed by a saboteur. Then, marooned on a pristine planet, they had spent months struggling against the planet's flora and fauna. Despite its benign façade, the danger had ratcheted up at every turn. Eventually, it seemed the planet's very nature was determined to trap and destroy the human intruders. Rescue had come in the nick of time.

Now they were almost back. In a few hours the Leviathan would drop from the Fold to reveal Sol and the familiar star patterns of home. After so much destruction, so many setbacks, were these green shoots? She allowed herself to believe.

'Here,' said Jamie, arriving at her side and proffering a coffee.

She took it and her smile revived. 'Thanks.'

At the peak of Earth's crisis, wayward humans had evaded General Dower's guards to attack and kill Weeman. In doing so, they had destroyed the one being who, even at that late hour, might have averted disaster, so leaving General Dower and his staff alone on Primo to attempt to resolve the wave of problems that had beset humanity.

Dower's people, isolated on Primo, had evaded the virus sweeping Earth but were alone: alone in space, equipped with a technology they didn't fully understand, tasked with galactic duties and responsibilities that she feared reached beyond human capacities.

Yes, they had managed to fend off the locusts, but who could guess what other threats lay ahead of them, and still, Earth's survivors needed to be rescued, if that were even possible. She leaned her shoulder against Jamie's, and together they stared at the star-streaked screen.

'We'll be at Primo in no time,' he said.

'Yes. The general's under so much pressure, I worry about him. So much to do, and we've lost so many people from our original Primo muster. It's going to cheer everyone that you and your crew are back.'

Chapter 2

Base Primo

General Dower leaned across the bed to kiss his daughter Fay's forehead, straightened and turned to leave.

'I have to go,' he said.

His wife Gail nodded without looking up from her chair by Fay's bedside.

Dower glanced to the bed opposite where her co-pilot Johnny also lay motionless.

A doctor appeared at the doorway. 'General, we're stumped. I'm sorry.'

'It's been a while now, doctor. Are there no signs? Anything?'

'There's nothing more we can do while they're both in comas. The only positive you can take is Fay's body is healing…' He waved a hand toward an array of equipment surrounding both patients' beds. 'Some of that stuff is a mystery to us. It might be helping, but we have no idea what most of it's for, much less how to use it.'

The general nodded an acknowledgement; several of the scientists, including his second daughter, Lily, had tried, but all had drawn a blank. Steph had rigged the current setup and briefed the medics before leaving on her rescue mission. That first phase had worked well, and now both patients were making steady progress physically but remained comatose – something more was needed. Steph and her advanced knowledge of the alien technology was needed.

'Do your best, doctor. I'm sure Steph will be back soon.' With a final glance toward his daughter, he left the ward and headed toward his office.

He paused at a viewing port and peered through into a docking bay where two locust vessels were still berthed. Cleared of locusts, they were safe for his people, and he could see several technicians walking about them. A chance to really learn about the aggressors' technology. This pair of vessels had been retained; all the rest had been dragged out into space and destroyed.

Stony-faced, he stared at the vessels and recalled the invasion – that day when scores of attacking locust vessels had almost overwhelmed the base. Even where he stood now had been surrendered to the invaders. His people had been forced back into the depths of Primo Deep, suffering terrible losses on the way.

Eventually, it had been Steph who pulled a rabbit from the hat. She had finally enabled their combat craft, the warbirds, to launch – the trigger for a last-ditch fightback against the locusts. He remembered his own part, the hand-to-hand engagement that had so nearly claimed his life. Everything had been bloody, so nearly lost. But his people had triumphed.

He resumed his walk along the concourse just as his collar-phone sparked into life. 'General, sir. Incoming transmission from O-3 – it's just emerged from the Fold.'

'I'll come to the control room now. Have Colonel MacMillan meet me there. What's its ETA?'

'Under three hours, sir.'

Chapter 3

Earth: On Board S-1

'The environment's still not safe for us,' said Celine, glancing up from her sleeve data display. 'It's getting better every day, but go out there now, and the virus will kill you: you're dead, plain and simple.'

Brigadier Smith-Brown grimaced. 'How much longer?'

'A week… ten days to be sure.'

'Very well, we wait. Any further life signs?'

'Our remote craft are doing visual surveying while sampling the virus load. Nature's bearing up, mostly doing better without humans. The virus is selective – it seems to be a primate killer rather than life in general. We've noticed a lot of domesticated livestock have died. I think not from the virus, though. Many of those enclosed in fields are dying of starvation or lack of water without human care. Those that have broken out are fending for themselves and faring better.'

The brigadier looked out through Leviathan S-1's viewscreen to the rolling green of England's Salisbury Plain. The bucolic scene was jarred by the serried ranks of huge sample craft. He'd brought the whole fleet down here, to his own familiar stomping ground. Anywhere in the world would have done, but ever cautious, he'd opted for the familiar. Pre-virus, pre-solar storm, Earth had fallen into civil turmoil and international conflict. At least here in Britain he could better gauge threats and anticipate the strength and reactions of any unexpected force; none had yet presented.

'Communications?' he asked.

Celine gave the same despairing shrug the brigadier had seen so often in recent days. 'Still no signals, no power signatures. The solar storm was massive; it must have fried everything. A coronal mass ejection of that size will have destroyed every active electrical device, and even induced massive destructive currents into passive devices and those switched off altogether, fried them all, everything, shielded or otherwise.'

'People?'

'As per my earlier reports. The observer craft continue to spot them occasionally. Not many moving about, but lots of bodies. I think Steph's ninety-nine percent fatality estimate may have been optimistic. We can't contact or help those we do see – no comms on the ground and we'd risk contagion to ourselves if we made physical contact. Wherever, whenever, we eventually go in, it's going to be tokenism; even a one percent survival means tens of millions needing help worldwide. There will be unbearable suffering everywhere. Where do we start?'

'Celine, you have to leave that decision to me. For now, just keep your craft doing global sweeps, testing the atmosphere. Wherever they go, keep them mapping survivors. Once it's safe to engage on the ground, we'll prioritise. Meantime, as you say, we're looking at only some tens of millions of survivors, max. Mostly, there will be sufficient tinned food and bottled water in the shops and houses to supply them all for a good while yet, maybe years. It's the poorest areas, that had little stocks to begin with, where survivors will suffer most. As it's ever been.'

Celine shrugged. 'Right, we'll keep going as we are for now.' She waved an arm toward the viewscreen. 'Meantime, I've been thinking about the fleet of sample craft we brought down with us. They'll be needed to rebuild the navigation tube, to open a safe route into space, when we're ready. You mentioned the other day that we might repurpose a few samplers, position them on the ground at strategic spots around the world: the US, UK and so on. They would seed the formation of regional hubs, secure bases around which to build a wider rescue mission.'

'Yes, I'm sure that's a sound approach, a good starting point. The rescue and recovery can radiate out from them, finding survivors and any local officials, support them in establishing order.'

'Well, how many do you need? I must have enough samplers available to be able to rebuild the tube, and I've been thinking about another plan to help get us back out through the atmosphere again.'

'I know you need the samplers to rebuild the tube shield. But you must have some redundancy in the system. How many can you spare?' said the brigadier, fixing her with a steady gaze.

'Oh, yes. There's some redundancy. Tell me how many you want, and I'll see what can be done. Meanwhile, I've got a temporary plan for the rest, which I'd like to run past you.'

The brigadier gave a long sigh. 'I'd like them all, get relief bases up and running around the globe. Truth is, I doubt we can skeleton crew more than thirty to start and that's stretching it – eventually, we can get the survivors themselves to help. After that, we'll need the atmosphere opened to get more equipment and rescue teams in from Primo.'

'I'll see if I can spare thirty craft from tube duties, but that might be asking a bit much. Certainly, freeing up twenty to start would work. I'll make sure they're ready when the time comes. But I know we don't have that number of trained sampler pilots among S-3's crew.'

'We don't. I think the captain and two or three of the officers. They'll have to fly each sample craft out to wherever we designate a hub should be and then be shuttled back here by observer craft, leaving the grounded sampler crewed by a handful of our people. Then they'll fly out the next sampler and so on. Once each hub craft is positioned, it'll be there for the duration, so they won't need sampler pilots, just regular crews. Even then, if you eventually find a way to spare more samplers, so I can scale up to thirty regional hubs, we'll still have only five or six bio-suited crewmembers to each, plus a medical orderly or nurse on some of the teams. That's going to limit the scope of our rescue activity, but it's the best we can do.'

The brigadier was acutely aware that the ability to operate shipboard technology was restricted to those with the personalised bio-linked bodysuits printed on Primo. Each suit was bio-linked to an individual crewmember; only they could operate equipment to progress the rescue efforts.

'Agreed. I'll detail one or two of my scientists to each craft you dispatch. That will give you more boots on the ground. It should help.'

'Brilliant, we'll be stretched very thin out there, so every hand will be useful. I'm going to speak to the major, see if we can allocate a couple of his soldiers to each hub too. Now. What's this plan you mentioned?'

'Yes, my plan. Whatever we manage to do down here with the survivors, my responsibility is to reopen the tube through the atmosphere so we can link up with Primo and the rest, get more help down here.'

'Agreed, I won't deflect you from that,' said the brigadier.

'Well, I can't rebuild the tube until we know for sure that the warbirds dealt with any surviving locust attack vessels above the atmosphere. We can't know that because of the mass of debris in the atmosphere disrupting our signals. Sitting waiting for a message to get through could take a very long time.'

'What do you propose?'

'I've been running some simulations. You'll recall how Lily originally suggested that rather than creating a safe navigation tube through the atmosphere we might try clearing the whole atmosphere from above. She thought of recalibrating the samplers' gravlifts and using them all together like a giant snow plough. But now we're all stuck below. I'm thinking of a variation on her plan. Recalibrate all the samplers' gravlifts from their current beams – long and vertical to form the safe navigation tube – to a broader shallow setting, with each beam set to face forward and down. Get all the craft airborne in line abreast. I might still be able to use them like that huge snowplough Lily envisaged, but from below, not above.

'Working from beneath the atmosphere, they could begin to clear it, scraping the debris field away from below. Orbiting the globe, clearing away the debris, circuit by circuit. Unlike the vertical tube shielding, which was simply waiting to deflect debris that came its way, the snow plough method would methodically sweep away debris – eventually clearing it all out.'

'That could take a long time,' said the brigadier, at once interested but sceptical.

'Yes, it'll take time. But hundreds of sample craft programmed to fly, say, ten miles apart, will make a plough blade several thousand miles wide and maybe ten miles high. I'll need to run some numbers. The craft can fly very fast. It will take time, and we'd need to redo the process several times to be sure we'd got everything, then climb up to the next level and repeat the process, and so on. If I can get the programming right, I believe it's doable.'

'Then you must try. The samplers are lying idle just now, put them to work. If nothing else, you might clear the atmosphere enough so we can get signals through, to find out how things are above before reforming the tube. Please, get on it. If it's feasible I'd like it underway as soon as possible.'

Celine smiled at him. 'I hoped you'd say that. The groundwork's nearly done. With your authority I can begin reprogramming the sample craft gravlifts at once. I'll have them in the air tomorrow. If it works, we may yet have a clear sky again. And if you need the tube reforming in the meantime, I can just revert the gravlift programming and redirect the samplers. As you say, if nothing else, whatever we can clear from the atmosphere might improve signalling.'

'Plenty of time right now, while we're all just sitting here waiting. Go to it at once.' The brigadier looked back out toward the fleet of grounded sample craft. 'Let's get them airborne and working!'

Chapter 4

Base Primo

Steph's first act on returning to Primo had been to visit the sickbay. There she had assessed the situation and made refinements to the equipment settings. Then she'd reassured Gail Dower that progress continued, and both patients' recoveries were going well – a little more time was the key component now. Then she set off to link with Jamie and head for the general's office.

By the time Steph and Jamie had reached the office, Gail had called ahead with the latest health update on the Dowers' daughter. Boosted by the news, the general rose from his desk and beamed at Steph before reaching out to grip Jamie's hand. 'Well, we're all glad to have you back, both of you.

'Steph, Gail has just called to say you think things are going well in the ward, thank you. And Jamie… what can I say? You're back; we need you and your crew. I'd like to give you and your people a break… you've had one hell of a shipwreck. But sorry, I need you on duty.'

'From what Steph told me, sir, you've had it worse than me – here, and out at Secundo too.'

'I don't know, different hells maybe. It's been bad for us all.'

'What have you got in mind for me, sir?'

'Colonel MacMillan will be going into the Perseus Arm, searching for signs of the other locust cones. It's a hunter-killer mission. I want you to go with him. You'll all stop at Secundo en route – deliver reinforcements and equipment.'

Jamie gave a brisk nod of his head. Secundo was the base MacMillan had established at the junction of the Orion and Perseus arms – the heart of his command. It had suffered very badly during the locust attacks. It needed to be restored quickly, just in case.

Steph bit her lip to supress her concern. She'd only just got Jamie back. She remained silent while Jamie told Dower of events at Osarus and the fate of his now abandoned Leviathan S-3. Finally, she could contain herself no more. 'General, Jamie's only just back. Let him catch his breath. There's plenty to do here at Primo.'

'I'm sorry, Steph. I know you've been apart a long time, but I need Jamie on the expedition; Colonel MacMillan will need him too. There's no debate.'

'What exactly have you got in mind for me, sir?'

'I'm sending two Leviathan squadrons into Perseus. The colonel will lead one squadron and have overall command of the expedition. I want you to lead the second squadron and be second in command of the whole expedition.'

'Thank you, sir, that's a real honour.'

The general stepped from behind his desk. 'How is the new Leviathan manufacturing coming along, Steph? That's your baby.'

'I'm on it, general. My team kept production on target while I was away – the Leviathans will be ready.'

The general's door slid open, and Colonel MacMillan stepped in. His face broke into a broad smile, and he reached out a hand. 'Jamie, welcome back. Good to see you made it. And welcome to the Hunter Fleet; I'm looking forward to working with you.'

'And me you, colonel. Though I understand it's still under construction.'

'Yes, but almost done, just a matter of days and we'll be off. I'll catch you up on the details later, just wanted to welcome you back now.'

***

Returning to Primo Main Base after a familiarisation tour of Primo Deep, which had been undiscovered when Jamie had last left Primo, Jamie followed Steph off the travelator and into the reserve control room. They passed its Goliath LPA – the enormous Light Processing Array that was the computing heart of the new technology. They acknowledged greetings from a cluster of scientists and technicians, all busy in an effort to calculate how long the debris field around Earth might persist; they did not look happy.

Past the Goliath, the pair carried on toward the silent sarcophagus room. The bots had replaced its locust-battered door, and there was no sign there had ever been an incursion. Beyond the door was the greatest Goliath. Now activated, spots of light pulsed, patiently waiting for instruction, radiating a warm white halo. Beyond it was the sarcophagus, cold and grey.

'So, what are we going to do about Weeman? And where exactly is he?' said Jamie.

Steph threw him a cautionary glance and remained silent, waiting for the door to slide shut behind them.

'Come on, his body's back there in the sarcophagus.' She led him to the rear of the chamber and triggered the controls. The opaque lid flickered and became transparent revealing the little body inside.

'It's like he's just sleeping,' said Jamie in amazement.

'I know. The sarcophagus seems to maintain the body in a sort of stasis, but it is dead… well, unrevivable.' She rested her hand on the surface and paused for a moment of reflection. Jamie stood in silence beside her.

'I want to bury him before you go to Perseus,' she said.

'How? Where?'

'We can have a little ceremony and launch him into deep space from an observer craft. I've got it all planned. The general and the others will come. You should fly us, and we'll send him away together, soon, in the coming days.'

'Okay, of course. But I really mean, *where* is Weeman. He's gone, dead. Yet, you told me he was in the Goliath over there, then your suit, or is it both, or none? I've still not got a handle on it.'

'I'm not sure exactly. He, or a bit of him, his essence if you like, was a little bunch of lights clinging on like a pilot light in the dormant Goliath – that's all that was saved, uploaded from the sarcophagus. Then he moved from the Goliath into my suit. Then, well, I've sort of lost track. Now, as long as he has direct contact, he seems able to flit from my suit to an LPA or Goliath and back when it suits him. I don't always know where he is until he decides to communicate with me. I can't explain.'

'What's he up to, dotting about? How do the other scientists feel about it?'

'I haven't said a word to anyone. They'd think I'm imagining things or mad. Probably both!'

'Should you keep it from the general?'

'I don't know. Maybe I'll tell him soon. Perhaps we can talk once you get back from the Perseus Arm. For now, I'm saying nothing.'

'Whatever you think's best. I'll take my lead from you on this. But Steph, I need to know – can you do that killer plasma thing with a Goliath?'

'I don't know. I've never tried. I know what Weeman did; he stirred up all the lights in the Goliath, and they bulged out like a burning flame to fry the locust that was trying to kill us. But that's different from doing it myself.' She gave Jamie an anxious look. 'There's so much I can do and access now, but I only understand a fraction of it. Weeman made you an upgraded suit too. It's time to give it a try. You need to understand; he wanted you to.'

'Okay, I'm up for that; we can test it out later today. What are the big differences?'

'Well, they look just like regular bio-suits – if someone doesn't know you have an upgraded suit they could never tell by appearance. But you'll find every process seems to be quicker and it gives access to so many other layers of knowledge, with much broader access authorities. Until you get started you don't realise there are so many things still to know. I'm sure you'll get a handle on everything at your own pace.'

'Right, let's test my new suit later today. I'll worry about using it when I get back from Perseus. Meantime, I'm to meet Captain Kingston. He said he'd show me round a warbird, take it for a run. When I get back, if you're free, we could spend the rest of the day together.'

'I'd love that, but Jamie, don't talk about your upgraded suit to anyone. It'll just create an immediate pressure of expectation, and believe me, you face a steep learning curve.'

'I doubt many will be expecting that much of me.'

'You'd be surprised. But it's not just that. Weeman warned me to be cautious. I'm not sure he's convinced humans are the right custodians of his technology. He's worried not all humans are trustworthy.'

'Based on his experience, I'm not surprised.'

Chapter 5

Earth: Sampler over USA

The sampler hovered high over its selected landing spot. Major Boucher looked intently down at the parade square. There was no sign of movement below. The brigadier and Celine had established criteria for placement of the regional hubs, and he was following that guidance to the letter.

Cruel as it seemed to avoid large centres of population, plunging direct into a major city such as New York would be counterproductive. With a one percent survival rate, his little team aboard the sampler would face an impossible task trying to rescue upward of a hundred thousand people. They would risk being overwhelmed emotionally and possibly physically by desperate survivors.

Instead, large military bases had been identified, east, south, north, mid and west. A base complex, ideally home to perhaps twenty thousand serving military and their families would offer a likelihood of around two hundred disciplined survivors and hopefully some dependents too – which would provide additional motivation for stability. It would provide people who were used to functioning within a chain of command with a purpose, people who could be readily drawn into service to multiply the rescue efforts. They in turn could use the sampler hub's piloted observers for local travel to find and embrace other satellite bases and local civilians: establish community self-help using the resources of the sampler. From that seed, a swift rollout delivered mostly by the rescued themselves was the best way to save as many as possible.

Weeks had passed since the counter-virus had been distributed, and Celine's team had reported steady reduction of the first virus' potency as virus and counter-virus interacted, until it was considered safe for crew members to expose themselves outside. To put the crew's mind at ease, Celine had stepped out first. She had been fine.

Great effort had been spent training as many Leviathan crew members as could be spared in flying the small observer craft, regardless of their skills background. Every sampler carried two observers as standard equipment. Celine's flotilla of unmanned samplers was parked all across Salisbury Plain, housing a whole fleet of observer craft in their hangars doing nothing. They were the perfect tool to expand local rescue and recovery.

She'd shuffled those resources, pulling observer craft from many of the unmanned samplers, adding them to the roster of observers that would work out of the samplers designated to be recovery hubs. She now had seven observers stowed in each recovery hub sampler, that figure limited more by the number of trained pilots available than by space in the sampler hangars.

Once a sampler had been landed, one observer would carry the sampler's pilot back to the main fleet on Salisbury Plain, leaving behind six more to serve as local transports flying out from the grounded hub sampler.

'It's quiet down there,' said Boucher.

'That's probably good for now,' said the sampler pilot. 'We'll make a clean landing without being mobbed. Then we'll make sure you're happy with the location before I head back to the fleet.'

Boucher looked back toward the dozen silent people ranged behind him; all were looking down on the base. They were a mix of service people: crew, soldiers, scientists, technicians and a med team member – this hub was lucky, there were simply not enough health workers on the Leviathan to allocate medics to every hub. He could see the tension in every face as they prepared themselves to begin the rescue.

'Interesting, there are no bodies about the base,' said Green, Boucher's second in command. 'We saw lots scattered around the English villages we flew over during preparation.'

'That's likely a good thing. Could indicate any survivors are organised. That's exactly what the brigadier had hoped for.'

'I've got some life signs in the LPA.' The co-pilot's voice sounded in everyone's collar-phones.

Boucher glanced at the pilot. 'Hold it steady here, please,' he said and hurried away to join the co-pilot.

'Show me what you've got.'

The co-pilot pointed into the LPA. 'See, beyond the parade ground, in the first line of buildings. Heat signatures, quite a few.'

Boucher watched the signals. 'They're forming up in a defensive pattern. I think we'll need to be careful. That lot might feel threatened. And they'll be armed.'

'Can we raise them?'

'Doubt it. All their electrics would have been fried in the solar storm. On top of everything else they've suffered, this big boy coming out of the sky is going to be one scary experience,' said Boucher.

He returned to the bridge where his crew waited. 'We need to communicate with them. Break out Celine's sign.' Several crew members left the bridge for the hangar deck.

'We'll land on the square as soon as the hangar squad is ready. Pilot, I'd like the hangar door to be facing that building where the people are holed up.'

The pilot nodded and altered the sampler's position so it hovered parallel to the buildings that lined the far side of the square.

'Hangar here. We're all set,' sounded a report in Boucher's collar-phone.

'Take her down, pilot. Let's see how they react.'

The sampler slowly descended, settling gently on the square. The stabiliser legs were deployed, and it was down.

'Standby in the hoppers… Open the hangar now,' said Boucher.

He watched on screen as the hangar opened to reveal two stationary hoppers, between them stretched a huge banner that read:

DON'T SHOOT. WE'RE HUMAN, FRIENDS. HELP IS HERE.

Nothing moved outside. The hoppers remained motionless, arms extended, the banner rippling slightly in a gentle breeze. This preliminary engagement an immediate step back to the low-tech world.

'What next, sir?' said Green.

'We'll give it a minute,' said Boucher. He activated his collar-phone. 'Any movement showing in the LPA?'

'Minor shuffling. Mostly they're watching us, I guess,' said the co-pilot.

'Well, here goes,' said Boucher, sending a signal to the hoppers. He glanced toward Green, and both men turned to focus intently on the viewscreen.

The hopper arms moved, twisting the banner, exposing the reverse side to any onlookers beyond.

BRINGING OUT A RADIO FOR YOU. SPEAK. WE'RE HUMANS.

Then the hoppers advanced down the ramp, one step at a time. At the foot they paused, one let go the banner and continued forward. Step by step, alone, it moved out of the sampler's shadow and toward the line of buildings. It halted before what had once been a neat line of flower beds bordering the buildings. One arm extended, then lowered a package to the ground.

The hopper backed off, all the way to the sampler, where it retreated with its partner into the hangar. The door slid shut behind them. Not a shot had been fired.

Boucher watched intently – nothing moved outside.

Hours passed, still no movement outside.

'They must have understood,' said Green.

'I think so. They'll be cautious, likely waiting for dark to recover our device.'

'They obviously don't know what to make of us. Don't trust us.'

'Would you in their shoes? Caution's a good sign. Shows control – somebody's exerting influence. Someone's in command.'

The sampler's pilot stepped across the bridge. 'Sir, are you happy with your landing position? Now things are grounded here, I really need to go. There are other sample craft to be positioned. The sooner I get back to the fleet, the sooner I can fly the next sampler to its location.'

'Okay, pilot. You've done your bit. Thank you. Get yourself away.'

'Thank you, sir,' said the pilot, as both he and the co-pilot offered up crisp salutes before hurrying away to the observer allocated for them in the hangar below.

***

'There's movement, sir,' said the technician whom Boucher had detailed to the LPA. 'I have someone moving from the building toward the radio.'

'Thank you. Just one?'

'Just one, sir.'

'Can we jazz up the low-light vision?' said Boucher, waving toward the viewscreen. It was nearly black, almost mirroring the darkness of night outside.

'Still working on it. Just another moment.'

The screen wavered slightly as shadows rippled through the black. Then it settled into a blend of shadows, broken by a heat signature.

'That's more like it. What do you think, Green?'

'The target's at the radio, sir. A male. Shall I broadcast a message?'

'No. Let him get back to safety first. He'll be sure to take it to the leader, whoever that may be.'

They watched the form of a man pick up the device and gingerly check it. Then, as content as he might be under the circumstances, the retriever hurried back for the cover of the buildings. Boucher and Green moved to the navigation room where the LPA was displaying the body signatures of those within the buildings.

'That's the carrier,' said the technician who was monitoring the LPA. He pointed at a moving signal that quickly approached a small cluster of other life signs and stopped.

Boucher and Green listened intently, but no message came from the device. 'They're still being careful.' He touched his sleeve to open a channel to the comms device.

'This is Commander Boucher. To whom am I talking? Hello?' He looked toward Green. 'I know they can hear us. The kit's not hard to operate. Perhaps I should broadcast an instruction.'

There was no need. Suddenly, a sharp, defensive voice barked across the airwaves.

'Hello, hello. This is Colonel Jamison. Who the hell are you? What the hell's going on? And what is that beast you've landed in?'

'Colonel Jamison, I am Major Boucher, commander of this craft. Part of an Earth rescue party. We have come to help you. My craft will act as a hub and tech centre to support recovery. How are you fixed?'

'How do you think we're fixed, major? I've three hundred people. Plenty canned and dried food, bottled water. Trying to push out a perimeter, provide support to survivors, but we've no transport, no comms, nothing. Mostly we've been burning bodies. God's sake, what's happened? Where are you from? What is that thing you're in?'

Chapter 6

Base Primo

General Dower and Steph stood together among the crowd at the viewing ports. She was struggling to raise a smile and a cheer for the passing craft. It was some days since she and her closest friends had flown out into open space and launched Weeman's body away into the void on an eternal journey. It had been difficult, even though she knew it was only his physical body and that Weeman's consciousness continued, if only in part.

From time to time, he would appear in the lights of an LPA she was working on. She'd reach her arm into the display, and the cluster of lights that was his essence would slip under the sleeve of her suit to communicate directly or just to spend time with her. Nonetheless, the physical goodbye had left her profoundly saddened. Today's event was doing nothing to raise her mood.

All about her, there was a buzz of anticipation in the air as the throng watched the Leviathans funnel past in a tight line astern. MacMillan was leading the two Hunter squadrons out of the Grand Canal on the first leg of their journey to the Perseus Arm. At last, taking the fight to the locusts. But taking Jamie away again. They'd had so little time together.

Gail Dower linked her arm through her husband's. 'Paul, was it really necessary to go on the attack so quickly?' she said.

'There are two more locust hordes out there. Both have captured sample craft, which gives them folddrive capability. With that speed, they'll find more and more planets to feast on, without any effective travel breaks to limit their progress. Before, they probably had to hibernate many decades, more even, while travelling between planets. Now they have open access. Steph thinks their reproduction pattern is governed by available food supplies. With unrestricted travel, they'll effectively have limitless access to food – their breeding will be unlimited. We must hit them now or they will swamp us.'

'How will you find them?' she said.

'Our systems harvested some data from the cone that attacked us here. It was the one that Colonel MacMillan originally discovered in the Pardamax system, in the Perseus Arm. From that we know in what directions the other cones set off from Pardamax – they are travelling in the Perseus Arm at present. How far they've travelled is another matter. The Hunter squadrons will just need to work on that in theatre. They'll start at Pardamax, the locusts' point of origin, work from there,' said Dower.

Steph pressed a hand against the viewport as the last of the Leviathans passed from sight. Nine craft. Each equipped with a flight of three warbirds. The first three Leviathans had been MacMillan's Alpha Squadron, followed by Jamie's Bravo Squadron. The final three represented a new refreshed Perseus Squadron. Their separate task: to rebuild and reinforce Base Secundo and maintain a protective force at the junction of Perseus and Orion.

Every craft was important, and with so many friends setting out on the expedition, Steph had a personal investment in each one. But in particular, the Hunter squadrons Alpha and Bravo, designated HA and HB – and most of all HB-1, Jamie's flagship.

The greater part of humanity's combat capacity was heading into Perseus. So was Jamie. Steph trusted his ability and the warbirds' fighting capacity, but couldn't help worrying. The locusts had shown they could overwhelm warbirds and take out Leviathans. Nothing was as certain as Colonel MacMillan and the general were suggesting. She just wished the conflict was over so she could focus on Earth's rescue.

'Well, they're on their way. You did a brilliant job getting the squadrons ready, Steph. Now it's down to them,' said Dower.

Gail Dower pressed her arm tight against her husband's. 'Pray it goes well.'

'I do, and I trust MacMillan and his warbirds. They pack a lot of firepower. Come on, I need to get back to the office.' They turned to leave, and Steph headed for the main control room and its Goliath.

***

Lily Dower was crouched on the top of the Goliath, oblivious to everything else. The younger daughter of Paul and Gail Dower had a brilliant mind and had quickly been drawn into Steph's team following her arrival at Primo. Her attention was flitting between the streaming lights and displays within the Goliath and her sleeve controls with which she was interrogating the giant computer.

'Lily, where are you? How are you getting on?' Steph's voice sounded in Lily's collar-phone, dragging her from the calculations she was performing.

'Hi Steph, I'm up top. Did the Leviathans get away?'

'On schedule, all good. I'm on my way up,' said Steph, hurrying past the line of standard LPAs that surrounded the Goliath. She couldn't see Lily but wasn't surprised. The Goliath was so big that, unless an operator was standing near the edge, they were hard to spot from ground level.

'Well, where are we?' she said as Lily rose to greet her.

'I've been doing as you suggested. Now the Leviathans are clear of the Grand Canal, we can give it a try... But I'm not sure we'll have enough sample craft to do the job.'

'Let me see,' said Steph.

Lily stroked her sleeve and the displays beneath them changed again.

'Damn,' said Steph, staring intently into the Goliath, 'you're right. Is that them all?'

'All that I can confirm are serviceable. You already took the best ones to create the tube down to Earth.'

Steph made a tutting sound and glanced up toward the ceiling. 'Okay, let's get the ones you've identified launched and mustering in orbit. Use the same auto program I created to ready the other old samplers for forming the first Earth tube. I'd hoped there'd be more that were serviceable.'

Lily nodded then stroked her sleeve to access Steph's original auto program and commence the process of reactivating the mothballed samplers she'd identified.

'Once you've got the process underway, let me know and join me in the concourse – we need to talk this through with the general.'

***

An hour later, Lily hurried across the concourse to join Steph who had returned to the viewing ports overlooking the Grand Canal. There she was, once more staring out into the vacuum.

'Have you seen any yet?' said Lily, coming to a halt at Steph's side.

'Yes, several have gone past. I can see others emerging from deeper in the canal,' said Steph, craning her neck to make out distant movements.

'I found a few more after you'd left, but most of those remaining in the hangars really are done, I wouldn't trust them to even reach Earth; they're only fit for scrap. I think we'll have just over a hundred flying once they're all out.'

'That's an improvement on your original estimate, but nowhere near enough to create a new tube thorough Earth's atmosphere. Look, here's more of them coming out now.' She pointed deep into the canal, and Lily strained to see.

'I see them. So, no second tube… It's plan B then.'

'Plan B it is. The general will be disappointed, but in the long term, I prefer this way. Your snowplough idea will take longer, but once it clears the atmosphere, it will be permanently clear. When we've brought the general up to date, we'll need to reprogram all these samplers' gravlifts. Get them expanded to a working max, pointing forward and down to start deflecting debris out of the atmosphere.'

'How long do you think?'

'It depends how long it takes to clear each altitude level. Right now, I'm only guessing, but I'd start by assuming we'll need to do at least five sweeps at each altitude to clear that space. Then drop down and repeat, and again and again. It's going to be like peeling a huge onion. Let's just set them to work and see.

'That's not going to help Celine and the brigadier down on the surface.'

'No, not at once, but it will in the long run. Meantime, we've got nothing else. Come on, your father's expecting us.'

Chapter 7

Earth

Brigadier Smith-Brown was pleased. Captain Harding's pilots had made great progress in distributing samplers to establish regional hubs. They'd established seven in the United States, two in Canada and four in the UK. The pilots were busy getting more out to Australia and New Zealand, then the remainder of the first tranche of samplers would go to allied countries who had also supplied Primo with crew in the last days before the atmosphere closed.

Though everywhere needed help in equal measure, Smith-Brown was forced to be pragmatic. Helping friends first would likely yield more willing hands more quickly to spread the rescue faster. 'It's going well, a great start,' he said.

'It is, sir,' said Harding, the Leviathan's captain.

'I just wish we had more people to populate each hub. A leader and a handful of supporters isn't much,' said the brigadier, glancing toward Celine.

Celine nodded wistfully. 'You're right. But some of the teams have made a great start. The idea of starting with military bases was a good move.'

'It was the logical move,' said Smith-Brown. 'And what progress with clearing the atmosphere?'

'We've started, slowly. But it's a start.'

***

Boucher looked up with pleasure as the canteen door slid open to admit Colonel Jamison. In no time, the army veteran had set aside his amazement at the giant sampler that had settled on his parade ground. Put aside, too, the pain of personal loss – his wife and teenage children had all succumbed to the virus. In only a few hours, the seasoned soldier had grasped the realities of the situation and invested every effort in getting all his survivors up to speed. He'd detailed staff to act as supporters on board the observers that Boucher's crew flew out, reaching a bit further every day.

'Colonel, come in. Coffee?' said Boucher. He was prompting the dispenser before the colonel could reply.

'Thank you.' In a single movement, the colonel sat and lifted the beaker to his lips.

There had been a few uneasy moments initially. Colonel Jamison outranked Major Boucher but found himself in the uncomfortable and subordinate role of the helped, not the helper. They'd worked it out. Boucher and his bio-suited team had absolute authority on board all craft and hoppers, while Jamison developed the local recovery plan, and his squads ran the face-to-face engagement and rescue.

'Today, I'm expecting to receive code instructions from Celine on the Leviathan to establish print manufacture of some freestanding resources – radios, portable lighting and power units. Our sampler has only a very limited capacity to print, and we carry few raw materials, but anything we can manufacture locally will speed things up, help us here and free the Leviathan's print capacity for bigger and more complex items like generators – they're needed everywhere too. Once we're printing some of our own resources locally, we can speed up distribution to all the scattered groups you've been linking together.'

'That's great, every little helps. What would also help is getting some of my people flying too, or at least driving the hoppers you've got sitting idle.'

'I know. Sorry, colonel, we're doing our best, but to operate equipment you need these bio-linked suits, and that can't be done here. Meantime, I have asked the science team to see if they can work out how to manufacture replacement circuits for some of your own transport equipment. But it's not looking hopeful, I'm afraid.'

'Okay, we'll keep pushing out, expanding our reach regardless. I know you're doing your best. I'm still not clear how it all happened.'

'Well, you and me both. A hell of a lot went on. Coincidence, bad timing, bad luck. Maybe some bad politics too.'

Boucher finished his coffee and looked again at Jamison. 'The big one was the missile launches – once that started, the debris closed the atmosphere just as the solar storm hit and fried everything... And you know all about the virus.'

Colonel Jamison grimaced. 'I do. Oh, I do.'

'You should know, Brigadier Smith-Brown is floating a proposal. He's eager to develop a network between the various hubs. Sharing ideas, problems, planning joint actions...'

'Sounds good to me. Let me know when a meeting's scheduled and I'll be sure to join you. For now, let's just keep your people flying the observers out, and mine making contact. I'm going out with one of my teams today. There's a bunker that's caught my attention. A ways south of here, army. It's closed up – we think pre-virus – and no sign of it having reopened since the virus came.'

'Do you think the virus got inside? Are the occupants dead? Could they have survived?'

'Maybe. Who knows? There's always a chance some people have made it if it was sealed before the panic set in.'

'What will you do?'

'Not sure yet. I'll decide when I get there.'

Chapter 8

Base Secundo

Colonel MacMillan stood on the base's rooftop, looking over the parapet and down onto the landing pads. Two of the new Perseus Squadron Leviathans were landed. The third was in the Fold, maintaining watch. Occupying the third landing pad was his own Leviathan, Hunter Alpha-1 – HA-1. The area surrounding them was abuzz with activity as equipment, stores and their payloads of construction materials were off-loaded.

He thought about the terror the locusts had brought to his command base, how close they'd come to being overwhelmed. How many people he'd lost in the battle to defend Secundo. Everywhere were signs of conflict. Several huge mounds of scrap marked where the shattered locust squadron had been cleared off the landing pads. A pit was filled to overflowing with black and grey ash, all that remained of the locust bodies, unceremoniously incinerated.

Spread across the building's roof were a handful of observer craft that were busy ferrying people up and down from the rest of the colonel's Hunter squadrons that orbited unseen in the sky above. He spotted Jamie emerging from the most recently landed and beckoned him across to the parapet.

Jamie let out a little whistle. 'This must have been hell.'

'That's an understatement,' said Delacroix, joining the two.

'They're hard to kill, that's for sure,' added Sarsen, arriving directly behind Delacroix.

'Jamie, meet Base Commander Delacroix,' MacMillan said. 'In my absence, he will also command the Perseus Squadron maintaining a watch over the Orion–Perseus boundary. And Major Sarsen. He and his troops were the ones who faced down the locusts here. Gentlemen, this is Major MacAulay, Jamie MacAulay – you're both aware of Jamie's involvement from the start. Today, he's commanding Hunter Bravo Squadron and is 2IC of the expedition.'

The men shook hands and exchanged brief pleasantries before MacMillan resumed. 'We'll be heading directly into Perseus as soon as the construction stores and kit are unloaded. I want this place rebuilt, tougher, thicker, stronger, higher, and better armed. We know some of the threats on offer, so let's be sure we can face them down if they ever come back.'

'Is that likely?' asked Sarsen.

'We're going into the Perseus Arm to hunt them down, so let's hope not, but preparation is everything.'

'And who knows what else might turn up one day,' said Delacroix.

MacMillan glanced at him and gave a grim smile. 'Ever the optimist.'

'Whatever happens next, we'll be better prepared, that's for sure. What's your plan of action in Perseus, sir?' said Delacroix.

'I'm leading Hunter Alpha and Jamie leads Hunter Bravo. We'll travel in the Fold together, direct to Pardamax. Radio silence at all times, just in case either of the cones is in the Fold and close enough to detect our transmissions – unlikely, but we're being careful. The information snatched from the cone destroyed at Primo gave us the course each cone took from Pardamax, so we'll split there. Each squadron will follow a course and track down their target.'

'You're splitting the force into two?'

'Only temporarily. Steph believes they will have used the folddrive to travel as quickly as possible to the next suitable planetary food source. Then they'll have likely begun their regular dominate and feed pattern. With a little luck, by now, they'll be busy feasting.'

'Won't they know to look out for signs of pursuit?' said Sarsen.

'Maybe, but we destroyed the first cone in regular space, so it couldn't get a message into the Fold to alert the others, even if they had been close enough to receive it. There was no way for the first cone to alert the other cones. In theory, they'll be oblivious to the threat we present.'

'Sounds good, sir,' said Sarsen.

'Once we've detected a cone, and hopefully its locusts are distracted in feed mode, our plan is to immobilise the cone and strand it wherever it is, provided it can be done without risking the squadron. Then, either way, withdraw to the Pardamax system and await the return of the other squadron, which will be following the same rule. Then we decide where first to attack, in strength.'

Sarsen and Delacroix exchanged quizzical glances. 'How will you link up while maintaining radio silence, sir?' said Sarsen.

'Trace, observe, surgical strike against the cone itself, damaging it enough to prevent it folding away, if possible, then retire to Pardamax. Both squadrons will do the same. We can't know yet how far either cone will have travelled, so the first squadron back to Pardamax will need to be patient, just wait for the other to return. Meantime, to aid comms, Steph has modified some of our homing buoys. We have some that are now set to return to a Lagrange point in the Pardamax system instead of Primo. They will be released by each squadron to deliver position and status reports to Pardamax for the other squadron to collect – not perfect, but it will enable some contact and comms.'

'Have you got beacons that could return to us at Secundo? That would keep us in the loop too,' said Delacroix.

'Sorry, no. There hasn't been time to do that yet. Maybe soon. For the time being, your Leviathans will just need to remain vigilant while on patrol.'

'Well, you travel with our best wishes,' said Delacroix.

'Thank you. But we won't be travelling alone.'

'Sir?' said Delacroix.

'Many of my pilots got a little experience fighting the locusts at Primo. I've got soldiers and marines who fought there too. But I'd like Major Sarsen and his unit to come along. If we do end up in on-the-ground fighting, his experience would be invaluable.' MacMillan looked from Delacroix to Sarsen.

After a short pause, Sarsen pulled himself to attention. 'Just say the word, sir. I'm ready. My troops will follow your orders.'

'You're the boss,' said Delacroix. 'Major Sarsen and his unit are a key component of the Secundo defence team. But I guess, needs must…'

'Thank you both. Major Sarsen, have your soldiers ready to come aboard ASAP.'

Chapter 9

Earth

Colonel Jamison stepped out of the observer's rear airlock into a stretch of knee-high grass. Unmown since before the virus, the once smart lawn had run wild. He faced two neat rows of single-storey buildings fringed by carefully parked cars and trucks – some civilian, some military. Immediately beyond, and overshadowing all, rose a small, isolated hillock.

In the other direction, beyond the observer and across the lawn was a tall security fence that ran around the entire location, broken only by the gatehouse. His previous reconnaissance team had reported the bodies of three dead guards. A burial detail peeled off toward the gatehouse to take care of them as best they might. They'd be ID'd and buried. He knew there were several more dead in the living quarters; they'd be similarly dealt with. Elsewhere, his people had resorted to mass cremations, just too many bodies to treat with the respect they deserved.

Jamison made direct for the buildings, flanked by half-a-dozen soldiers, all holding their weapons at the ready. They were being careful – the site had been scouted the day before, but elsewhere there had been some instances of individual survivors panicking and opening fire on his teams.

Passing the vehicles and the first row of buildings, he led the way to the second. These were built tight to the hillside. He wasn't fooled by appearances and knew exactly what he was approaching. It was a bunker. The little hillock was manmade, part of the blast defences.

Selecting the middle building, which abutted the hill directly at its rear wall, he tried the front door; it was locked.

'Sergeant, get this door open,' he said, stepping aside.

'Yes, sir.' The sergeant waved forward two men who put their shoulders to the door. It resisted for a few moments then gave. Its lock was largely cosmetic; the real security lay beyond.

Jamison led the squad through an innocuous anteroom, past a tidy reception desk and into a corridor. Striding past several doors to reach the end, he slapped the door in front of him. 'Sergeant!'

Once again, the door was forced open, though this one took far more effort. Eventually it gave to reveal a dark space.

'Lights,' demanded Jamison, and squad members activated hand-held torches. At the end of the darkened room was a staircase almost as wide as the room. It ran down into the hill. 'Forward,' said Jamison, and the squad moved down the steps and beneath the hill. Ahead of them was a steel door, locked tight shut.

He pointed toward a metal locking wheel set in the face of the door.

The sergeant stepped forward to turn it. It was frozen tight. 'Won't budge, sir. Locked solid.'

'Thank you, sergeant. You know what I want.'

'Yes, sir. You two, step forward.' With their rifle butts, two privates struck the door ten blows. Paused, listened and, in the absence of any response, repeated the blows. Several sequences passed with no response.

'Not looking good, sir.'

'We'll see, sergeant. If you'd been locked on the other side of that door all this time you'd want out. And you'd want to be careful too. Keep the men going.'

Five minutes of drumming on the door had brought no hint of a response, when during a regular pause, the faintest clicking carried through the steel door.

'There's a response, sir. Tapping back.'

'Excellent. Where's my signaller?'

'Here, sir,' said a young soldier, stepping forward.

'Got your hand device ready? Good, go to it, soldier!'

The signaller stepped forward to use the tool he'd manufactured with the help of a technician on board the sampler. He pressed it against the door. Running a charge through the device, it vibrated hard against the steel to generate a buzzing sound in the enclosed space. Content, he looked back to Colonel Jamison. 'All set, sir.'

'Go for it. You know what to send. Do it slowly though, I doubt there's a signaller on the other side. It may take them a while to realise you're sending a message.'

The signaller transmitted a series of long and short buzzing sounds as he sent a four letter morse code signal, SAFE:

Dit, dit, dit—dit, dah—dit, dit, dah, dit—dit

He paused then sent it again before waiting for a response – nothing.

'Keep going, man. Twice a minute and listen out carefully for a response.'

For several minutes, there was no coherent response. Then, in one of the pauses, a rhythmic tapping sounded.

'What's the message, soldier?'

'Not sure there is one, sir. They might know what they're trying to send, but I sure as hell don't. Whoever's tapping is no signaller.'

'Okay, they know we're here, and someone will likely have enough basic training to make out your message. Let's leave them to mull things over for a while. Sergeant, let's get out for some fresh air. Detail two men to stand by here, the rest with me.'

***

Sitting on a chair he'd had pulled out from the anteroom, Colonel Jamison enjoyed the still of the morning and waited in hope to see what the bunker would offer up. From his pre-calamity duties, he knew it was one of many secret regional command posts scattered across the country. He hoped it would yield up a senior commander who might assume overall control. Jamison was a good officer and leader of his men – he thrived on organisation and tactical activity – but deep down, he was not so comfortable with strategy and hoped someone suitable for that role might be found.

'Sir, sir! The door seal is opening,' a soldier's shouted voice sounded from within.

Jamison was up at once, hurrying indoors. 'On me, sergeant. Let's see what we've unearthed.'

Hurried steps brought the whole squad back to the steel door, just as the wheel lock completed its opening turn. The door cracked ajar, and Colonel Jamison called out. 'Attention bunker, American military rescue party without. Come forward in safety.'

The bunker door swung open, just enough to let a slim figure squeeze out. Colonel Jamison watched as the combat-fatigued woman emerged. A captain, her features displaying the same gaunt tension Jamison had now seen scores of times on rescued survivors' faces. She raised a hand to shield her eyes from the torchlight that shone in her face.

'Drop that beam, soldier,' said Jamison. 'Come out, captain. Report your status.'

Long days of darkness mixed with spells of chemical light had sensitised her eyes. She continued to blink even as the beam cut away, leaving just the shadowed daylight that reflected down the passageway to the bunker door. Then, giving in to the urgent need, she closed her eyes and pressed the palms of her hands over them, gently rubbing to soothe away the brightness that seemed to linger behind her eyelids.

Jamison waited.

'Sir, Captain Parsons, sir,' said the captain, stepping fully clear of the door. She stumbled very slightly and one of the waiting soldiers reached out a hand to grab her.

'Steady, captain. You look in a bad way. Are you alone?' said Jamison.

'No, sir. I was the bunker's duty officer when it all kicked off. My duty detail were inside, but others were on guard duty or stood down in the accommodation blocks. I'd have been too, but had just been ordered to open the bunker for political visitors on an inspection. We'd only been inside a little while when the technician monitoring the CCTV spotted the soldiers outside going down. It was horrible. I was ordered to lock down immediately. Then shortly afterward, our power dropped out and every piece of electrical technology failed. What's happened, sir?'

'Hell happened, captain. A virus has killed most everyone. Coincided with a mega solar storm that fried every circuit on the planet. Hell!'

'Everyone dead?' The captain slumped to the floor. 'My children? My husband? Dead?'

'I'm sorry. Take a minute, captain. You were lucky to be sealed in the bunker.'

The captain looked at him. 'Lucky? This is lucky?'

The colonel jerked his attention to the bunker door where another figure was suddenly framed deep within the doorway.

'Colonel, did I hear you right? A virus? Why did you have us open up? You have put our lives at risk!' The authoritative voice came from the figure framed in the open doorway. The man jabbed a finger toward the nearest of the colonel's soldiers. 'You, soldier, close this door!' The soldier didn't move.

Jamison peered into the bunker, shone his torch on the figure within, seeing it back away from the bright beam, a shielding hand raised.

'Cut that light, damn it!' said the man. 'Don't you know who I am?'

The voice was familiar, but the colonel couldn't quite place it. In the bunker's gloom, the silver haired, unkempt figure was hard to recall, but the bearing and voice were authoritative, the kind of authority honed by a lifetime of privilege at the top table, the kind the colonel had not heard since before… 'Identify yourself please, sir. There is no further need for concern over the virus; it has been neutralised now.'

'I am Senator Longthorn of the United States Congress. With me are my grandson, Representative Longthorn III, and General Pashman, the vice chairman of the Joint Chiefs of Staff. We were conducting an informal visit to this facility when things went bad.'

Jamison's mind raced. What the hell had a senator and representative been doing in this bunker? And with a four-star general, to boot? That was a lucky break for them. Now given the man's name, recognition came swiftly. Colonel Jamison pulled himself to attention and presented a salute. 'Senator, it's safe to come out, sir.'

Chapter 10

Earth

Senator Longthorn emerged from his cabin on board the sampler and strode along the passage. He paused at another cabin door to collect his grandson. Together, the two men headed for the bridge deck where they found Boucher deep in conversation with one of his technicians. The viewscreen showed a busy scene outside. Two observers were taking off, a third was making ready, while a little way off, a pair of hoppers moved away on another local expedition to collect store goods and water and deliver where they were needed among the now growing communities beyond the base.

'Senator, I trust you're settling in well,' said Boucher, with a nod of acknowledgement toward Longthorn III.

'All good, thank you. A marked improvement on bunker life, that's for certain.'

'Great. Colonel Jamison is coming up shortly. I'm sure he'll want to speak with you.'

'I'm sure he will,' said Longthorn, stepping calmly beyond the craft's commander to stare intently out at the scene below. He was smarting with anger at the lack of respect shown by Boucher and Jamison, both of whom should have been waiting to attend him.

Unaware of any slight, Boucher returned to his earnest conversation with the technician.

'Grandfather, you shouldn't be waiting for anyone,' muttered Longthorn III. 'That's a damned insult – who the hell do they think they are?'

Longthorn nodded and raised his hand slightly to silence his grandson. 'You're right. From what they told us yesterday, it seems you and I are the only national politicians known to have survived. That puts us in a very special situation, but let's hold off a little, keep our powder dry until we better understand everything that's going on.'

Longthorn III stepped closer to his grandfather and spoke quietly. 'Yes, sir. But the disrespect makes my blood boil. And Boucher's a damned Canadian. What's he doing in charge here? This is America. Yet Colonel Jamison seems to be playing second fiddle to him.'

'You're right. But let's wait and see. There's so much we don't understand yet. Ignorance is dangerous. Let's be quiet a little while longer.'

Chapter 11

Perseus Arm: Pardamax d.

Six Leviathans spread across the sky above Pardamax d. When the Hunter squadrons first dropped from the Fold, the planet had come into view, distant, calm, blue and brown,. Careful monitoring of frequencies had confirmed what was expected. The system was abandoned. No radio signals, no space traffic, no locusts. The fleet had quickly closed on the planet and now hung waiting in the sky.

At the surface, a wind gusted off the sea and across the beach to rustle reed grasses that waved and bowed on the dunes behind. Just a little inshore, stunted trees, shaped and pruned by the prevailing weather, stood like sturdy dwarfs braced for whatever would come.

Standing atop the dunes, Jamie could see over the tree-line toward gently rising land beyond. He shielded his eyes to scan the horizon. He saw what his various scouting groups were reporting from every corner. Nothing. No living animals of any size. The planet was almost dead, devoid of any large life forms.

Yes, there were insects, and smaller birds that fed off them. Probably rodents still scurried about safe in their runs below ground. But nothing of substance survived – everything was dead. Eaten.

He looked back at the beach. Dotted in one area were little boats, neat constructions of wood, iron nails and pitch. Once, the planet had supported life capable of intelligent thought, of construction and simple manufacture. He walked down to the nearest boat. There were nets, oars, and what he assumed was a sail stowed neatly on the bottom boards.

In human terms, this society, whatever the creatures had been, would have been late dark ages to early medieval. They wouldn't have stood a chance against the locusts and their technology, not a chance in hell.

His mind darted far away to another coastline, to Reahlagh, his own remote island home, nestled quietly amid the Scottish Western Isles. He guessed those he had left behind were all dead too. It wasn't just a cruel world; it was a cruel galaxy. His thoughts were pulled back to the moment by a voice sounding in his collar-phone.

'Sir, we've found something odd in the settlement. You might want to have a look.'

'On my way,' he replied, and hurried off the beach.

Beyond the dunes, he cut through the stunted trees and emerged into a clearing surrounded by huts. Shutters and doors swung in the wind, banging against their frames in the occasional stronger gusts. There were partially dismembered skeletons scattered all about the village. Far more than might reasonably have been accommodated in the huts. This must have been a feeding station for the locusts – a place where the settlement's inhabitants were gathered and held together with those from the hinterland – for easy feasting.

On the far side of the clearing, an enclosure fitted the bill. Here the locusts would have corralled their prey until ready to feed. One of his soldiers was beckoning from a large hut beyond the corral. It was Sergeant Grant, he'd transferred to Jamie's new command. Almost all the crew of S-3, the crippled Leviathan they had abandoned on Osarus c, had joined too. Crewmates, once again, on board HB-1, but novices no more. All were experienced in alien environments and threats.

'What's up?' said Jamie.

'Inside, sir. It's different.'

Entering the hut, he guessed it was some kind of communal meeting hall of the now extinct indigenous population. The soldiers had activated some portable lights, and he had no problem spotting what was causing concern. The rudimentary furniture had been swept to the side of the space and the earthen floor scraped up to form volcanic cone shapes. Waist-high craters, uniform craters, row upon row, each a man's pace long and the same wide. He peered into the first and winced. Looked into the second, then a third – then he stopped. He knew what would be in the scores of other craters.

'What do you think, sir?' said the sergeant.

'I think this is why we're hunting them.'

'Yes, sir. Evil. Do you think they felt anything?'

Jamie shrugged, turned, and made toward the hall's entranceway from where emanated the sound of an observer landing in the clearing. 'Probably. These locusts are not noted for their mercy. What do I think? I think those poor mites felt a lot.' They reached the entranceway and spotted Ossie hurrying from the landed observer. 'And here's the man who will tell us for sure.'

Ossie, Leviathan HB-1's chief scientist, had been dotting up and down the coastline in response to a series of calls from search parties.

'Ossie. Come see. Tell us what you think,' said Jamie.

The scientist joined them. With a nod of respect to Jamie, he turned to Sergeant Grant. 'What have you got?'

'Inside,' said Grant, leading them all back into the building where the rows of cones spread to the far end of the hall. Ossie was silent for a moment, took a few steps amid the cones then bent. He gingerly prodded about the contents of a cone with his gloved hand while shaking his head.

'Well?' said Jamie. 'What do you think?'

'There's nothing alive here. I've seen this same phenomenon in settlements up and down the coast. Brutal.'

'Is it ceremonial in some way?' said Grant.

Ossie gave a dry laugh. 'Not quite, but the queen's been here for sure. This is a hatchery. I think, once an environment is subdued, the queen is brought down and lays eggs in these earthen shapes. Or maybe the eggs are just carried in and placed. The corralled prisoners are a steady food supply for her and the locusts. Probably, once the food is exhausted and the egg cells filled, the queen moves on to the next location.'

'But that doesn't explain what's left in the cones,' said Jamie.

'No, it doesn't. But this does,' said Ossie. He fished back inside the cone and pulled out the remnant of a little skeleton. 'Judging by the size and shape, it's safe to assume this is the offspring, a child of the skeletons scattered about outside. And look at the limbs – the flesh and skin are mostly gone, but see how there are ligatures still binding the bones.'

'They were alive in there?' said Grant.

'For a while. I'm thinking there's an egg and a living food source is added, bound tight so it can neither get out of the cone nor damage the egg. The living body warms the egg. The egg hatches and a larva emerges. It feasts on the prisoner. A living death.'

'Hell, that's a nightmare,' said Jamie.

Ossie nodded and reached back into the cone. Deeper. He pulled out another skeletal form. Smaller than the first but bound just the same. 'A long nightmare. In some of the other settlements, I've found four, sometimes five, skeletons in any one cone. The larvae must be tended by adult locusts. As the first meal dies, which could take some time, a fresh living captive goes in, and again, and so on.'

'But why?' said Grant. The more he saw of the galaxy, the crueller it seemed.

'That's how they've evolved to reproduce. An extreme case, but insect larvae eating a living host is known back on Earth. Just here, it's on a massive scale.'

'So, Ossie, these larvae couldn't be much more than an arm's length in size. Are we looking for much smaller locusts than we'd expected?'

'I'm not sure. But it wouldn't make sense to produce young immediately before setting off on a long interstellar journey. They might well all starve en route. I think we're looking at a multistage process. Eggs laid, hatch into larvae. Larvae feast and grow. Then larvae pupate, wrapping themselves into cocoons where they lie in diapause, or dormant if you will, waiting for something to trigger their emergence as adults – and I'm thinking, yes, small adults. But based on everything else we know about these monsters, I'd be happy to bet, hungry and very fast-growing.'

Jamie looked through the entranceway and out across the clearing. It must have been hell for those adult life forms imprisoned in the corral. Trapped, waiting to be eaten and all the while assailed by the desperate cries of their own young trapped inside the cones being slowly eaten alive. He made for the sunlight. Sergeant Grant and Ossie followed him.

In the fresh air, he stopped and turned to his companions – all three found it easier to breathe in the clear air. 'That's a brutal process, Ossie,' he said.

'It is, but you know the real tragedy? It's not the individual lives butchered. Almost everything is gone. I doubt there's anything left bigger than a rabbit. They have wiped out millions of years of evolution. Whatever had evolved here is lost forever. Whole gene pools destroyed.'

'Surely, things will recover here, given time?' said Sergeant Grant.

'Oh yes. But nothing of what was. The species that built these huts, cleared the ground, planted those crops, built the boats – they're all gone. The animals they farmed, gone. The wildlife, gone. Whatever these creatures and their society might have become has gone. Destroyed completely. As though they had never been.'

Jamie placed a hand on Ossie's arm. 'Alright, Ossie. We can't undo what's been done.'

'No, we can't. But we can make sure it never happens again elsewhere. We've got to stop these locusts, Jamie. No matter what.'

'Agreed. I need to meet with Colonel MacMillan right now. If they are going to start hatching out a new generation once feeding starts again, we need to catch them before they get that far. This suddenly got a whole lot more urgent.

'You stay down here for now. Learn what you can, but be ready to have all the teams recalled at short notice. I think we will need to move fast.'

Chapter 12

Perseus Arm: Pardamax System

On HA-1, Colonel MacMillan was listening intently to Jamie's report. They had all known the locusts must have a breeding mechanism. Known it had to exist. But the process was as barbaric as every other aspect of the locusts' life cycle.

'So, they've bred. I agree we need to move fast now, breaking their breeding cycle is likely one of the best ways to rid us of the problem for good. But one thing I don't understand: you didn't find anything that might have remotely resembled a pupa nor any juveniles among the cones, or in their combat vessels back at Primo and Secundo. Where are the young?'

Jamie scratched the side of his head. 'Yes, I've thought about that. All I can come up with, and it's pretty scary, is the cone you met was making for Earth, hell for leather. They didn't want the burden of young to care for. So, what you faced back at Secundo and then Primo was a hunting party. What do you think?'

'That would certainly explain the absence of any pupae, which probably mean the other cones are transporting them. Let's leave it for the scientists to sort out. What we do know is one, or both, of the remaining cones must be carrying pupae or juveniles ready to launch a new generation of fear on the galaxy. That can't be allowed to happen.'

'Agreed,' said Jamie.

'Then the plan stands. We know the direction the two cones set off in. I'll take my squadron in pursuit of one. You take Bravo

Squadron and chase down the other. But Jamie, remember, at this stage avoid full-blown conflict at all costs. Locate the locusts and send one of the buoys with a detailed message back to the Pardamax Lagrange point. Then you observe from afar, make sure you know exactly what's going on. If there is a clear opportunity to destroy the cone and its embedded sampler do so before returning here. That will leave the locusts trapped in their locale, until we are in a position to close in with strength and destroy them, at a time of our choosing. Remember, neither squadron is to engage in a full-blown battle alone. When you are ready, return directly here to Pardamax.

'I'll do the same with Alpha Squadron. First one back here will meet their own beacon and hopefully one from the other squadron, which will signal their imminent return too. Once back together, we'll decide which cone to attack first.'

'Colonel, I think we should send occasional beacons, regardless of finding the locusts. If for any reason either of us does not return here, it will make sure the other knows why.'

'Agreed. Now, unless our recon teams have come up with anything more on the planet surface, I think we need to get started.' MacMillan rose and extended his hand. 'Good hunting, and be careful.'

***

Jamie stood on HB-1's bridge. Every vessel in the class was identical, and he felt quite at home. The biggest difference between this trip and his former commission on S-3 was he now commanded a full squadron: three Leviathans. He looked across to where Casper Wills, his former first officer on S-3, stood foursquare, staring intently into the viewscreen while listening carefully to a host of voices that were reporting in his collar-phone.

The grizzled mariner now had his first full command as captain of HB-1. He turned purposefully to look toward Jamie. 'Colonel MacMillan is leading his squadron off, sir. He sends his regards, and we are to fold directly behind.'

'Thank you, captain,' said Jamie. He stroked his sleeve then spoke into his collar-phone. 'This is Major MacAulay aboard HB-1 speaking directly to all Hunter Bravo Squadron crews. Captain Wills will be leading us into the Fold imminently. There will be dangers ahead.

'I know most of you signed on at Primo for science, technology, adventure even, certainly not any sort of conflict. This is something none of us wanted, but if we don't stand now, take on these monsters while we can, they will grow in strength, and there is every risk they will come back at us and overwhelm us. You are aware of what happened down on the planet we've just left. We can't let that level of destruction continue. They must never again have the chance to reach Earth. That is down to us alone. Good luck to each of you; good luck to us all.'

Jamie tapped his sleeve, closing the channel, and looked back at Wills. 'Over to you, captain. This is your craft.'

'Very good, sir.' Wills stepped across the bridge issuing a string of orders. The great screen displayed the action outside where Hunter Alpha was already commencing its fold, the telltale milky discs forming to allow each in turn to slide smoothly into the Fold.

Then a similar disc began to form in front of HB-1. The hunt had begun.

Chapter 13

Perseus Arm: HB-1 in the Fold

'What do you think, Ossie?' said Jamie.

Ossie's fingers drummed on top of the navigation room's LPA. For days, they had been running along the course they knew the cone had taken. Once, they had dropped from the Fold to check on a system that included a life planet. It had been a watery world that sported just a few isolated islands.

Those modest outcrops of land had hosted fauna on a scale to support only small indigenous predators; they offered little to sustain a host of locusts. The seas had been a different matter. They had teemed with life, including many marine mammals – all safely beyond the reach of the locust predators. The locusts had not chosen this planet. Ossie logged their observations – the planet was worthy of a detailed assessment sometime in the future.

Bravo Squadron had pressed on.

'What do I think? I… *we* know the cone has incorporated a sampler that provides the power to transport a fleet of their attack vessels in the Fold. That sampler can only be flown by someone wearing a personalised bio-suit. So, Weeman's compatriot is enslaved and compelled to pilot the craft. If they're in his mind, which they have to be to control him, they must know what he knows. I think they are on a direct route to a substantial food source. To a planet that offers high levels of fauna. That's knowledge Weeman's compatriot would have, and the locusts will have trawled his mind for it. That's where we'll find them.'

'What happens if they changed course in the Fold?' said Captain Wills.

'If they changed course, we've lost them. Unless they broadcast a signal in the Fold, which they would have no reason to do. But I'm confident they have no reason to do anything other than make directly for the nearest feeding planet.'

'Can't you dig into the archives and work out what's available locally?'

'Locally? That has no meaning here. We've already travelled a distance the locusts would have required a hundred Earth years to cover without the sampler's folddrive. To do that under their own steam, they must previously have hibernated for long stretches.'

'So what's next?'

Ossie jabbed a finger toward the LPA. 'The course they set from Pardamax passes another life planet. I think that's their destination. After that, this course will run for a long time before going anywhere near another life planet. It must be this next planet, and if not this one, they could have set off on any number of courses that would have got them to other life planets sooner.'

'How long until we get there?'

'A little over an Earth day.'

'Okay. How does this system lay out?'

Ossie tapped his sleeve and the LPA display changed to reveal a planetary configuration that was becoming quite familiar. A single sun at the centre. About it rotated five planets of various sizes and compositions, from small rocky dwarf planets to gas giants. As normal, they spread out across the system's flat planetary plain as they rotated about their sun.

'The Pelesius System. The third planet, Pelesius d., is the life planet,' said Ossie, pointing it out with an extended finger. 'It's a truly typical system layout. Nothing remarkable at all.'

Jamie and Wills studied the layout carefully.

'From records made during the regular auto sampler visits, we can predict where the planets are on their orbits right now.'

'Just how accurate are the predictions?' said Jamie.

'Pretty good.'

'Okay, Captain Wills, can you put the squadron on standby? We will drop out of the Fold on arrival. Same protocol as before. I want your navigator to calculate an entry point on the far side of the sun from where we expect the life planet to be. We'll hold station there, scan for signals and then send an observer out to reconnoitre the situation. Best remind everyone, once we drop from the Fold there will be complete signal silence. Once the observer returns, there will be a captain's conference on board here.'

'Very good, sir,' said Wills, and he stepped out onto the bridge to get his officers busy.

Chapter 14

Earth

Together, Colonel Jamison and his second in command, Major Coral, stepped off the observer. They hurried across the parade square and into the sampler, making directly for Senator Longthorn's cabin. Jamison tapped on the door.

'Who is it?'

'Colonel Jamison and Major Coral, sir.'

'Enter.'

The colonel swiped open the door and the two officers stepped inside. Their grim faces told Longthorn all he needed to know.

'Tell me, colonel, what did you find?'

'Bad news, senator. I've left a team setting up a satellite operation in DC, but I can confirm the president is dead. As are all his key staff, including General Troy.' The colonel paused to allow Longthorn to react to confirmation of the death of the president and the chairman of the Joint Chiefs of Staff – nothing. 'There are some survivors in Washington as we would expect. Civilians, but no politicians that we could find. I'm afraid we found a lot of your colleagues' bodies. You may be the only surviving senator, sir.

'I see. Tragic. And the House of Representatives, what news there?'

'Equally dark, sir. No survivors found. Perhaps there will be some who were away in their constituencies when the disaster struck. The virus did not kill everyone; we may yet find some, given time, as we widen our rescue mission. We're making steady progress, spreading our net wider every day.'

Longthorn was silent for a long moment, thinking. He came to a decision. He'd played the grateful survivor long enough while he gathered information. Now, this was his moment. 'Could you fetch General Pashman and Representative Longthorn, please, major? I think now's the moment to discuss certain matters relating to governance. Thank you.'

Only five minutes later, Longthorn was sat at the desk in his cabin, his grandson sitting on the bed. Pashman stood to one side and the two more junior officers stood by the door, at once attentive and apprehensive. In the days since he'd rescued the Longthorns, more and more snatched memories of Senator Longthorn's previous public pronouncements had returned to the colonel. With each recollection, his sense of disquiet grew. There were good senators, there were great senators and then there were less inspiring senators; Longthorn fell into the latter category. Jamison wasn't sure about Longthorn III, but he suspected the apple had not fallen far from the tree. There was still the niggling question about how they and General Pashman had found themselves in a safe bunker when everything hit the fan. But right now, they were the most senior leaders America had, so he had to respect them.

Longthorn glanced from the soldiers to his grandson, then back. 'So, I have to say, colonel, you are doing a great job: every day more people brought under our protection, inducted and redeployed as part of the widening rescue mission – admirable work.'

'Thank you, sir. Everyone's doing their bit in hellish circumstances.'

'Yes, agreed. Now, I'm not seeking to apportion blame for this catastrophe – what's done is done, almost doesn't matter how it happened. But it's clear to me that those presently controlling events are the ones closest to the disaster's cause. I'm not very comfortable about that.'

'Well, senator, you've had the backstory from Boucher. I don't think anyone living can be blamed,' said Jamison.

'You're right, of course, colonel,' said Longthorn with a languid wave of his hand. 'These are tragic days, and certainly I for one would never seek to apportion blame for the sake of it. But one day, I trust we'll have an inquiry into these events. Then's the time for identifying culpability, not now.' Longthorn raised his hand sharply, cutting off Colonel Jamison who made to interrupt.

'Colonel, please. Believe me when I say I'll be delighted if an investigation eventually delivers a clean bill of health to all those involved in this near extinction event. For now, we need everyone on board pulling together. Me, you, Congressman Longthorn, General Pashman, Major Coral. Boucher too. Everyone.

'That brings me to my first point of concern. Why is a French-Canadian heading this regional hub? Why not you? Why not any American? This is America; we are the most powerful country in the world. At the very least, the recovery operation here should be headed by an American.'

'It's just how it is, sir. The teams from Primo's own crew are drawn from a number of countries. We just happened to get Boucher; other regional hubs established elsewhere in America do have Primo Americans in charge,' said Jamison.

'Do they, though, colonel? Really in charge?'

'Oh yes, senator. I know – I've visited some of the other hubs in person. Very much American commanders. But that doesn't matter. It appears Primo never makes any distinctions based on nationality. They're concerned only that the best person is appointed for a job.'

Jamison glanced toward the bed where Longthorn III was sat. The representative had just released a dry laugh.

'The nub of it, colonel,' Longthorn III interjected, 'is who decides who's the right person for the job? An anonymous committee? A bunch of foreigners? And who is this Brigadier Smith-Brown? Some Brit, based in the UK and organising the rescue of America? I don't think that's right. Do you?' Longthorn III looked toward his grandfather.

'He's right, colonel,' said Longthorn. 'No way any outsiders should be organising American affairs.'

'But sir, Boucher is doing a great job here. He's working only to rescue survivors – American survivors. Helping us put infrastructure in place – we're getting better every day. We make a great team, hand in glove. And anyway, even if we wanted to change the controlling structure, my people can't fly the observer craft, drive the hoppers, can't work the equipment here on board the sampler. There is nothing we can do about that.'

'So we are led to believe, colonel.' Longthorn pulled out his cigar box and paused to light up. Puffed vigorously, then drew long and slow. He blew the smoke out in a streaming cloud. 'So we are led to believe.'

'I don't see what you are getting at senator. Everyone is working flat out for the common good – everyone,' said Jamison.

'Colonel, I agree. Today, saving people and creating structure are all that matters. You, Major Coral and Boucher are doing a fine job. It's noted. But following the death of the president and General Troy of the Joint Chiefs, House Representative Longthorn, General Pashman and myself are the sum of American political, civil and military leadership and control. American officers have a duty to protect America's position in this troubled world. You do agree? Or would you prioritise foreign powers over America?'

'Sir, I am an American officer – you know where my loyalty lies,' said Jamison.

'I do, colonel, and I'm glad you recognise that too. Knowledge and technology are the tools of power. I'm worried that this new technology is being distributed too widely, a policy that may one day put American interests in peril.'

'Senator! There's been a major international conflict. Missiles fired, a devastating plague, all our electronic technology wiped out by a solar storm; the atmosphere is closed off, and there are some extra-terrestrial threats. American interests must be exactly those of the whole world, surely?'

'Thank you, colonel. You're a soldier. When I want a strategic geo-political overview from you, I'll ask. Meantime, remember you are a servant of the United States of America. As of now, I am America's surviving senior politician. I, together with able assistance from our sole surviving member of the House of Representatives, and General Pashman of the Joint Chiefs, represent the sum total of the strategic leadership of America. Do you understand...? Do you understand, colonel?'

'Yes, sir, I do. But the whole Primo operation is commanded by General Dower – he's American, through and through. There's Colonel MacMillan and many more. They will have America's interests at heart, for sure.'

'Americans, yes. But sadly, together with others, British and God knows who else now, they are the very people who so spectacularly let us down. Listen, colonel, now's not the time, but when it comes, I expect you to do your duty. Is that clear?'

'No, sir, not clear. Are you suggesting a change in the control of rescue efforts across America?'

The room fell silent as Longthorn subjected Colonel Jamison to an extended glare.

'More than that, colonel. I intend to seek an urgent meeting with this Brigadier Smith-Brown. I believe he should be subordinated to my command.'

'I see, sir. Are you sure that's the right thing to do?'

'Colonel! When Senator Longthorn wants your opinion, he'll ask for it,' said Longthorn III, standing abruptly. 'You are a servant of the United States; you do the senator's bidding.'

Colonel Jamison stiffened. 'Are you sure the constitution says that, sir?'

'The senator is the only senior politician remaining. The constitution could not be expected to cover this eventuality: intercontinental war, plague, a solar storm, alien entanglements and a closed atmosphere. In these circumstances, Senator Longthorn is the only candidate to lead America at this moment.'

'What about democracy?'

'Colonel, the senator and I love our democracy. We serve it unswervingly. Under the circumstances, the only legitimate vote we Americans can point to is from the last election – the term of which is still current, of course. If you think different and can organise a legitimate vote by the people, go ahead. But don't think to divert any resources from saving our citizens. Is that clear?'

Jamison recognised the hopelessness of holding his position. 'Yes, sir.'

Longthorn blew out another long stream of smoke. 'Colonel, I know you'll do what's needed. This conversation is of the highest confidentiality. I want you to make sure your chain of command is stalwart and await my instructions. Now, I need to request a meeting with Smith-Brown. You can go.'

As the cabin door slid shut behind the retreating officers, Longthorn looked from General Pashman to his grandson and drew again on the cigar. 'Well, gentlemen, what do you think?'

'I think Colonel Jamison may prove a weak link,' said Longthorn III.

'Yes, pity. He's done a good job organising his people and spreading the recovery work, but he seems a little overly scrupled for my liking.'

'Soft. God knows how he made colonel,' said Pashman.

'It takes all sorts. But did you notice Coral?'

'He stayed silent, not a peep,' said Pashman.

'Right, but his body language was screaming. He's our man – I'm sure of it. We'll have to speak with him. I think, if Jamison proves a weak link, Coral could fit the bill.'

Chapter 15

Perseus Arm: Pelesius System

The observer scout craft had returned to HB-1 with confirmation that the Pelesius System was their target. The locusts were here. Shortly afterward, Leviathan HB-1's hangar door swung shut behind the two observer craft that ferried the captains of HB-2 and HB-3 to the squadron's flagship.

Captain Wills greeted his opposite numbers and ushered them into the Leviathan's navigation room. Jamie, Ossie and the scout craft's pilot looked up from the flickering LPA.

'Captains, welcome,' said Jamie, straightening. 'Come right over. The lieutenant here has done a good job. He got the information we needed.'

The captains nodded approval. 'Well, what have you found?' said Stewart, captain of HB-3.

'I'm afraid it's exactly what you might have expected. A cone in orbit around Pelesius d. but then the unexpected, only a handful of their combat vessels registering on our sensors.'

'Why so few?' said Stewart.

'Assuming this cone is similar to the one we engaged previously, it would have been carrying upward of three hundred combat vessels, but in fact, Ossie here thinks it would be considerably higher. Some might be in the moon's shadow or on the far side of the planet. But the only reason so few are showing is that the overwhelming majority have likely entered the planet's atmosphere and started their takeover process,' said Jamie.

Stewart jabbed at the LPA. 'Did you detect any indigenous signals traffic?'

Ossie shook his head. 'Nothing. Only locust communications. If there is intelligent life on that planet, it has not yet developed far enough to employ radio.'

'It'll be a walkover for them on the surface,' said Stewart, 'but that cone is almost defenceless. Shall we hit it quick?'

'We must, but let's be careful,' said Jamie. 'Experience tells us the locusts can rally fast enough when a cone is threatened. As soon as our cover is blown, there will be swarms of them coming up from the surface. This is what we'll do…'

***

The space around Pelesius d. was quiet. The cone slowly orbited the planet. Locked deep within the cone was a giant sampler. Just half-a-dozen combat vessels were attached to the cone or hovered attentively close to the sampler. Everything else was still.

Once again, and as close as the navigator dared, HB-1 slipped quietly from folded space – this time tight behind the system's third planet, exactly on the opposite side of the planet from where they calculated the cone would be.

The Leviathan's hangar door swung open, and two warbirds flew out, each sporting their mothership callsign and individual combat craft designation: HB-1:C1 and HB-1:C2. Radio silence observed, they headed away, quickly settling into an orbit, while HB-1 set a course to get above the plain of the system and beyond the orbit of the outermost planet as fast as it could, allowing it to move safely into the Fold when the moment came.

As the retreating Leviathan broke the planetary horizon it became visible to the cone on the opposite side of the planet. For just a moment, Jamie thought they had not been noticed. Then the dawdling combat vessels attending the cone shook into life. Three immediately broke away and began chase. He smiled.

'That's halved the cone's defences. Captain Wills, ease back the speed. With a bit of luck, they might just think this is a routine auto sample craft that they can chase down and capture.'

'Very good, sir. One quarter ahead it is.'

Both men watched intently as the locust vessels slowly closed on their Leviathan.

'Any closer and they'll likely chance firing off a missile to stop us, sir,' said Wills.

'Agreed. Best pick up the speed a little, keep drawing them on.'

Almost at once, the Leviathan moved ahead, establishing a safe gap, retreating while still playing a broken-wing gambit. The locust combat vessels powered on determinedly.

'What about the warbirds?' said Jamie.

'They're tight against the atmosphere. We've lost them in the curve of the planet, sir.'

'That means they will become visible to the cone on the far side just about now.'

'Yes, sir. Then it'll hit the fan, for sure. Sparks and his team are monitoring every channel. We'll know as soon as our craft are spotted – the comms console will light up like a Christmas tree.'

Jamie nodded, silently wished his warbirds Godspeed, and stood quietly waiting. Everything that could be done had been done. Now he was a spectator.

***

Ali, the lead warbird's co-pilot chanced a glance backward to check the little LPA located behind the crew seats. 'Cresting the planet, Jill. You should see the cone any moment now.' He turned to face forward again as she acknowledged.

'Got it… Holy Moly, it's a big boy!' She glanced toward her co-pilot. 'Way bigger than the one we destroyed back at Primo.'

'Nearly twice the size.' Ali was frantically trying to calculate what that meant for combat vessels. He gave up as the open airwave receiver crackled into life and the locusts aboard the cone transmitted a warning. 'They've spotted us!'

'So I hear,' said Jill, tapping open a channel. 'All stations, all stations. This is C1, we're in play. Radio silence ends. C2, follow me in.'

'Roger that, C1. Wilco.'

Jill accelerated the warbird, making a beeline for the cone. Close to her starboard quarter, the second warbird mirrored her, maintaining its position in formation.

'Two minutes to contact,' reported Ali.

'Arm two missiles. Lock on the cone's nose. If they hit the framework, it'll disrupt its movement. If they go through the frame gaps, there's a chance of a direct hit on the sampler itself.

'C2, you do the same. Four missiles on the nose will likely do some damage for starters.'

'One minute to contact, missiles locked on target,' said Ali.

'Fire!' said Jill, and she watched with satisfaction as her missiles were joined by a salvo from C2. The four missiles streaked away from the warbirds making direct for the cone.

The cone had been settled in orbit with no expectation of conflict. Its manoeuvrability functions simply could not react in time. Two missiles connected with the nose, which was immediately obscured from sight in a flash of light. The other two sailed through the open lattice framework of the cone and kept going.

Both missed the sampler within and continued on. An explosion signalled a contact with the far side of the cone's framework. The fourth missile passed through the lattice and drove on toward the atmosphere where it would soon burn up or explode harmlessly.

'Winged it,' reported Jill. 'Now for the kill. We'll arc round the cone, come in from its open aft end and hit the sampler with everything we've got.'

'On you now,' reported C2, following Jill as her craft rushed past the cone. 'I see bandits breaking off the back of the cone. Three bandits.'

'We see them too. I'll take them on, C2; you continue with the mission. Hit the sampler. Keep hitting it until it's done.'

'Wilco.' C2 veered off, its course describing an arc that would bypass the three locust vessels and bring it in behind the struggling cone.

Jill stared ahead at the locust combat vessels as they rushed to assemble in attack formation. 'Too close for missiles already. Activating laser now.'

A beam of light jetted out from the nose of the warbird. It swept left and right, precisely tracking Jill's eyeline. 'Here we go!' she said as the locusts powered toward her.

The lead locust vessel cleaved in two under the laser's burning touch. She registered locusts spilling out into the void. One or two sported their great domed helmets and glided off quite composed. Most, unprepared and helmetless, flailed briefly in the cold vacuum as they died.

The second vessel lost half its nosecone to the laser and, with it, controlled navigation. In a feat of courageous piloting skills, its captain cut one wing engine, the other continuing to power forward, driving the crippled vessel into a manic turn that brought it so close to Jill's warbird it burred against the hull, slightly altering the warbird's direction of travel.

Still focused on attack, Jill looked about to locate the third locust. It was closing fast on a suicide run. It had fired a raft of missiles that proved just a futile gesture of aggression – they were past the warbird long before any target detection system could lock on. For the locust combat vessel, there was no such remission as the laser beam swept across it. The bridge area vapourised. As Jill maintained her gaze, the vessel split in two and the threat was over.

'Bandits down. Clear space. C2, report your status.'

'Hello, C1. Nice work. We thought it was getting a bit too close to call for a moment. We are astern of the cone now. Clear sight of the sampler within, about to launch missiles.'

'Go for it. We'll come about and join you. Give it everything you've got.'

It only took moments for Jill to bring her craft alongside C2. By that time, it had fired two double salvos directly at the sampler. Each had hit home, and sections of its hull were fractured with flames visible within. C1 fired its own salvo to complement more from C2. Soon, a dozen missile strikes had wrought havoc on the rear of the giant sampler, but locked within the cone, it still retained some integrity.

As the first shroud of blast debris began to clear and filter away through the cone's gaps, the crews' initial enthusiasm for their task began to fade.

'It's not enough,' said Jill. 'Why won't it break up?'

'The cone is holding it in place, but it's burning. That should be enough; they'll never power that up again, surely?' called C2's pilot.

'You'd think,' said Jill. 'But the order was precise. It must be destroyed.'

'So what do we do?'

'We'll get inside the cone. It's connected to the sampler by arm struts. Use our lasers to cut them away and the sampler will crash up against the inside of the cone – breaking itself and the cone permanently.'

'Jill, look.' Ali was directing her toward the LPA.

'What have you got?'

'Locust combat vessels coming up through the atmosphere.'

'Hell, they're reacting faster than I'd hoped. How long have we got?'

'Three, maybe four, minutes before the first of them get here,' said Ali.

'Look at them all,' sounded C2. 'Zeus! How many of those monsters are down there?'

'More than we could cope with,' said Jill. A single glance into the LPA had told her enough. Too many to count. 'That's a real swarm. Let's do this now and get away while we still can. C2, you go inside the cone framework to port, we'll go in to starboard. We'll burn the forward stabilising struts first, fall back to burn the rearmost ones then get out at once. Let's move. Now.'

The two warbirds moved quickly ahead. Like two raisins dropped into a mixing bowl, they were dwarfed by the enormous cone. The warbirds parted company, with the sampler between them. C2 was out of sight, but Jill could see light glowing from its laser reflecting off the inside of the cone. Then her own laser triggered, and its bright light banished the distant glow.

She made short work of cutting the forward strut. Then, retracing her movements, she lasered the rearmost strut. It burned apart quickly. Satisfied, she retreated, exiting the cone. The sampler was already beginning to drift within the cone. It would smash into it soon enough.

Nudging clear, she noted with satisfaction that none of the rising fleet of locusts was in range yet.

'How's it looking Ali?'

'Looking good. We'll get clear well ahead of the locusts.'

'Great, C2. Close on me and we'll exit together then run for the hills.'

'Wilco, C1.'

As Jill's warbird turned away from the crippled cone, she saw C2 emerging from its other side.

'I see you, C2. Let's go now.'

The two warbirds accelerated clear from the cone's tail just as the newly loosed sampler bumped into the cone's inner side. The collision was not great, but with no power source nor means to counterbalance the effect of the collision, both lurched to the side and slightly down. The wrecked cone, trailing an exhaust stream from the burning sampler within, began a slow and inexorable response to gravity – their orbit began to decay.

Rising from the surface, locust attack vessels swarmed about it unable to dock or affect the trajectory. With each orbit, the mass of scrap would pass lower, and its descent would accelerate. Jill's LPA estimated only four unalterable hours until the atmosphere's resistance burned at the metal framework and hull, dragging sampler and cone together down in an uncontrolled atmospheric dive – mission accomplished.

Far off in open space, Jill called a halt to the escape run. Her warbird was not responding as it should. She struggled, then accepted Ali's analysis that the almost forgotten hull scrape had done more than cosmetic damage. Bit by bit, she was losing control. Though the locusts had quickly given up the chase to attend their cone, if a locust patrol should come across the warbird now, it was a sitting duck.

'Hello C2, this is C1. We've a problem. Must stop now. Come alongside us. We're going to need to abandon ship, collision damage.'

'Hunter Bravo-One, did you hear that?'

A moment's delay was ended by Captain Wills' voice: 'Message received C1. Have you any injuries?'

'No. All good here. We will transfer to C2 and destroy my craft. Then rendezvous with you as planned beyond the outer planet.'

'Roger that C1. Be aware we did not engage the three chasing locusts. Left them far behind. Just keep a wary eye out for them. You've done a great job. Hurry back.'

Chapter 16

Earth

The lights within the LPA were churning as they had been for some time. Celine waited impatiently for them to settle. The regular LPAs were standard on board every Leviathan; they were fast and efficient but struggled with the biggest of calculations. This was a big calculation. *Oh for thirty minutes on one of Primo's Goliaths.*

'Any answers yet?' asked Brigadier Smith-Brown.

'Shouldn't be long now, brigadier.'

'Well, keep me posted – good news is at a premium.'

'Yes. I just wish we could establish more regional hubs, start to rescue more people. All the places we can't reach, they will be dying. Hopeless.' Celine gave what was quickly becoming a trademark shrug.

'We're doing what we can, and you've delivered more than anyone could have expected of you. Thank you for that, Celine. It's going really well across North America. Here in Britain, we're making steady progress, and things are progressing in the Antipodes and much of Europe. We're getting more and more people into the system; they are helping, networking, supporting. Survivors know there is hope. But we just don't have enough crew with bio-linked suits to run transport, equipment, LPAs – everything we need to support expansion. There are whole swathes of the world still left untouched, and right now, it's beyond us; we simply don't have the capacity.'

'I know it, and I'm sorry. The thing that would change the game right now is the capability to create bio-linked suits but that's just beyond me. It's absolutely another Primo task. If I could, I would – you know that.'

The brigadier nodded. 'I guess we should all be pleased with the progress made so far but not be complacent. Where we have been able to place sample craft as regional hubs the rescue effort has taken off. People really want to network and help.

'Talking of which, you know the senator who survived? Longthorn. He's asked for a conference. An observer craft will have him and two or three others here in the morning. You should attend.'

'Great. I don't recall him, but then I've never bothered much with politics. It might be nice if I could get the chance to go home for a bit too…' She bit her lip gently. She already knew from one of the regular reports coming from Boucher's regional hub that none of her family had been found alive. 'Then again, I've a lot to do here.'

The brigadier understood and nodded. His silence was sympathetic. He turned to go and stopped short as the LPA's churning lights suddenly slowed and settled into some form of rhythmic order. 'What's happening?' he said, turning back to Celine.

Celine stared into the display, carefully tweaking the scale and display as she circled round. Looking up, she smiled. A warm smile, not the social nicety variety that she and many others so frequently forced onto their faces.

'Well?' said Smith-Brown.

'Progress. Real progress at last. Look!' She jabbed a hand into the display, lights darted away from and around her moving limb before settling back to their previous positions.

'What am I looking at?'

She pulled her hand out of the LPA and swept it across the top. 'See, this half of the display shows the density and distribution of debris through the lower atmosphere when we started the clearance work. This half shows the debris as of yesterday. We've deflected a huge amount. It's reduced by almost a third.'

The brigadier beamed. 'Celine! Your plan is working.'

'Better than I'd ever hoped,' she said. 'It seems clearing from below is quicker and more efficient than Lily's original proposal to clear from above. But there's a long way to go. The sampler fleet have been round and round in the lower atmosphere, but it's really not like ploughing snow – clear it and it's gone. Every piece of debris is in a unique orbit, a few of which are nice, neat circles at a set height

– we got them first time around. But most are following their own unique elliptical orbits, so much of the time they're not at the altitude we're clearing. It will take many more circuits to be confident we've got it all.'

'How long? How long to get the atmosphere cleared?'

'Sorry, brigadier, I can't speculate yet. It's real progress but still early days. We've got the easy stuff so far, and there's a long way to go. But it is definitely thinning.'

'Keep the samplers at it, Celine. That's all you can do for now.'

'Well, I'm wondering. As the debris field thins some more, perhaps we'll get a signal through the atmosphere to the warbirds that were arriving as we came down. At least we'd know for sure if the locusts have been cleared away and it's safe to rebuild the tube.'

'Keep checking. You didn't say how long. Even a guestimate?'

'Until the atmosphere is cleared with our snowplough method and safe for navigation? I really don't know. Just can't say.'

Chapter 17

Perseus Arm: Pardamax System

Leviathan HB-1 was accompanied by HB-2 on arrival at the Pardamax Lagrange point. There, they found their own signal beacon and a second one from Colonel MacMillan's Alpha Squadron: they too had found their quarry. HB-3, meanwhile, with Captain Stewart at the helm, had been left behind to continue monitoring the activity of those locusts stranded in the Pelesius System.

It was only a day later that two of the Alpha Squadron craft arrived at the rendezvous. MacMillan, like Jamie, had left a solitary Leviathan monitoring the locust swarm they had traced to the Prenar system.

A senior officers' conference was convened immediately on-board HA-1. MacMillan looked about his officers. 'Well, it seems Bravo has been successful in trapping one locust swarm in the Pelesius System while we have done the same with ours in Prenar. It seems neither swarm considered they might be being hunted, so thought there was no risk to them or the cones – big mistake. I think we can put their complacency down to generations of learned impunity. It's a great start to the campaign. Yes, Bravo Squadron lost one warbird, but no casualties. Two cones for one warbird? We'd gladly take that every time.

'Now let's consider what we know. We can outfly them, we can outshoot them, but they still present a real threat, particularly in close-quarter dogfights where they have repeatedly shown their willingness to sacrifice a combat vessel to take out a warbird. So, the question is, which swarm do we hit first?'

'Colonel, I've had a look at readouts from both expeditions. It's clear our assumption about all three cones being similar in size is just wrong,' said Ossie. 'When you first flew past that cone here at Pardamax, we thought it was a solitary entity, cone one of one. But they had captured and repurposed three sample craft for three cones. I think what we first encountered was the third cone preparing to leave. The other two had already departed.'

'Okay, but what does that tell us?'

'It tells us we know nothing about what a normal cone size is. Based on the number of locust combat vessels that swarmed up from the atmosphere when we attacked the cone at Pelesius d., I'd consider it quite possible they number about six hundred combat vessels. Way more than were carried on the first cone.

'For the numbers within the other swarm at Prenar? The cone encountered there is less impressive in scale than at Pelesius but bigger than the original cone we destroyed beyond Primo: perhaps five hundred combat vessels.'

MacMillan gave a slight nod and looked around the room. 'Thank you, Ossie: noted. So, we have two targets. Both are trapped in their respective systems without a folddrive, neither can run far even if they choose to. I must decide which we attack first. Does anyone have anything to add?'

The captain of HB-2 spoke up. 'Do we know what the locusts are doing now? Since we hit the cones, they will know a threat exists; they must be preparing for a greater attack. What about their queens? Did we destroy them on board the samplers?'

'We have received further beacon reports from the Leviathans we left on duty at each system. In both cases, the locusts milled about the space debris for a while before dropping back into the atmosphere. In both cases, a handful of combat vessels have remained in space. Likely maintaining a lookout duty. I'll let the scientists talk about the queen situation. Ossie?'

'Thank you, colonel. While our warbirds were in proximity to their respective target planets, and prior to destruction of the cones and samplers, automatic data-sharing took place between the warbirds and the ensnared samplers. We are certain that each originally had a queen on board and both queens had left their respective craft for the surface before we attacked.'

One captain jerked his head back slightly and tutted. 'So, they survived then. Pity.'

'Yes. We can't speculate how the locusts would have reacted had the queens been killed, but there we are – they're still in play. Sadly, both Weeman's colleagues were captives aboard the respective samplers. They died in our attacks,' said Ossie, turning to look at Colonel MacMillan.

'Not so sad. We all know the conditions they suffered. It will have been a mercy for them,' said the colonel.

A circle of grim-faced heads nodded solemn agreement. Everyone knew how the locusts had overpowered the little aliens. The transferred data reports told of how they had been overpowered and physically controlled by locusts' antennae sliding into eardrums or eye sockets to engage with aural or optic nerves to assimilate their brains, to control and manipulate – pure torture. Exactly as happened on the first cone. The locusts kept their victims alive and enslaved in agony on the bridge of their own craft in order to control their movements and, through their bio-suits, pilot the samplers.

'Yes, a relief for them, certainly. But with their passing, the last opportunity to engage with Weeman's race is gone. We are truly on our own now. We can only learn more of the ancient technology by our own efforts. Meanwhile, the locusts have probed directly into those pilots' minds. Let's not kid ourselves – they know more about our technology than we do,' said Ossie.

'Thankfully, they can't operate the technology directly without bio-suits,' said Jamie. 'Colonel, I'm ready to go for either attack option. However, I favour attacking the locusts at Prenar first.'

'Noted. The smaller cone; why so?' said MacMillan.

'We have as strong a force here as we could reasonably assemble. We know from experience we can outgun them, and I'm confident, but they do significantly outnumber us. If we first attack the larger swarm at Pelesius and fail, for any reason, that will leave the surviving locusts of that battle to breed and expand unhindered. And the other swarm at Prenar would be untouched.

'That's two surviving swarms. Without our technology, we might assume it would take them hundreds of years to spread to threaten Earth directly, perhaps thousands. But now they know about our sample craft, and know they can sometimes commandeer them, it's a certainty they'll try again. They're very clever, so there will always be a risk of them eventually bypassing the need for bio-suits; the samplers work on autopilot while travelling the spiral arms – if the locusts manage to override that autopilot, they could turn up at Earth any time.'

MacMillan nodded. 'Good points, Jamie. But why does that determine we hit the smaller cone first?'

'Hitting the smaller first offers a better certainty of destroying a swarm. During which we can learn and hone tactics before going on to attack the bigger one.' Jamie stopped talking and looked from MacMillan around the gathered captains. Several were nodding in agreement. War was seldom democratic, but this field of combat was new, and MacMillan wanted all his best minds to contribute.

'Thank you, Jamie. Does anyone else have a view?'

A brief silence was broken by Captain Wills. 'Do Science have any inkling about the tactics the locusts might use? Will they come up to meet us or fight on the ground?'

'We have no idea,' said Ossie. 'At the battle for Secundo, they seemed equally happy to fight on the ground or airborne.'

'Correct,' said MacMillan, 'but both there and at Primo, the locusts were on the attack. What their defensive tactics are we have no idea. Any more contributions?' Macmillan looked about the group. Silence.

'Fine. Return to your vessels. I will take a little time to weigh up our options and we will then move on one swarm or the other. For now, thank you all, and make sure all your crews and equipment are ready for imminent action.'

Chapter 18

Earth

The observer touched down on the flattened green beyond the Leviathan. Its stern airlock opened and Senator Longthorn emerged. He paused to look up at the monstrous vessel. He'd heard talk of them before Earth's collapse, seen pictures, but seeing a Leviathan for real was breathtaking. He composed himself before turning to speak to Longthorn III, who was immediately behind him and quite visibly awed by the sight.

'Well, here we are. Let's find out what's really going on.' He stepped onto the grass and reached a hand toward the approaching Brigadier Smith-Brown.

'Welcome, senator. Welcome to you all. Delighted to meet you in person. I'm Brigadier Smith-Brown. I thought we'd meet here and walk in. We don't want to do anything to slow down distribution. The landing bays are constantly in use for recovery work: funnelling out stores and newly manufactured power units and electrical equipment. Come this way, please.'

Longthorn III scowled behind the brigadier's back. *This man didn't have his priorities right. Observing the niceties with a political delegation from the world's most powerful country should have taken precedence over any routine works.*

Beside him walked Major Coral, saying nothing but looking with excitement at the huge craft and the buzz of observer craft coming and going about the open side hangars.

'You know, brigadier,' said Longthorn, 'I'd thought the sample craft used to support the regional hubs were enormous. But my, this Leviathan is in another league altogether. It's a true monster.'

'It is, senator. Of course, it's not designed for sitting on the ground. Its design is perfected for deep-space travel.'

'Well, it's welcome here today, for certain.'

'Come on inside, everyone. Senator, I've allocated personal rooms for each of you. I thought you might appreciate a couple of hours' break, before we talk.'

'Thank you, brigadier, that's good of you. These observer craft certainly move fast; crossing the Atlantic now is not the long flight I'm familiar with from before. But nonetheless, a chance to gather ourselves is welcome.'

***

Two hours later, Smith-Brown was comfortably settled at the end of a conference table in one of the Leviathan's workrooms. To his right sat Celine, to his left, Captain Harding.

'Brigadier, do we have an agenda? I'm not sure what the purpose of this visit is,' said Harding. He was careful to mask his irritation at being called away from facilitating the Earth-wide rescue plan, the heart of which was his Leviathan.

'Senator Longthorn was… still is a senior American politician. He's due respect for that. America will be central to Earth's recovery. If he can help focus efforts, I'm sure he will. Celine, what do you think?' said the brigadier.

'Well, I don't know Senator Longthorn. Nor his grandson. I can't shed any light, never having followed politics. Incidentally, isn't it amazing that two from the same family survived? That must be a really unusual thing. I'm guessing they'll have political leadership skills that will be useful as the recovery gets underway.'

The brigadier nodded. 'Perhaps, that would be useful. Let's hope so…' His voice drifted off as he looked down and intently scanned a sheet of old-school handwritten notes he'd prepared. He folded it away into his pocket. 'The senator requested the meeting, so I expect he'll have an agenda.' Smith-Brown's demeanour was calm, but inside he had a nagging anxiety. He knew the trouble Longthorn had caused General Dower in the days before Earth's politics went into meltdown. *Why him? Any senator but him.*

Trust was a common and essential commodity between the Leviathan's crew and the many Earthbound survivors who had enthusiastically joined up in support of the global rescue mission. But Smith-Brown knew of Longthorn's previous machinations. He couldn't share his concerns with his subordinates, so he kept quiet. *Perhaps Longthorn will have changed in the light of recent events?*

The door slid open, and the senator entered.

Freshened up, he displayed all the airs of a senior statesman. Choosing the seat at the opposite end of the table, he sat facing Smith-Brown. Longthorn III and General Pashman sat to his either hand. Major Coral stood behind the general's seat.

Pleasantries complete, the brigadier gave his visitors a full briefing of progress and future plans for expanding the recovery mission, for regaining access through the high atmosphere and, with that, access to the resources that Primo could channel down to boost the rescue – provided the locusts were actually defeated. After an extensive Q&A, the senator seemed content. He leaned back, produced his trademark cigars and made a half-hearted gesture of offering them round the table.

'Senator, people don't normally smoke on the Leviathans or any other craft,' said Celine. 'It's unhealthy.'

Longthorn nodded while selecting a cigar from his pack. He examined it intently. 'Thank you, young lady. I believe in today's climate, *unhealthy* has whole new degrees of meaning. And I for one will not take a health lesson from one of the scientists that allowed a killer virus to sweep our globe.' He lit the cigar and puffed contentedly as Celine stared ferociously down at her clenched hands.

Senator Longthorn spoke directly to the brigadier. 'Events have been awful across the globe. It seems your Primo team has had quite the adventure too. I'm impressed with your rescue and recovery efforts so far, and clearly there's a long way to go. Of course, there's a lot of management and coordination work still to do. I know you are aware, brigadier, that I was put in full charge of the Primo project shortly before the wheels came off.'

Still outwardly calm, inside the brigadier tensed. *Here it was.*

'As such, and I'm sure you'll agree, under that authority, today I remain in sole command of the whole Primo project, and by extension you, this Leviathan and the whole rescue and recovery mission.'

The brigadier remained tight-lipped. Longthorn III could not contain a smile, almost a smirk, reading silence for acceptance. His grandfather continued.

'You've done well, brigadier, a good start for which I'm sure we will all want to thank you. But now's the time for a more considered, a more politically strategic… a more holistic perspective. Now is the appropriate moment for me to relieve you of your stand-in duties and assume full control—'

'It was all the damn politics that caused this problem. We've been mopping up the mess ever since,' said Captain Harding, his voice calm but the statement firm.

Longthorn III leaned forward to rebut Harding's observation but was cut short by his grandfather's hand gripping his forearm.

The old senator delivered a languid smile. 'Captain, err, Captain Harding, isn't it? Well, captain, you too have done a good job to date. I admire your efforts, really, I do. But this task is well beyond a captain, even the captain of a ship as big as this.' He raised his hands and glanced about the room. 'I'll thank you, captain, to remember what you are and who I am. Authority sits where authority aught, is that clear?

'Now, brigadier, where were we?'

'I believe you were asserting a seniority claim over my command.'

'Exactly, brigadier. Now I'm happy you should continue in post, under my control and direction. And of course, with your diligent Captain Harding ably assisting you. For now, I think only two immediate changes are required. One, I require you to move this Leviathan to the United States from where I will be better able to oversee and direct operations. And two, I consider your dispersed approach to rescue is misguided. All as yet uncommitted resources and any further regional hubs to be deployed should be refocused on the United States…'

The sudden silence was broken by Celine's shocked intake of breath, quickly followed by Harding's anguished protest.

'Impossible! We've been building up regional hubs across Europe and Australia, New Zealand. I've got teams just ready to commence opening up in North Africa and the Middle East. Then still further east. You can't pull support for the hubs we've committed to installing – it would be a betrayal of the people we have linked with. And delaying support elsewhere is barbaric. Just plain barbaric.'

'Captain, watch your language,' said Longthorn III sharply. 'Right now, Senator Longthorn is the elected democratic leader of the free world – your leader. You treat him with the respect he deserves.' Longthorn III banged his fist on the table. 'Is that clear?'

Harding didn't flinch, held the young congressman's gaze for a moment, and turned deliberately to look at the brigadier. 'What are your orders, sir?'

The brigadier was gazing up; he let out a long slow breath while slowly shaking his head. He pursed his lips and made eye contact with Senator Longthorn.

'Brigadier Smith-Brown, I suggest you clip your captain's wings before I do it for you,' said the senator.

'Senator, I and all my crew recognise that you may be the most senior surviving American politician. That automatically accords you a level of respect and, where appropriate, deference from us as demonstrated by the granting of this meeting…'

Longthorn was nodding along in agreement with the brigadier's words. He took a celebratory draw on his cigar and slowly expelled the smoke – his head angled very slightly to one side, ensuring the smoke carried toward Celine.

The brigadier continued. 'It is reasonable to recognise you are undoubtedly a key political leader in America today. Indeed, the nearest thing to a legitimate elected leader. I acknowledge that without question.'

Harding sounded an irritated exclamation of protest but immediately fell silent as the brigadier's open hand rose to cut him off.

Longthorn drew again on his cigar as he sensed power shifting toward its rightful place.

'However, while recognising your status in the United States, senator, my understanding as to who controls Primo is somewhat different to yours. The week before it all fell apart, you certainly were appointed, jointly by the US president and the UK's PM, to have oversight of planet-based and space aspects of the Primo Project. But General Dower's experience was different. He informed me you were declared missing at the point of collapse, and he had to communicate directly with the secretary of defense in Washington. I understand the general's last order from there was to assume sole and continuing independent command in space, and thereafter his command was to act independently in whatever way best suited the fast-changing circumstances.'

'Rubbish. I wasn't missing. I was visiting a military facility in my constituency, as was my grandson. We're politicians; it's expected that we attend our constituencies regularly – it's part of the job.' Longthorn jabbed his cigar toward Smith-Brown. 'Your General Dower should have tried a bit harder to get in contact with me, instead of running for safety. Now, the command structure is clear, you will submit to my authority at once.'

Once again, Smith-Brown released a slow breath. His head shook again, and he looked about the people seated at the table, everyone waiting for his response. He tutted once, the quietest of sounds, but it seemed to echo about the silent room.

'Senator Longthorn, again, I must, and I do, acknowledge you have a certain political authority in matters relating to the United States. I'm afraid, however, my command does not fall under your jurisdiction. I am operating under the direct orders of General Dower, whose Base Primo command is presently operating independent of all Earth-based authorities. And it remains so in the absence of any direct contrary order issued jointly from the British prime minister and your president.'

'But they're both dead. They're all dead. There's only me!'

'I'm afraid, therein lies your problem, senator. You have no jurisdiction over me, my crew or our assets. None whatsoever.'

'You can't do this!' Longthorn banged his fist on the table. 'Damn it, I'm a United States senator. You do as I say Smith-Brown, or I'll break you. Believe me, I'll break you good.'

The brigadier offered a tight smile. 'I was afraid it might come to this, so I took the precaution of noting down one or two points where I can help you. Undoubtedly, getting America on its feet fast is essential, which is why I gave your country such a high priority at the start of the process. And along with my own country and our other joint allies, that will continue as planned, for obvious reasons. But you should note, I will not sanction cancellation of our promised support missions anywhere, nor will I stop the expansion of rescue missions into as yet unsupported territories.'

'You're finished, Smith-Brown, finished,' shouted Longthorn III, as he lunged toward the brigadier, swinging a fist.

Captain Harding, who sat between the two men, grabbed the flailing arm and forced it down onto the table with one strong hand; with the other, he pressed Longthorn III's face onto the surface. 'Steady now, young man. That's no way to behave. Stop struggling or your wrist will snap.' Harding was struggling to hide the glee behind his deadpan voice. Deep down, he'd known the brigadier would make a stand.

The brigadier reached into his pocket, withdrew his handwritten note and slid it across the table toward Longthorn. 'This details my understanding of our relative positions. It details the continuing support that will be ferried to you and the American regional hubs as fast as is practicable to support the extension of continental recovery efforts. All my crew members and assets currently in place will remain and support the mission exactly as has been previously specified. They will continue to work harmoniously with your regional leadership as any reasonable person might expect.

'America is and always has been at the heart of the Primo project. Rescue and recovery in the States is of paramount importance. But you have no jurisdiction over Primo or General Dower, from whom I take my command. In the circumstances, I must do what I believe to be right and what I consider would have been ordered by General Dower were he here or able to communicate his orders.'

Longthorn scanned the paper. He glared at Harding, who still held Longthorn III pressed against the tabletop. 'Let him loose. Brigadier, you have acted against your own chain of command and against the interests of the United States. Today, you have the upper hand, but it will not always be so. When the time comes, there will be a heavy price to pay, and be sure you will pay it.' He screwed up the paper and pushed it into his pocket.

'Come on,' he said, making for the door. As he moved off, he dropped his cigar butt, only half standing on it, leaving it to trail an angry smoke stream from the deck. The senator suddenly stopped, he half-turned and pointed at Celine. 'And you, young lady, should be ashamed of yourself. You're American. Where's your patriotism? God's sake!' And he was gone, making directly for the observer craft that would transport him and his delegation away.

Chapter 19

Perseus Arm: Prenar System

The mix of blue and green colouring showed Prenar b. was almost equally split between deep waters and rich fertile lands. The four Leviathans had travelled from Pardamax to join HA-3, which had been maintaining a lonely vigil. Now, all five circled the planet. Only HB-3 was missing – it still maintained its watch on the other locust swarm at Pelesius.

Above Prenar b., a flight of two dozen locust combat vessels had remained in space to maintain a watch, and they quickly assembled into an attack formation when the Leviathans appeared. MacMillan immediately ordered HB-2 to launch its warbirds to engage the attacking locusts and had HA-1 launch its own warbird flight to provide a safety screen for the Leviathans.

Locust missiles flew in toward the fleet, but the advancing warbirds of HB-2 swatted them down with their lasers. Most were taken care of; those few that slipped past were intercepted by the protective screen of HA-1's warbirds.

'Form on me, tight chevron formation. Let's punch through and turn one eighty to hit their rear,' said the lead pilot on warbird HB-2:C1. They knew from past experience where their relative advantage lay. These locusts didn't.

The three warbirds bunched in tightly. The leader on point. 'Loose missiles now,' he ordered.

Six missiles raced away ahead of the warbirds; the gap continued to close as they registered four locust kills. 'Good start. Watch out, they've fired another salvo!'

The warbirds' lasers burred out again, cutting through metal; all so easy. Then disaster struck. Debris from a damaged incoming locust missile adopted a fast cartwheel spin while continuing to hurtle forward. C1, on point, could not take evasive action without ramming one or other of the warbirds flying tight to either hand. The scrap missile ploughed directly into its cockpit and detonated.

The surviving pair of warbirds were past almost before the explosion registered in the pilots' minds. Instinctively, they knew their leader was gone.

'HA-1, HA-1. This is HB-2:C2. We've lost C1. Repeat C1 is down.'

'We see it, C2. Assume command and press on with the attack. We will move forward HA-1's warbirds in close support.'

'Wilco.' The pilot kept his eyes ahead as he spoke. 'C3, close on me. Lock laser on live, and good luck.'

The pilot scarcely registered C3's reply because the pair were suddenly among the locust combat vessels.

He'd heard awed messroom talk of a pirouetting warbird wiping out half-a-dozen locust vessels in one go during the fierce space battles above Secundo.

Let's see. Let's just see…

A twitch of his finger across the joystick had the warbird spinning, its laser following the pilot's gaze to touch and split one locust vessel after another. He lost count of his kills, three, four… In the rapid spin it quickly became impossible to differentiate between first hits and subsequent strikes on the same vessel.

Then there were no more immediate targets, the warbird was rotating in the centre of a smoking circle of broken vessels.

The pilot glanced toward his co-pilot. 'How many?'

'Reckon we broke the record—'

'C2! C2! Get out of there! Above you! Look out!'

The pilot didn't have time to look up before an attack vessel, trailing a stream of evacuating locusts behind it, drove down and smashed directly into the warbird. The explosion destroyed both warbird and attack vessel instantly. A fiery plume reached out to envelop the escaping locusts.

'C2's gone,' reported the pilot of C3.

'We see it, C3. Standby, reinforcements coming forward to join you now,' responded the captain of HA-1.

As HA-1's reinforcing flight of warbirds moved forward in support, the remaining locust vessels dived into the atmosphere.

'Warbirds, hold your positions. Let them go,' Colonel MacMillan's voice sounded across all the fighters.

Bridge crews on every Leviathan were stunned. This was not how things were meant to play out. They had lost two warbirds in as many minutes.

'HB2:C3, HB2:C3. This is Colonel MacMillan. You did well. Stand down, return to your mothership. All HA-1 warbirds, establish a protective flight pattern about the fleet and hold for further orders.'

Prior to the first engagement, MacMillan had hoped the locusts would rally support and come up in force so he could deploy his warbirds as a big wing. They had not. For several hours afterward there had been no further sign of the enemy, and on reflection, he was relieved. Warbird losses were not sustainable at the rate they had just experienced. Two birds in almost as many minutes. At that rate they'd lose the whole warbird fleet in under half an hour. Something had to change.

The alternative to dog fights in space was ground combat and aerial dogfights in the atmosphere. That wouldn't be good for the soldiers. The locusts had some physical advantage on the ground – putting soldiers down was the least attractive option but it seemed that was how it was going to be.

MacMillan consoled himself with the knowledge that the advantage of gravdrive would be multiplied tenfold and more in the lower atmosphere. There the locust vessels would struggle with gravity and atmosphere, which would have no impact on the warbirds – they would dominate supreme in the planetary atmosphere and could provide close and unrivalled ground attack support to the soldiers.

As a precaution, in the event of a sudden locust swarm attack, MacMillan pulled the Leviathans some distance away from the planet before convening a meeting. Now, once again mustered on the bridge of HA-1, all the captains gathered along with Jamie and Ossie. Also there were the ground force commanders and warbird flight commanders. Everyone stared out at the distant planet.

To one side, Sevrine, the chief scientist based on board MacMillan's Leviathan, was in deep whispered conversation with Ossie. Head shaking and arms gesticulating hinted at some contested issues just as the meeting was called to order.

Sevrine rested her hand on Ossie's shoulder. 'We are agreed then?' she whispered.

'Agreed,' said Ossie. He smiled to himself – she was a kindred spirit, albeit more fiery.

'Attention, everyone! Attention.' Colonel MacMillan stepped out in front of the gathering. All eyes were on him, every ear straining so as not to miss a word.

'They know we're here, and it seems clear they are not coming up to meet us. So we must go down to them. It's going to be very difficult. This is how we will proceed.

'Initially, we'll concentrate our attack in one area. A flight of warbirds will descend first, pick off individual combat craft either on the ground or in the air around our attack zone. The locusts will have to rise to meet us soon enough or be destroyed on the ground – equally, in the atmosphere, they will struggle against the warbirds' gravdrive.

'Then other warbirds will escort observer craft to land troops. They will seize and hold ground, establish a bridgehead, expand. Thereafter, the process will be repeated to extend our line, and we'll ferry in more troops to secure and link the holdings.'

'Where will we go in, sir?' said Jamie.

'Phase One: there's a wide expanse of open steppe-like terrain bound by two rivers. We'll establish bases at each river then spread across the land to link up in the middle. Once linked, all will sweep downstream to clear the whole area between the rivers. When we have established a hold on that ground, the remaining locusts will be obliged to attack us in force, when they will again be vulnerable to our warbirds.'

'Where are the locusts concentrated, sir?'

'Clusters here and there, dispersed right across the landmass. However, the greatest concentration is between the rivers, spreading out a good way downstream from our landing zone.'

'You'll all have your detailed orders shortly. And people, we must prevail. Now, before we disperse, Sevrine and Ossie, you have something to suggest?'

'Thank you, colonel. We have been working on an idea that Steph floated to us before the squadrons left Primo,' said Ossie.

'Yes,' interrupted Sevrine. 'It's an idea for a new weapon, but we haven't been able to do a practical trial yet. We'll need to come down and see how it works; calibrate and reset it in action.'

MacMillan frowned. 'That'll be dangerous. I'm not happy with that suggestion. Are you sure it's worth the risk? You two are essential to the overall mission.'

'It could be a game-changer if we get it right, colonel.'

'Well, anything that helps is welcome. But you have essential duties up here. Let's get a better feel of how things are on the ground first. I don't want to put civilians down in the middle of a fight. When the time's right, I'll see what can be done. If practicable, I'll allocate you to Sarsen's unit. They are very experienced.

'Major Sarsen, you understand I don't want to lose any scientists. We can't afford mishaps?'

'Yes, sir. We'll take care of them. What exactly is the weapon?'

'It's a sort of laser. Could be useful, we hope. But we're not ready to talk it through until we've tested and analysed the results,' said Ossie.

'Well, we need something. When push comes to shove, our small arms just don't cut it against a locust,' said Jamie.

'You've brought heavier weapons, I thought,' said Ossie.

'Oh yes, but not many. They're weapons we'd never have imagined needing to use off-Earth, so only a limited number had been ferried up to Primo before the atmosphere closed. We'll likely be hand-to-hand and bayonets again.'

'Oh,' said Ossie. He looked toward Sevrine. 'We'd better get to work then.'

Chapter 20

Perseus Arm: Prenar b.

Three warbirds issued from Jamie's Leviathan and swept down into the atmosphere, wide apart and line abreast – the previous tightly grouped formation abandoned to cut back on ramming risks, and no more chevron formations, which had prevented one lost warbird from manoeuvring away from the missile debris that downed it.

They knew their targets. Time spent scanning from above had identified the signatures of the many attack vessels distributed about the planet. Right now, the warbirds' focus was on the wide plain between the rivers, identified by Colonel MacMillan as the initial target zone.

Breaking through a thin layer of high cloud, the three warbird pilots suddenly had a panoramic view across a quiet landscape. They could see animal herds grazing as they moved slowly across the terrain. LPA signals confirmed locations where a number of locust vessels were landed, scattered all across the plain, the locusts themselves presumably engaged in feeding and tracking the herds.

Readouts showed almost thirty vessels in the immediate area between the rivers. Odds of nearly ten to one, but the enemy were all on the ground. The warbird pilots were confident they would outfly the locusts to provide air cover for the landing. Better still, the locusts showed no signs of getting airborne to engage the warbirds. It would be like shooting fish in a barrel. On every Leviathan and every warbird, the same question was being asked – why no resistance?

'Jill, it's odd – I see the locust vessel signatures in the LPA, but I can't see the locust vessels,' said Ali.

HB-1 had collected a warbird from Leviathan HB-3 prior to leaving it on surveillance patrol at Pelesius. So HB-1 had a new C1, and once again a full complement of warbirds, ahead of the anticipated locust battles.

'Are they camouflaged? Surely, they realise our scanners will find them regardless?' said Jill.

'Why aren't they coming up to meet us?' said Ali. 'It's weird.'

'Don't know, but let's make hay,' said Jill, opening a public channel. 'All HB-1 warbirds, this is HB-1:C1. Maintain the extended line abreast, on me. We'll fly over the plain, river to river. As we go, lock on and fire missiles at the grounded vessel targets showing in the LPA. Let's take out as many as possible before they get their act together.'

'They must see us,' said Ali. 'It just doesn't make sense to stay on the ground. Why do it?'

Jill shrugged. 'We know they're always up for a fight, so who knows? Anyway, let's not waste an opportunity. All HB-1 warbirds, select targets, fire at will; hit them while we can.'

The attack began, and in only moments, Jill had loosed her first missile. It raced off into the distance, locked on the signal of a grounded locust vessel. She registered the distant vapour trails of more missiles fired by the other warbirds.

She whooped as her missile struck home and immediately locked on to a further target, firing another missile that also hit home. 'Where's next Ali?' she said, searching for the next target.

'Coming up about four miles ahead. I'm feeding coordinates through to you from the LPA. Why aren't they launching? I don't understand.'

'Their problem. I have the location, thanks. Firing now.'

'Hello. Hello, all HB-1 warbirds. This is Major MacAulay, we're above you ready to land troops. C1, how are things progressing?'

'Major, this is C1. We're hitting them on the ground. For some reason they are not getting airborne,' said Jill.

'Okay. Are we clear to descend?'

'Yes, sir. No enemy airborne. We've hit everything close to the western river's bank, now working our way across the plain toward the eastern river.'

'Thank you, C1. We will come down at the riverbank behind you. Request one bird from your flight doubles back to provide us with some dedicated aircover, just in case. Stay alert.'

'Wilco, sir,' said Jill. She detailed C2 to break off and double back to patrol the riverbank landing zone.

***

Jamie piloted the observer in to land a hundred paces from the riverbank. Crowded in behind him was Major Baz Browning and a troop of his marines. Tight-packed, they had filled the central passageway all the way to the airlock. The last on board were first to lead the hurried exodus as the airlock doors opened.

One after another, three more observers landed close by, and more marines hurried out to join those who had already disgorged from Jamie's observer craft.

Lieutenant Grieves' troop formed a perimeter, and he prowled about pointing out risk spots and keeping everyone on their toes.

'All quiet, sir,' said Lieutenant Grieves, hurrying back to report to Jamie and Major Browning where they stood amid the four landed observers. Overhead, the warbird roamed to and fro, ready to respond to any aggressor. Nothing. All was still.

'Where the hell are they? It's too easy, too easy by half,' said Browning.

Jamie couldn't help but agree, but they had to push on. 'Lieutenant Grieves, I want your troop to hold this location as our beachhead. Establish defensive positions, set up air defences. Then we'll ferry more troops down to this point for onward dispersal. Baz, I want you to take two troops, sweep the ground in that direction.' Jamie pointed directly away from the riverbank. 'I will jump ahead about a mile in the observer with Sergeant Grant and the remaining troop. We'll establish a forward base there that you will work toward. That's where we'll link up and keep leapfrogging from there. Once we have a pattern in play, Colonel MacMillan will begin to ferry down more troops to take over and hold the line you've swept.'

'It's nearly twenty miles between the rivers. That's going to take a while, sir,' said Sergeant Grant, who had just joined the officers.

'You're right, but only ten miles for us. Once we've tested the ground here, Major Sarsen and his teams are to mirror our action by coming from the other direction; we'll meet in the middle. Then everyone moves downstream as one, dealing with any locusts as we go.'

***

'Jill, this isn't making any sense,' said Ali. He had twisted right round in his seat to peer intently into the LPA.

'What's up?' she asked.

'We've hit more than a score of locust targets already, but the signals are still there. None of the vessels have been destroyed.'

'That's not possible. We saw them blow.'

'The LPA doesn't lie, boss.'

'So what's going on?'

'I don't know. Our missiles hit the targets, but once the dust has cleared, they still show as live.'

'Right, I'll swing back across and check some out,' said Jill, pulling the warbird's heading about and racing back to review her most recent hit.

'Over the target now, and it's reading live,' said Ali, turning back from the LPA to peer down a thousand feet to ground level. 'There's nothing there. What's going on? Are they dummy signals? Are we being duped somehow?'

'Let's go down a bit lower, take a closer look,' said Jill, as she opened a channel and reported the anomaly to the bridgehead.

Chapter 21

Perseus Arm: Prenar b.

Jamie flew his observer away from the bridgehead and dropped back to land at the spot planned for the first forward base. It was a slightly raised hillock covered with grasses and a scattering of bushes coated in blooms of vivid yellow flowers. The land behind stretched back to the river, peppered with tall trees in full leaf. All around them were spread a variety of bushes flowering in a riot of colour. Every inch of ground unclaimed by tree or bush was covered by thigh-high grasses that rippled gently in the breeze.

On landing, a herd of big black herbivores had bolted away in the company of smaller fleet-footed creatures. Sergeant Grant and his troop had quickly disembarked to establish a perimeter, and now everything was still, barring the rustle of branches in the gentle breeze. The animals had gone.

'What do you think?' said Jamie, joining the taller man.

'We're good here, just now, sir. We should send out a patrol to scout about.'

'Okay, sergeant, do it. Major Browning's just set off from the bridgehead to scour the land between us on foot. Provided they don't encounter any difficulties, they should be with us in about half an hour. But hold off a moment, something's come up I'd like to check out.'

'What's up, sir?'

Jamie quickly briefed Grant on the combat vessels' anomalous signals. 'The first target they hit is only about a quarter-mile from here. I think we should check it out on the ground.'

'Very good, sir. I could take a section out now.'

Jamie raised his arm to reveal a local scan map displayed on his sleeve. 'Okay, here's the location – you should come across it soon enough. It will be easy to spot a big hole in the ground where one of our missiles hit a little while ago. Be careful. Look and report back; don't initiate engagement. There's every chance of a live locust crew too. A warbird will come in to cover you from above. Should be with you by the time you reach the bombsite.'

***

Grant's section made steady progress, pressing through the high grasses, eyes alert and scanning the ground ahead. The regular scattering of flowering bushes offered frequent danger spots from where ambushes could be launched. Ten paces to his either hand was a marine, mirroring his wary advance. Ten paces wider still, two more marines, and a further ten paces out, two more to complete the wide line abreast.

Some twenty paces behind and a similar distance apart came two hoppers. Both drivers focused every faculty ahead, the hoppers' stature affording them the height to see over many of the bushes that were so concerning Sergeant Grant. Marines in the shotgun seats divided their attention between flanks and rear. The wildlife had fled. Spooked. Nothing moved as the marines continued to advance.

'I see the blast sight, sergeant,' said one driver. It's dead ahead in a clearing beyond the next clump of bushes.'

'What do you see?'

'A broad clearing. At its centre, a blast crater with broken earth, flattened grasses – all natural, no metallic debris field. Whatever the warbird hit, it wasn't a combat vessel. No sign of any locusts.'

The section continued to move ahead, clearing the intervening line of low trees and bushes to give Grant a clear sight of the location. In the centre of the clearing was a mound of fresh earth, marking where the missile had exploded. The displaced earth had settled to form the raised edge of the blast crater.

'Sergeant Grant, HB-1:C3 will be overhead shortly to provide you air cover. How are things looking now?' Jamie's voice sounded calm in Grant's collar-phone.

'Quiet, sir,' said Sergeant Grant. We're approaching the blast crater, but I don't see any sign of locusts.'

'There's definitely a locust combat vessel signature there, sergeant. Stay on your toes and keep me posted.'

'Very good, sir,' said Grant while signing the line of marines to continue forward and encircle the crater.

He reached the lip and stared down. It was deep, perhaps two or three times his height, and at the bottom, just earth. He reported back to Jamie as the rest of his section closed around the hole.

'Sarge! Sarge, I'm getting something!' said a hopper driver.

'Getting what?'

'It's a signal in the hole. There's something down there. Something big.'

Grant stared intently down into the hole. 'I don't see anything.'

'Big signal, sarge. For certain. I reckon it's a combat vessel.'

'Scan again,' said Grant.

'Still down there, no doubt.'

Grant opened a channel to Jamie and reported.

'How did it get underground, sergeant?'

'Can't say, sir. It must have some burrowing capacity.'

'Why though? It's trapped itself down there,' said Jamie. 'And it's happened all across the land. Look, sergeant, hold tight there, wait for the warbird to arrive, then we'll stir the hornets' nest.'

'Very good, sir,' said Grant. He looked up and about. This was not a good position. The blast crater was at the centre of a naturally formed clearing filled with waist-high grasses, though all of it was flattened near the crater – no cover. Beyond the blast zone remained a modest fringe of high grass that quickly gave way to a border of bush and low trees that stretched away into the distance. He stroked his sleeve.

'Corporal, you and one man stay here at the hole. Any sign of activity down there, raise the alarm and double back to join us immediately. Don't try to engage on your own. The rest of you, fall back with me and the two hoppers to the bush-line. We'll have some cover there to establish a holding position.'

On the edge of the crater, his section corporal raised a hand to acknowledge the order, then pointed out one marine who was to stay. The pair watched the rest of the section retire, then settled down, intent on the hole where all remained still.

Reaching the surviving fringe of long grass, Sergeant Grant began to feel more comfortable with their position. The hoppers had immediately been put to good use, scraping their great feet across a section of ground several times to demonstrate their versatility as effective mechanical trench-diggers.

The air was calm, warmed by the sun's rays, the stillness belying the tension that prevailed among Grant's marines. All silent, all watching, waiting. Birds returned to swoop around, filling their beaks with the endless supply of insects that swarmed about the flowering bushes.

Sergeant Grant saw the warbird swing low across the clearing, coming to a hover directly above the hole. The two marines on lookout at the blast crater's edge stepped back slightly as the craft began an intensive scan.

'Sergeant Grant, this is C3. Confirmed – we're definitely picking up a combat vessel signature down there. Can't analyse it completely. Still too far beneath the surface. Have your guards fall back. I'm going to put another missile directly into that hole, blast in deeper. If there's a decoy signal down there, we'll nail it. If there's something else, this will flush it out for sure.'

'Very good, C3. Give my forward marines a couple of minutes to get back here before you start.' Grant recalled the guards and then signalled their readiness to the warbird which quickly climbed to a thousand feet and tilted its nose, so the craft pointed directly down into the hole.

'Firing now.'

Grant watched the exhaust trail extend out from beneath the warbird, following the missile toward its target. 'Down!' he called. Instantly, he and the marines ducked their heads deep into the slit trenches.

There was a roar, a pattering of blasted earth returning to ground. Grant looked up to see a billowing plume above the original crater. 'Stand to!' he shouted, and all the marines focused their eyes and weapons on the thinning cloud.

The lip of the crater was wider and higher, reflecting the effect of the explosive excavation. The warbird swooped down and again hovered directly above the hole as the pilot struggled to get a clear sight through the smoke.

'I see something down there,' said the pilot broadcasting on open channel. Not sure what. Stand by, I'll drop down further. The smoke's clearing now. I should be able to identify what we've got here.'

'C3, pull away. Do not close above the blast hole yet,' ordered Jamie.

The warbird had already descended to just a hundred feet over the crater. Sergeant Grant watched it steady, heard the pilot acknowledge Jamie's order, saw it begin to rise then closed his eyes as a flash roared across the ground and the warbird exploded, hit from beneath by two missiles that had raced up from the crater.

'Warbird down, sir! Warbird down. They hit C3, hit from inside the crater,' reported Sergeant Grant, ducking involuntarily as the warbird's payload of missiles detonated, firing out debris in every direction.

'We heard that blast back here, sergeant. What's your status?' said Jamie.

Grant lifted his head and quickly scanned his command; his heart sank. 'Not good, sir. Our hoppers have been destroyed.' The fierce air blasts had flattened the grasses and swept away the bushes for two hundred yards in every direction. Of the trees, a handful of branch-stripped trunks remained upstanding. The two hoppers were bowled over, one had been speared directly through the cab by a piece of warbird wing; it lay flat out with the wing sticking up toward the sky. He knew at once, the two marines on board could not have survived.

The other hopper had lost a leg to flying debris and lay awkwardly on its side. Grant pointed toward it. 'You two, get over there, see what you can do.' Two marines darted across the wasteland while Grant and the remaining marines turned their attention back to the crater.

Scorched earth, scattered with wrought chunks of warbird, filled the space between.

'Sergeant Grant. Update me,' said Jamie.

'Bad, sir, very bad. The warbird is down, destroyed. My hoppers are down and'—he glanced back toward the broken hoppers where two dazed marines were being hauled from the wreckage—'I have six fit marines and two walking wounded. Two dead.'

'What's happening at the crater?'

'No sign of movement, sir. I'll try to get closer.'

'No, hold your position, Grant. Stand by.' Jamie broke off and issued an urgent call to all stations.

All the buried attack vessel signals that had been hit were not to be approached. Monitored from afar only, pending further instructions.

***

Standing in the observer's shade, Jamie could smell the acrid smoke of the burning warbird as the gentlest of air flows wafted it across the green landscape. Just a quarter-mile away, Sergeant Grant's section was in a mess. And the loss of a warbird had punched another hole in the expedition's strike capabilities.

Jamie contacted Colonel MacMillan, whose voice crackled back, anxious for news. He listened intently to the report, interrupting occasionally to fire a quick question. When Jamie had finished, MacMillan took a few moments for thought. The warbirds were great craft – they should be virtually invincible – but for all their superiority in the field and the pilots' enthusiasm, there was no accounting for lack of experience.

'Jamie, there are scores of these buried combat vessels spread across the plain. We can't do much until we know the purpose of this tactic. Certainly, it would be foolish to engage with any of the other craters before we've learned more. Your crater is already engaged – let's use it to learn what the locusts are up to.'

'Yes, sir,' said Jamie. 'First off, they must have gone to ground as a defensive response, surely. Perhaps they realised they can't out-fight the warbirds in the air, so they developed this tactic to draw our craft down into vulnerable positions then hit them.'

'If you're right, it worked perfectly. But they can't expect to repeat that result at every crater, can they? Deep underground, I doubt they can transmit or receive comms with any certainty – they are all isolated from one another. Could there be something else behind this?'

'Possibly, colonel… I don't know. Look, things are starting to develop here. I'd better go,' said Jamie as incoming signals heralded in his collar-phone.

'Okay, keep me in the loop at every stage. If we can't sort out one buried vessel, we have no chance with the rest.'

Jamie dropped the colonel's call and picked up the next. It was a further warbird he'd summoned. 'Hello C1, this is Major MacAulay, where are you now?'

'Just holding off your position, sir. Awaiting your orders.'

'Thank you, C1. Confirmed, a combat vessel is hiding at the bottom of the blast crater. I don't know why. But it did manage to destroy C3. Whatever its underlying purpose, it clearly presents a danger to us. I'd like you to be ready to provide any support necessary to the ground troops, but stay well clear of the crater. If the vessel tries to take off, you blast it. That's your core task.'

'Wilco, sir. Moving toward location now. I can see your people – I count a sergeant and six – looks like they have a couple of walking wounded too. They are falling back clear of the blast site, just settling into grass cover now.'

***

Grant called a halt and had the men hunker down in the tall grass. The two injured hopper survivors were taken to the rear. The fit spread out along the grass-line, concealed from the crater but able to watch, unseen.

'Something's moving, sarge,' said a marine.

'I see it. Hold your fire, everyone. Let's just watch,' said an unflinching Grant. He put a call through to Jamie and the warbird.

Just wavering above the crater rim were four wafting strands. They twitched this way and that, detecting whatever they could. Then two great heads appeared. Up and over, the locusts slid down the cone of debris surrounding the hole. They stayed still, cautiously waiting. After a short while, they rose and looked about. Then moving away from the blast site with increasing speed, they quickly reached the broken hoppers.

One stooped to peer inside the first hopper. It prodded at the lifeless bodies of the marines. Dead meat was unappetising on all but the leanest of days. It checked the second hopper. No bodies. This was more interesting: survivors. It straightened to full height, head turning, huge black eyes and antennae working in harmony to scan the grass-line for movement. Everything was still.

The second locust scoured for clues in the nearer flattened grassland. It looked toward its partner and hissed. A clicking sound answered it. Then both locust scouts straightened up and clacked loudly while rattling their carapaces in unison.

'That can't be good,' said Grant.

He had hardly got the words out before a dozen locusts hurried over the lip of the crater and made directly to join the two scouts.

'Sir, locusts emerging from the hole. Coming our way. What are your orders?' said Grant into his collar-phone.

'Stay where you are, sergeant. Major Browning has just arrived. We'll advance to support you now.'

Grant called to his men. 'We stand here. The major is coming to support us. Make ready.'

***

Jamie waved the newly arriving marines to him. Baz at their head.

'Baz, I want you to squeeze a troop of your marines into the observer now. See that smoke plume deeper in the bush? Locusts. Sergeant Grant and the remains of his section are there. We're going in to provide support and rescue. Have your second troop go cross-country, fast as you like – they're to catch up with us there ASAP.'

Jamie hurried aboard the observer, and the marines filed in behind him. Reaching the bridge, he opened a collar-phone channel.

'Hello, C1. I have reports of locusts on the ground, coming from the crater. Our second missile has unearthed them. Watch the crater carefully. If the combat vessel tries to take off, blast it before it can engage. Do not let it get airborne. That is your priority task. And do not fly over the crater under any circumstances – they can fire missiles vertically, and we've seen what that can mean for a warbird. Move in now. I'm bringing forward more marines to support the ground position.'

Baz Browning pressed past the throng of marines to reach Jamie on the observer's bridge. 'Jamie, sir. The other troop's set off at the double. They'll catch us up, soon as. We're all on board, ready to go.'

Jamie nodded. He raised the observer just high enough to clear the trees that dotted the grass and bush terrain and flew forward. Almost at once, they passed over the hurrying troop of marines. Dropping to grass level, Jamie wove a careful course amid the patchwork of bushes and trees, hoping to arrive at Sergeant Grant's location unseen. He soon settled the observer on the ground. 'Grant is just beyond that next clump of bushes, thirty, forty paces at most.' he said to Baz.

Baz turned and raised his voice, so it carried over the heads of the marines squeezed into the bridge to reach down the passageway as far as the airlock. 'Listen up, marines. You know the score with these monsters. They will kill you if you do not kill them. No quarter. As you exit, pair up, grenades at the ready. We move fast, we move silent, we close, we kill. Let's go!'

***

Sergeant Grant stood up. The grass almost reached his waist. In his hands, a small block of metal, a counterweight, attached by strong line to a grenade in the hands of his supporter who remained unseen, kneeling in the grass.

Two more marines, similarly armed, rose five paces to his either side.

Not far beyond them, exposed in the flattened zone from where the soldiers had just retreated, a line of twelve locusts had caught up with their two scouts. They all stopped, perhaps surprised at the sudden appearance of their new prey, perhaps puzzled the newcomers were not attempting to flee. They eyed the three men: a modest meal for fourteen locusts, but living flesh, nonetheless.

Grant's heart sank. Emerging over the lip of the crater were a dozen more locusts. They hurried to join the attacking line. He activated his collar-phone. Sir, if you're coming to help, now's the moment.'

'Coming now, sergeant. You do your bit; we'll do the rest,' called Baz.

'Pull pins,' ordered Grant, nodding to his companions. He felt a slap on his leg and launched his grenade. Readying a second before the first made contact. He was launching the third as the first exploded.

This swarm of locusts had no experience of human grenades, nor did they know human scientists had replicated the properties of the binding tendrils employed in the locusts' own nets.

The marines now had plenty of training and experience in deploying the grenades, and the first salvos made lethal contact with locusts, most locking tight, tendrils wrapping about limbs, before exploding, dismembering locust bodies. *Six down*, thought Grant as they readied their fourth round for launch. But locusts learned quickly. Realising the danger, they began to leap forward, fast. One jumped into the wrapping embrace of a grenade and was blown apart in mid-air. The rest landed and jumped forward again. Now there was no time and no distance to throw grenades.

'Bayonets ready!' shouted Grant, bracing himself.

The crouching soldiers stood armed with their sharp knives, all watching the locusts' trajectory as they hurtled through the air.

'Ready now!' Grant's voice filled the space.

***

Jamie flew the observer up and over the screening line of bushes. He took in the scale of the problem. 'Corporal, are you ready yet?'

'Nearly, sir. Nearly.'

'Well, I need you now, corporal. Right now.' Jamie watched the viewscreen where the remnant of Sergeant Grant's section was grappling with a swarm of locusts. Outnumbered more than two to one, they had no time.

'Baz! Get your marines into action now! Sergeant Grant has only seconds before they're overwhelmed.'

Looking down through the viewscreen, he saw the marines standing back-to-back, surrounded by locusts. The locusts had corralled the remnant of Grant's section into a tight circle and seemed to be savouring the moment, baiting their prey before closing in for the kill. Beyond them, a third line of locusts hurried forward across the blast site. Emerging from the crater was a fourth.

'Two more ranks of locusts closing. I'll do what I can to slow them.'

Jamie swept the observer forward, whooshing close over the heads of those locusts surrounding Grant. They flinched slightly but were not distracted from the attack. He pressed on, making direct for the oncoming line. Three collided with the observer and were instantly crushed, the other nine continued toward the anticipated feast. Jamie swung the observer round to face the rear of the locust line, which continued quickly toward the fight. There was nothing more he could do at such close quarters.

Eyes fixed on the viewscreen, he opened a channel and called out, 'Corporal, are you ready yet? It's over to you now. Do your damnedest.'

'Working on it, sir. Just another minute to have it secured and ready,' came back the corporal's answer from within the observer's airlock.

Jamie didn't think the corporal had a minute. He looked beyond the remnant of the third locust line, closing fast on where the leading locust ranks had stopped toying with their prey and were readying to move in for the kill. He turned away from the viewscreen; there was nothing he could do for Sergeant Grant. Instead, to minimise the risk of a shoulder-launched missile strike while he was away from the bridge, he brought the observer down to a hover just a metre above ground and engaged auto control. Then he hurried aft, making for the observer's airlock.

***

'Remember, don't waste your effort – go for the antennae. That's the only place we can hurt them,' shouted Grant, as the locust commander rattled its carapace and lunged forward. The other locusts mirrored the attack.

Feet planted firmly to ground, Grant jerked his arms and body back as the great head and jaws swept down in front of him, just missing their bite. He heard the clack of the locust's jaws as it expressed annoyance. Still lowered, head twisted, its jaws opened wide to close on Grant's thigh and commence the feast.

Grant reached down with one hand, grasping at the antennae that swirled about his waist. His other hand swept in, and the bayonet sliced off both at once. The locust reared up in an agony of hissing and clicks. Its head caught between Grant's legs, launching the sergeant up as it straightened. He wrapped his legs about the locust's neck to avoid being propelled high into the air. Suddenly disoriented, it stumbled aimlessly, and Grant dropped to the ground.

The sound of screams and the splashing red all about told how his team was not faring so well. Marines were down, several locusts already feasting. His combat partner was holding a blade out toward two locusts in a defiant gesture that belied the odds. The stump of his left arm spouted a flood of blood – unstemmed, it was a toss-up between him dying from rapid blood loss or the next locust bite. The warrior had not surrendered his arm easily and one locust had wandered off in aimless distress, sporting only one antenna. The remaining two locusts were cautiously eyeing up the wounded marine while readying a second assault, aware now this food source could bite back.

Grant sprung up on to the back of the nearer locust. He reached up and grabbed for the antennae. They evaded his grasp as the locust jerked its head to one side, antennae swirling to assess this new threat. It seemed unconcerned, but twisted its whole body so its companion could pluck Grant from his perch on the monster's back.

The companion turned from the wounded marine to oblige, clicking its jaws in excited anticipation. Little arms reached forward and gripped Grant's flailing wrists, drawing him away from the first locust about whose thorax Grant still kept his legs locked. The bayonet dropped from Grant's grasp as his arms were pulled back, stretching his body out and away from the first locust, who clacked in frustration that its hard exoskeleton prevented it from reaching round to bite at Grant's exposed belly.

Then its little arms reached down to pry loose Grant's wrapped legs. Trapped, Grant could do nothing as a thudding sound heralded the landing of the next locust wave. He looked in anger at the locust gripping his wrists, its compound eyes staring expressionlessly back at him. Then the antennae that had almost caressed his face jerked up, twitched, and he could tell the compound eyes were looking beyond him.

Amid the sound of blood pumping in his ears, Grant heard a noise he knew well. A troop of marines yelling themselves on as they hurtled into the charge. Thirty fighters poured into the scene. Over the din of shouts and alarmed carapace rattles, he heard Baz Browning's shouted orders, directing pairs of marines against individual locusts.

The locusts that had begun to feed died at once. Heads down, mouths full and red with flesh, they had no chance as blades swept across their antennae, severing them, many down to the stump.

Baz propelled himself up to swipe at the locust that gripped Grant's arms. It clicked angrily and released Grant to intercept and deflect the major's attack. In that moment, its antennae twitched, confused and immobilised. The monster looked down at its arms to see Grant had reversed the situation, and he now held the locust's arms locked tight.

The sergeant lost sight of the puzzled monster as Browning's body flew over him. He saw the major's arm arc, saw the glint of steel, then only combat green fatigues. He lost his wrist grip on the locust as it erupted in distress when Browning slashed away its antennae.

Sergeant Grant suddenly found himself flying through the air as the locust around whom he'd locked his legs also came under attack. It leaped up with an anguished cry. Its carapace flew open with such force it flicked Grant off like a passing leaf. He landed with a bump.

The locust came down a little further off, its normal agility wrecked by severed antennae. As it moped about, a marine hurried behind and fired several shots through its open carapace. It died. More shots sounded, confirming that the marines were dispatching all the wounded. A handful of survivors had leaped away and were hurrying back to join with the oncoming waves.

Between them, Jamie's unguarded observer.

Chapter 22

Perseus Arm: Prenar b.

Jamie hurried into the open airlock and crouched down to help the corporal tighten the last of the securing bolts.

'Nearly done, sir,' said the corporal.

'I see that, corporal. This job should have been finished hours ago. We need it sorted now,' said Jamie, while lending his weight to the arm of a large shifting spanner, squeezing the last fraction of a turn from the nut, tightening it against a bolt set in the deck.

'Sorry, sir. I've had troops running in and out the airlock all morning. This has been my first chance to complete the fitting.'

From outside the airlock came sounds of small arms fire and exploding grenades. They could not see the action as the aft airlock faced toward the blast crater, so couldn't judge how the fight was going. They could see an oncoming line of locusts was clear of the crater and closing on the conflict, with yet more emerging over the rim – the observer bang in the line of their advance.

'What do you think, sir?'

'I think, corporal, we're set. Let's get this bad boy working before we're overrun. There's more advancing now.'

Jamie straightened up and focused again on the advancing locust line. 'I'm going back to the bridge, to get us higher. I'll pilot round and you let them have it.'

'I'll be ready by the time you get there, sir.'

'Good man.'

But just as Jamie turned to go, two of the retreating locusts appeared at the airlock. They both peered inquisitively in, antennae twisting and scanning. Hissing and clacking, the first locust thrust its head and shoulders forward into the airlock. Little grasping arms moved immediately to seize the kneeling corporal, jaws opened to savage its prey.

Taken about the waist and lifted up off the deck, the corporal could do nothing to defend himself. Without a weapon, Jamie was also in a bind as the second locust tried to press through the outer airlock door. Taking a half-step back, Jamie tried to close the airlock, it slid partially shut, bumping to a halt against the locusts.

The pressing door could not close, but it did restrict the attackers' movements. They hissed in anger. The leading locust was trapped with its head, upper body and arms inside, the rest out. The second locust was outside but trapped where one small arm was pinned between its companion and the closed door.

Jamie swung up the heavy spanner to crack the locust's jaw as it made to bite the corporal. The blow did no obvious damage but distracted the beast, and its head pivoted to face him. Jamie swung again landing a fierce blow against the head. With an angry hiss, the locust dropped the corporal and reached its arms out to grasp Jamie.

Gripped tight at the shoulders by two grasping claws, Jamie was suddenly being drawn directly toward the locust's snapping mouth. He could do nothing to prevent himself being pulled inexorably into the great mandibles' biting range. Looking desperately about, he realised there was nothing he could do to stop contact.

With a prayer in his mind and a curse on his breath, he raised his arm toward the locust and pointed the long-handled shifting spanner straight ahead, thrusting his arm forward as hard as he could. The locust's claws drew him on to its mouth, first the spanner then his arm up to the elbow and beyond, all disappeared into the maw. Powerless to respond, Jamie watched as the jaws closed over his hand.

The bite never came. The spanner jarred against the back of the locust's mouth and tilted up to block the locust's closing jaw. It hissed in pain as the pressure of its own closing jaw forced the hard metal spanner through soft inner tissues and locked against the inside of its crusty hard jaw and skull. It could not close its jaws. Furious, it pushed Jamie away, a claw cutting into his uniform and throat as they parted company. The spanner remained wedged in place. Jamie dropped, landing, winded, with his back flat on the deck, momentarily dazed. Then his hands swept up to his neck in response to the pain. Blood ran across his hands from his neck wound, but he could tell it wasn't a death cut.

The second locust, still trapped by its arm yet eager for feasting, poured out a torrent of enraged hisses, clicks and carapace rattles while repeatedly thrusting its head forward into the little space above its mate's head and beneath the airlock's doorframe.

A metallic clunk sounded as the locust spat the spanner out onto the deck. Angry clicking signed it was not finished with Jamie yet. Its short arms reached out and down to catch Jamie just as he began to slide away. A claw caught his boot, clamped on and pulled. Jamie's hand flailed about seeking a purchase point. Touching the bracket he and the corporal had just secured, his fingers curled tight around it and a tug-o-war ensued, testing his grip against the locust's.

'Hold tight, sir,' said the corporal, shouting to be heard over the enraged calls of both locusts. Having recovered from the terror of the initial attack, he had scrabbled to the airlock's inner door and out of the monster's reach. Now he was rallying.

Clinging on for his life, Jamie scarcely registered the words, nor did he hear the metallic slap as the corporal locked in the belt and cocked their newly mounted heavy calibre machine gun. Then the roar of rapid fire overwhelmed every other sound. He didn't hear the corporal's maniacal scream of anger as he unleashed a torrent of heavy calibre rounds straight at the head of the locust.

Deafened by the percussive roar, blinded by the sudden release of smoke in the enclosed airlock, Jamie struggled for a moment to understand what had happened. The sudden release of the locust's grip on his boot triggered him into action, and he scrabbled back. One hand up to protect his face from the spent cartridges that were raining down onto him, he slid behind the machine gun and pulled himself up, slapping the corporal's arm to halt his fire.

The noise of the gun stopped, replaced by fierce ear-ringing that continued for several moments. Then silence. Vents sucked away the smoke to reveal a new horror.

The heavy calibre rounds, designed to destroy defensive structures as much as life, had done everything that their regular calibre assault rifles had failed to do in previous campaigns with the locusts. The rounds had punched through the locust's exoskeleton: head, shoulders, everything above the chest was pulped. Behind it, the second locust, still standing, trapped by its locked arm, but decapitated, its upper body peppered with yellow oozing holes.

'Thank you, corporal; you saved my bacon there.'

'And you mine, sir. Thank you too.'

Jamie nodded and grinned. 'Stand by the gun,' he said, and stepped forward to open the outer airlock door. It slipped back and released the trapped corpses. Raising his boot, Jamie pressed against them, and the bodies slid unceremoniously out and down to the ground. The airlock door slid shut.

'You know what to do. I'll get back to the bridge and get us up. Once we're in position, I'll open the outer airlock. Be ready.'

Jamie exited the inner airlock door and sprinted for the bridge, leaving the corporal to check the weapon and prepare himself in anticipation of Jamie's next move.

As he hurried along the passageway, Jamie put a call out to Baz Browning. Nothing happened, and he realised his collar-phone was broken. A raised hand confirmed the locust's claw had slashed more than his skin. Reaching the bridge, he paused to catch his breath and review the scene outside before opening a channel via the observer's comms system.

'Hello, Baz. I see you and your team – good work there. Hold your position while I get some altitude, then we'll soften them up before you advance. Stand by now.' Jamie piloted the observer up about twenty feet above the ground. As he did, he split the viewscreen display to show both forward and aft.

Assembled ahead were Baz Browning's marines. Aft of the observer, there were now two full ranks of locusts massed before the crater. He could make out yet more just emerging above the rim. *That's way more than the compliment of a combat vessel. Where are you all coming from?*

With no time to dwell on the anomaly, he again opened the observer's comms channel.

'Hello, corporal. You have around thirty targets on the ground. I've lined the airlock door up and our marines are holding off. You'll have a clear line of fire. Opening the door now. Give them hell.'

'Airlock door's opening, sir.'

***

Baz Browning and Sergeant Grant stood together watching events play out ahead of them. Deeper in the bush, the wounded were being treated, readied for evacuation. Meanwhile to their either hand, marines were spread in pairs, all prone, concealed behind a line defined by what little remained of the grass. They saw the observer manoeuvre slowly. They couldn't see the opening aft airlock, which now pointed directly toward the advancing locusts.

A cruel rat-tat-tat roar reached them a fraction of a second after they saw dust flick up about the front locust rank. Quickly, the gunner got his aim, and they saw locusts quiver as rounds hit their bodies. A locust head exploded; the body swayed then toppled over. A ripple of confusion ran along the front rank; it wavered. Then, with a rattle of carapace, the leader pulled itself up to full height and leaped forward. The remnant of the front line followed suit, and they advanced rapidly toward the waiting marines.

The observer carefully manoeuvred, keeping the stern airlock aligned with the advancing locusts. As it turned, Baz saw the open airlock, which emitted an almost constant flash and glow, and with it a hail of death.

'Take that!' shouted Sergeant Grant, punching the air. On the ground ahead of the marines, the locust line was cut down as though by a scythe. 'Take that!' Cheers sounded from the grass to either side as the marines recognised a shift in the balance of power.

'Hello, Jamie, that's working great,' said Baz into his collar-phone. The message reached Jamie via the observer's PA system.

'Yes, this is a game-changer. Hold your position now. I'm going to come round, and we'll have a go at the other lines, then you come in fast to mop up.'

'She's turning now,' said Baz to Sergeant Grant. The observer turned, the airlock vanishing from view as it came to bear on the new locust lines. Once again, the rat-tat-tat sounded, and the next line of locusts took fatal casualties but far fewer. As ever, they learned quickly, breaking formation to reduce the quality of target offered while still advancing rapidly toward the marines.

'They're coming our way, sir.'

'Yes. Stand by everyone. Here they come!'

Overhead, the observer continued to turn as Jamie tried to give the gunner an angle to hit the advancing locusts. Further casualties were inflicted but not enough.

'What's that over there?' said Baz, pointing toward the crater lip.

Grant followed his gaze and groaned.

Touching his sleeve, Baz called a warning. 'Jamie, look out! Ground-to-air! Ground-to-air! At the crater lip. Get out of there!'

The two men watched the observer bank and break off; Jamie's combat helicopter skills delivering an immediate response to the warning. An arc of tracer shells spiralled harmlessly away, high into the sky, highlighting where the gunner had continued to fire for a moment, surprised at the observer's sudden evasive movement.

'Oh God,' said Grant, his voice suddenly despondent.

The locust at the crater rim had got the ground-to-air missile away. Its exhaust trail stretched out behind the streaking bolt. Both watching men knew their warning had come too late. With a brilliant flash, the stern airlock was enveloped in a destructive shockwave. The gunner died instantly.

The observer rocked under the blast, orange flame jetting from the airlock, morphing into a black billowing trail that spread across the scene. For just a moment, the observer seemed to stabilise, then the machine gun's ammunition blew, and the airlock lightshow erupted to a whole new level.

'Here they come. Stand to! Stand to!' The sergeant's shouted command brought the marines to their feet. The marines faced off against the oncoming locusts. For the first time that day, they actually outnumbered the attackers.

'Launch tendril grenades,' ordered Browning.

Strong arms swung and twenty grenades flew across the divide. Some missed. A dozen made contact where the tendrils coiled about locust limbs and necks before blasting them off, dropping the victims, wounded or dead.

'Steady!'

The locust line was just bracing for the final leap that would carry them in among the marines when providence intervened. The observer wheeled about the clearing, blackening the sky in its trail. It dipped, attempting a controlled landing but ploughed across the locust line, catching several as they jumped, swatting them down even as the observer itself dropped to ground.

The surviving locusts landed among the marines, eager to fight but confused by the mid-air thinning of their ranks. The lead locust landed between two pairs of marines. It had stuck a leg out as it landed, sharp talons on hardened foot slashing through a marine's body armour as though it were paper. The man screamed and dropped to his knees, his combat knife dropping from his hand as strength instantly drained from his dying body.

With a shout of rage at the loss of his partner, the surviving marine faced up to the monster. It towered over him. One short arm swatted away his blade while the other grabbed him by the throat. The monster lifted its victim up and drew the marine toward its opening jaws. Antennae swept about the helpless marine's head and shoulders while the locust assessed its prize. Carapace rattled and the jaw gave a short clack of pleasure as it savoured its moment.

Sergeant Grant ran in close. Tried to jerk the suspended marine down and away from the predator. The effort had little effect. This was a big locust – Grant knew the antennae were beyond the reach of his blade. But he couldn't leave the marine to die. He jerked again at the marine's legs.

The locust looked around at Grant, irritated but unthreatened. It kicked out a leg, but Grant had seen the monster's weight shift and anticipated the strike, throwing himself to one side and down as the sharp clawed foot flashed to where his chest had been a second before.

Rolling beneath the captured marine's flailing legs, Grant rose as the locust turned its head toward him, shifting its weight again to aim a second kick. Grant jumped, scrabbling in his flak jacket holster to pull out a flare gun. Thrusting it forward he fired the cartridge. At less than an arm's length, the incendiary hit its target before the locust could process what was happening.

The angry clicking sound stopped abruptly as the flare careered into the back of the monster's throat. Its head recoiled at the shock of contact, and it involuntarily swallowed the foreign body. But it remained standing. Now super angry, its antennae swept over Grant's head, big black eyes surveyed him, suddenly its full attention switched to him. The marine dropped, forgotten, and the locust's arms shot out toward Grant's throat. Then stopped, still in mid-grasp.

Grant took the opportunity to duck backward but stumbled. From the ground, he looked up at the locust. Something was wonderfully wrong. It tilted its head back, opened its mouth and released a long cry of agony. The distress call was accompanied by a stream of bright coloured smoke pouring from the locust's mouth. Grant fancied he could see flashes of light from the burning flare showing amid the cloudy stream.

He rolled over and grabbed the grounded marine by the shoulder. 'Come on, there's plenty more like that one.' He picked up the marine's knife and shoved it into his hand. 'Let's move; support the next man along.'

Chapter 23

Perseus Arm: Prenar b.

With no communication from Jamie's observer, the warbird closed in, C1's pilot looked anxiously at the scene below. She glanced toward her co-pilot. 'Ali, I think we're getting the upper hand down there.'

The ground was littered with dead or dying locusts. Many marines were down too, lost to the fight. The initial battle line had dissolved into a dozen or more separate desperate duels where individual locusts grappled with knots of two, three and sometimes four marines.

'I think you're right, Jill, but that observer's a mess. Could anyone have survived that?'

Just beyond the fighting was the downed observer, smoke billowing from its airlock door – no sign of movement there, human or locust. A little further off was the blast crater, mostly obscured by wafting smoke.

'Squadron Commander MacAulay? Major MacAulay, this is HB-1:C1 can you hear me?' said Jill through the comms system. There was no reply. 'C1 to Major MacAulay, please reply.' She glanced toward Ali, her eyes full of concern. 'No answer. The observer's comms are down.'

'It's not looking good – look at that smoke.' said Ali.

'Oh hell,' said Jill, while stroking her sleeve. She attempted to open a direct collar-phone link with Jamie. There was no pickup.

'Can we do anything to help the marines?' said Ali, looking down to the other side.

'No, they're all in too close; our weapons can't differentiate.' She tried to raise Jamie again then shrugged into the silence. She opened another channel.

'Hello, HA-1, this is HB-1:C1. Report for Colonel MacMillan.'

'Go ahead, C1.'

'Major MacAulay's observer is downed sir. Seems intact but a lot of smoke coming from the airlock. Nobody's got out, and I can't raise him. There's a fight going on between our troops and the enemy. I think we're getting the upper hand, but it's all close quarters, so we can't assist.'

'Thank you, C1. I'm in direct contact with Major Browning. I have ordered another section up in support from our forward post; they should be there any moment. Can you see them?'

Ali jabbed a finger beyond the skirmish line. Approaching fast through the bushes was a section of ten marines. 'There they are!' he said. 'That'll swing it our way for sure.'

Jill reported the news to Colonel MacMillan who responded with a satisfied grunt. 'Okay, C1. Keep me posted. And stand by. If any locusts fall back from the fight when our reinforcements arrive get in tight and laser them. I don't want any surviving. Keep trying to raise the observer. And C1, remember, keep clear of the crater rim. If any vessel comes out, blast it – that's your focus, first and last.'

'Wilco, sir.'

She looked across the cabin toward Ali. 'This is a mess; it's gone right off script. Way more casualties than we can sustain.'

They watched as the supporting section of marines burst from the surrounding undergrowth and charged toward the fight. The locusts wavered. Already outnumbered and on the back foot, the arriving reinforcements convinced most that it was time to retire, and they began to break away.

'Ho, we're up,' said Jill. She backed the warbird around in the tightest of turns, tilting the nose down to give Ali clear sight of the retreating locusts. 'Burn them!' she said.

Ali locked the laser sight to his gaze and began to trace individual locusts as they jumped for safety. A single glance was enough to bring the laser to bear, a touch of burning light sufficient to vaporise the monsters.

***

Jamie stood in the passageway leading directly to the stern airlock, his hands stroking and tapping on his sleeve. Ahead of him was the inner door, shut and sealed but peppered with holes that marked where heavy machine-gun ammunition had detonated, firing off in every direction.

The observer's fire control system had got the airlock flames under control now – once fully doused, that would help. Meantime, the passageway ventilation sucked out the smoke that still streamed through the pepper-pot surface of the inner airlock door.

The armoured rounds had punched through decks and bulwarks as well as the door, doing significant damage, which he was trying to assess. Comms were down, as was propulsion, though localised emergency power circuits were beginning to power up. Bots were hurrying about, assessing and prioritising what needed to be repaired. He allowed them to continue in auto, knowing they would handle recovery best if he didn't attempt to impose any personal priorities.

Content there was no continuing fire risk, Jamie turned and headed to the bridge. Entering, he looked at the display screen – it remained blank. Comms were still down. Not knowing who, if anyone, might still be outside, he tried a collar-phone call. No good. His collar was well and truly wrecked. He stood quietly, hands clasped behind his back, staring at the blank screen. *Come on bots, get a move on.*

Chapter 24

Perseus Arm: HA-1 over Prenar b.

The deadlight curtain isolating bridge from navigation room was twitched aside by Sevrine as she hurried onto the bridge.

'Colonel MacMillan, we need to speak,' she said, pacing toward him.

'Go ahead,' he said, waving away a cluster of officers who were discussing the marines' progress on the surface.

'Ossie and I have been conferring about the strange combat craft signal we are picking up from the holes we blasted. The one we hit multiple times has got a deeper crater of course. That's allowing our sensors to sweep deeper.'

'And?' said MacMillan. The officers who had just been side-lined all edged closer.

'Now we've exposed it, it's clear there's not just a single combat vessel in the hole. We think there is a stack of four, perhaps five, one sitting on top of the other.'

'What? Why would they do that? How do they even do that?'

'We don't know, colonel. But if they were going to hide in burrows, why not hide several in one? It would be more efficient.'

'Until we found them.'

'Yes, sir, but we think maybe they didn't appreciate how efficient our scanners are. Or perhaps when they burrowed down it was for another reason altogether, and nothing to do with expecting an attack – perhaps they were buried even before we hit the cone. Ossie is wondering if this behaviour has nothing to do with our presence.'

'Well, we'll find the reason soon enough.' The colonel pointed to one of the officers. 'Get a signal to the warbird. Warn it that there are multiple combat vessels in the crater… and inform all units. If one site has multiple vessels, likely they all do.'

'Colonel, I'd like permission to temporarily transfer to Ossie's Leviathan. You know the project we have been working on; we need to finalise things.'

'Now's not a good time, Sevrine. We're at battle stations. I need you here to advise as required.'

'But colonel—'

'No buts, Sevrine. Do what you need to do with Ossie remotely.' The colonel turned back to his officers. 'What's happening with that downed observer? Any sign of Major MacAulay?'

'Nothing, sir. We're monitoring it closely.'

***

Ossie leaned back in his seat, ran a hand through his hair and grinned at the screen. 'I think that's it.'

'Agreed,' said Sevrine, grinning back through hers. 'Though it'll still need some in-situ fine tuning.' Her grin relaxed into a smile, and Ossie felt it warm his laboratory as though she were actually there. Both believed they had done it.

Each scientist had identical versions of the machine in front of them. They had worked in parallel for weeks, snatching time when they could to refine the initial idea that Steph had suggested back at Primo. Now, at last, it was ready for testing – something they dared not do on board.

Her face dropped slightly. 'Question is, how will we test it? Colonel MacMillan has insisted I stay on board in case he needs advice.'

'Well, you can understand that,' said Ossie. 'However, with Jamie down on the surface, I'm not facing such a barrier. Why don't you head up to the bridge and let's set up a conference over the network with the colonel. He needs to authorise this, and it needs to be tested now. One of us has to go down, for sure.'

Chapter 25

Perseus Arm: Prenar b.

Stuck until the bots could effect repairs, Jamie was sitting down on the bridge deck. His mind turned over every conceivable scenario as he tried to imagine what was happening outside. *Had Baz and his marines prevailed? Were locusts surrounding the observer, even now working out how to break in?*

One bot appeared on the bridge and started bothering him. It extended little probes, nudging, almost nuzzling. He kept swatting it away and it kept coming right back. He gave up. *Hell, if the bot wanted to sit next to him, let it.*

The bot's extensions again reached out and suddenly Jamie twigged. The bot was attempting to repair his suit. *Who'd have thought they did that too?*

He sat still as the fabric and collar were tweaked and snipped, short blasts of heat telling of bonding work. Finally, with a stroke and nudge that Jamie felt was almost like a craftsman's self-satisfied pat on a finished job, the bot retired.

He looked at his sleeve, the collar-phone was live. Immediately he made a call.

'Hello, Baz! Jamie here, do you hear me? How are things out there?'

'Jamie! Thank God! We'd begun to think the worst. How are you?'

'I'm good. The observer's sustained some damage to the aft end, mainly our own munitions detonating. Happily, most went out through the airlock.'

'We saw that from out here. But by God, you and Corporal Bruce did some damage first. You really thinned those locusts out. We managed the rest.'

'That's good. But Baz, I'm sorry, Bruce didn't make it.'

There was a short pause before Baz responded. 'Yeah, we assumed he was in the airlock when the RPG hit. He was a good man, and brave. He'll be missed… But we've lost a lot of good men today.'

Baz delivered a full status update, and Jamie took it all in while moving back toward the aft end to check on repairs to the main power supply and around the inner airlock – the bots were making progress, but it would clearly be a while before he could get airborne. Finishing with Baz, he called the colonel.

Chapter 26

Base Primo

Steph had left the main control room; she was deep in thought as she made her way toward the sickbay. Though the general had broad shoulders, an awful lot fell to her. So much expectation, so many needs. Increasingly, she had begun to treasure the quiet times, and they were in short supply. Most of all, she needed a confidant. She gave a rueful smile – most of all, she needed Jamie and the unquestioning support he always gave her.

She'd rescued him from his shipwreck, but they had hardly caught their breath before he was whisked away again. Once more, he was light years away, this time hunting down their enemy. Her face clouded a little at the thought of the danger he might be facing. Then she forced a smile, taking a little comfort from his new role. At least as a squadron commander he wouldn't be in the thick of the fighting – thank God. She set her face in a confident expression and turned into the sickbay.

Only one bed was occupied at present. Fay Dower was sitting up and chatting busily to her visitors. The bed opposite her was empty now. Johnny, her co-pilot, had just been discharged to his cabin to continue his rehab from there.

Gail Dower noticed Steph first and stood up as she approached. They hugged, and Gail kissed Steph's cheek. The older woman knew that her daughter was alive only because of Steph's abilities – the operation of Primo's advanced medical technology had been pioneered by her, and Fay was the living proof of her success. Lily reached out and took Steph's hand, a warm expression of their friendship.

'So, how's our patient?' said Steph, untangling herself from the other visitors.

Fay beamed at her. 'I'm doing great. Reckon I'll be out soon. Johnny got out this morning.'

'I know, and you know your physical injuries were worse than his. You may have a bit to go yet.'

'Come on, Steph, give the doctors a nudge. I can rehab in quarters just as easily as here. I'm feeling way better than I did before.'

'That wouldn't be hard – you were pretty well dead before.'

'Well, I don't know.' Fay looked from one visitor to another and found no support.

'You'll get out when the doctors say so,' said Gail. 'There's plenty of time and plenty of other pilots to cover your duties.

'That's just it – they're my duties. I need to get back…'

***

Back in her cabin and alone, Steph lay on her bed and tried to still her mind. She knew she had friends, yet she was still lonely – *why?* The Dowers were close; she could count on them and plenty others too. She began to count off names in her mind, forcing herself to be positive. *Maybe things weren't so bad. Once the Hunter Expedition was over, the threat removed and Jamie back, maybe then they could start to look ahead – together.*

Just as her mind was settling, she caught a movement out of the corner of her eye. She'd had an LPA installed in her quarters, and as she turned, she saw a flurry of lights. She rolled over to focus on the display. After a moment, she jumped up and crossed to the device.

'Weeman, where have you been?' she said, reaching her hand into the display and allowing the glittering cluster of lights to swarm around her sleeve. The first unforced smile of the day crossed her face.

'Busy,' said Weeman, 'just busy.' His voice sounded clearly in her collar-phone.

She watched the lights swirl as they began the journey under her cuff and into her bio-suit. Then the LPA stilled, and she felt the strange sensation of the lights busying within the suit. She returned to her bed and lay down.

'Busy doing what? You've been gone for days.'

'Just checking the system. All the remote samplers coming in from the life planets are backing up, with no samplers going back out. It's never happened on a scale like this before, ever. I wanted to know how long before we start to risk bio-divergence among the planets.'

'Oh, I hadn't thought too much about that with everything else going on. Where are we?'

'A good margin of safety still applies. I've also seen what you are doing, using Lily's plan to clear the atmosphere. It's clever as long as you keep at it. There will be enough time after to preserve the homogeny of the life planets.'

'Well, at least that's one thing less for me to worry about. So, Weeman, I've been working through some of the information layers in my upgraded suit. There are so many things that don't quite add up. Lots of new information then dead ends. What's that all about? What does it mean?'

There was a long pause. 'When I upgraded your suits, I gave you what I thought you would need. There is more to be revealed but not until you understand what you have now.'

'Come on, Weeman. You know what they say, "a little knowledge is a dangerous thing".'

'And too much knowledge could be a disastrous thing. One thing at a time, Steph, one thing at a time. Now let me talk you through some adjustments to Lily's plan that I think will speed things up…'

Chapter 27

Perseus Arm: Prenar b.

Things had been quiet for some time, as though both sides were catching their breath, trying to understand what was happening. The warbird had made repeated sweeps of the clearing. Having picked off the last of the retreating locusts, Jill had established a slow circular course that ensured she could see the lip of the blast crater at all times but was never so close that a missile launched from within could surprise her. She and Ali continued to wait for the enemy vessels to emerge.

'Do you think they'll come out?' said Ali.

'Have to. Otherwise we've got them trapped down there. Once the top brass work out how we approach this, we've got them; they're sitting ducks.'

'Wow! Wow! I just saw something at the crater lip – over there, see?'

Jill followed Ali's line of sight. For a moment she saw nothing unusual. Then she spotted a movement. 'It's a locust hiding at the rim. And I think that's another one a bit further round.'

'It is!'

They kept their eyes on the two locusts who quickly became more visible as the warbird continued its circuit around the crater.

She changed the warbird's heading slightly, tightening the circuit, edging a little closer. 'None of the retreating locusts made it back to the crater, so these must have come up from below. What are they up to?'

'Maybe just doing reconnaissance. Finding out what happened to the ones they sent out,' said Ali. 'What shall we do?'

'We're losing sight of them behind the rim again. Wait up. We'll see if we can burn them off with the laser as we circle round to the other side.'

She allowed the warbird to continue its circuit, once again bringing the two locusts clearly into view.

'There they are. Hit them when you're ready. Damn! Damn them!' As Jill spoke the two locusts had hopped out of the crater and dropped behind the cone of debris that surrounded it – they were hidden from view again.

'I'll continue round. As soon as you see them, just fire.' Jill and Ali focused on the spot where the locusts had gone to ground. The warbird continued to circle, all the while Ali was poised ready to blast them with the laser. 'Nearly there…'

As the warbird flew round, with eyes fixed on the spot ahead where the locusts had vanished, neither saw the movement in the crater astern of them. From deep within, three locusts leaped up. The first raised a launcher and dispatched their version of an RPG. The other two raised weapons but held their fire.

An alarm sounded in the warbird cockpit. Jill glanced at the display ahead of her. 'Hell! Incoming! Look out.' The slightest touch of a finger had the warbird turning. At such short range and slow speed, the warbird could not outrun the danger. It just might evade. Executing a pirouette, the two breathed a sigh of relief as the missile flew past.

'There's the culprit,' said Ali, pointing across the crater to a locust holding an empty launcher. I'm on him now.' He activated the laser which followed his gaze to burn into the locust, melting it to nothing in an instant.

The other two locusts fired their weapons and fine mesh nets flew into the sky. One directly in front of the warbird which travelled gently into the trap, as the second settled from above in a further layer of entrapment. Even before the warbird had been fully ensnared, the locusts had fired further lines deep into the crater. There they connected with a combat vessel's cargo bay, which began to draw in the lines. Ali's gaze switched to the two locusts who were immediately incinerated.

'What the hell's happening?' said Jill.

'We've been trapped in nets. They're attached to something beneath us.'

'Hell with that,' she said, feeling the slightest downward movement as the cables began to winch the warbird down and over the lip of the crater. She pushed up the power to accelerate away from the problem while pulling up the warbird's head, struggling for altitude.

The strong metallic cables immediately stretched as the pilot used raw power to move away from danger. They began to vibrate in protest while the strain on them mounted. Sensing resistance, she upped the power, and one of the restraining cables snapped. The whole load transferred onto the second cable and the craft slewed round.

'Nearly there,' said Jill ramping up engine power still more. 'That other cable will give in seconds.'

Ali nodded. Then felt sick to his stomach. Beneath the rim of the crater, he registered another locust. The monster had already fired its RPG. He opened his mouth to call a warning while trying to reactivate the laser. Too late. The incoming rocket exploded. The warbird rocked, power cut and it slumped to the ground with a crash, landing beyond the outer rim of the crater. Both pilot and co-pilot were still. Unconscious, they didn't perceive the gentle pull of the surviving cable as it struggled to haul the warbird up to the crater's lip. Inch by inch, it drew in the prize. Waiting just below the lip of the crater were locusts readying to force entry into the warbird to harvest its technology.

Chapter 28

Perseus Arm: Prenar b.

The viewscreen flickered several times then burst into full display. Immediately, Jamie leaped up, touched his sleeve and the observer responded. Slowly at first, but as each part of the power system linked in, the observer became more responsive. He tried the power drive, and the observer began to rise off the ground. The readings had made clear the observer's stern was compromised and could never make it into space; it would be a death trap without an atmosphere-tight stern door.

Orienting the craft toward the crater, he tried to make out what was happening. His heart sank as he spotted the downed warbird – another! Then he realised C1 was being drawn by a cable toward the crater where several locusts were preparing to force entry.

Jamie watched intently as smoke began to belch from within the crater – it suddenly began to present like a mini volcano.

'Hi Baz, do you see the smoke? What is it?' said Jamie.

'No idea.'

Colonel MacMillan's voice overrode the collar-phone conversation. 'Hello, Jamie, Major Browning, I'm getting reports from Sevrine about the smoke. Her detectors are reporting activity inside the crater. The combat vessels are firing up their engines. She thinks they are about to launch.'

'Why now? They've been happy to sit tight, managing to take out our warbirds in the process,' said Browning.

'She's speculated they have seen the observer recover and worry what weapons you're carrying. Decided now's the time to break cover.'

'Hell's teeth! Are there any more warbirds in our vicinity?' said Jamie, knowing his observer was unarmed.

'C2 is providing air cover at the bridgehead. I'm having it divert, but you're on your own for the next few minutes.'

Jamie looked at the growing plume of exhaust fumes streaming from the crater. He knew if the locusts got airborne, they would all be dead long before air support arrived. 'I've got an idea.'

'Yes?' said MacMillan.

'Sorry, I need to act now – no time to explain. I'll give you a live feed from my viewscreen here and talk you through as I go,' said Jamie.

'Carry on and good luck,' said MacMillan, realising he was in no position to influence events directly.

Jamie pushed the observer forward, doing a full circuit of the crater, checking out every feature. He saw the warbird inching ever higher up the sloping debris cone. He nudged closer to the lip. Smoke was belching out. Deep inside, he could see flashes of flame as thrusters prepared to lift the topmost off the locust stack. Or perhaps they were all coming up at once? He couldn't be sure.

Opening a channel, he broadcast. 'Baz, I'm going in. I see three… no, four locusts about the crater rim. Have your people close up and destroy; rescue the warbird's crew and then get your people well back in case it all goes pear-shaped. There's every chance. And Baz, I need that rim to be locust free as soon as you can.'

'Roger that, moving in now. Good luck,' said Baz.

'Jamie, what are you doing? You can't face down combat vessels in an unarmed observer. Come away now. Stand off!' said MacMillan, cutting in on the channel.

'I've got this, colonel,' said Jamie, ignoring the order. 'If those combat vessels get airborne, neither the marines nor this observer will stand a chance. I must stop them.'

Very carefully, he nudged the observer forward. As it crossed over the crater rim, huge turbulence from the locust thrusters rocked the observer, and he struggled for control before stabilising within the updraft, allowing him to continue forward. He hoped the locusts were too consumed by the need to take off to notice him slide overhead.

Suddenly he was relying on sensors alone as the exhaust thickened to an impenetrable fog, broken only by the dull red from the thrusters burning far below. Jamie lowered slowly into the crater – very slowly. He gauged the narrowing distance to the vessel beneath, refining his descent path and praying the locust pilots would not detect him or even think to look until he'd got into position.

Having dropped into what was now a cauldron of flame, he was truly alone. The observer's viewscreen lit up bright orange as the locust vessel beneath ignited its main thrust engine. No backup, no plan B. Comms with the surface lost, Jamie pressed on. With a final touch to his sleeve, the observer dropped the last ten feet and stopped with a jolt, landing on top of the uppermost vessel. He breathed a sigh of relief.

He was safe for a few moments. Even if the vessel beneath could direct a missile at zero range, it could never launch properly, doing more damage to the firing vessel than his craft. The glow from the viewscreens intensified as the locust pushed its power to the max. Jamie was disappointed, though not surprised, to see the sensors report he was beginning to rise again, lifted by the locust. Whether they realised it was him on top or thought something else was blocking their progress, the locusts were determined to exit. He was determined they wouldn't. *Time for phase two.*

Splitting the viewscreen display to get fore and aft views, he scanned through the confusion of images blowing and burning around the observer. He searched the wall of the crater, looking for something he knew was there, somewhere. Nothing. While maintaining the observer's position hard on top of the locust vessel, he began to slowly rotate. Metal ground and screeched and the whole craft vibrated and jarred as it pirouetted against the upward pressing locust. Trying to blank out the chaos, Jamie continued to scan the walls, searching. And suddenly, there it was. He kept turning the observer until what he had found was close to the stern, then he stopped.

He keyed an order against his sleeve and tapped for execution. The gravity brake engaged. At once, all the observer's power focused on locking the craft to its position on the surface – nothing would move it. As the locust pushed up, the observer's gravdrive pressed down. The upward motion slowed to a halt, then, as the observer drew more deeply on its power reserves, the direction of travel reversed, pressing the locust vessel back the few feet to its starting point.

The locust struggled against the press, and the observer's viewscreen displayed an ever-growing fireball as the vessel maxed its fuel burn to no avail. The locust had no power source great enough to overcome a gravdrive.

Jamie felt an overwhelming sense of elation; the whole locust flotilla – four, perhaps five, vessels – was trapped beneath his observer, each pressed down, one on top of the other like a stack of pancakes.

He thought the orange glow faded a little, but then it redoubled and more, as other desperate locust pilots within the stack began firing their own engines. Getting trapped in their hidey hole was not part of their plan. The series of orange bursts, progressively less organised and each more vigorous than the last, prompted him into action. The heat the vessels were generating would soon ignite their own explosive armaments.

Leaving the bridge, Jamie tried again to open a comms channel to Baz. The confusion of burning fuel and screaming engines below combined with the rising heat envelope to blur out the comms. He remained isolated. At the end of the passageway, he stopped and looked closely at the inner airlock door. The bots had filled the pepper-pot holes, but he knew they had stopped work when it became clear repairing the outer doorway was beyond them.

A deft flick of his hand deployed the helmet from his collar; it enveloped his head, sealed and firmed. He tweaked the gloves out from his sleeve cuffs, and at once, he was enclosed in a safe environment. He tapped his helmet, offering up a thank you to the bot that would not be deterred from fixing his collar. Without that, he'd be going nowhere. He took a deep breath – once he opened this door, there was no way back.

He slid his hand over the door, and it opened smoothly, as though there had never been any damage. The inside of the airlock told a different story. There were no functioning lights, so he triggered his helmet beam to complement the red glow that pulsed against the crater's side and reflected in through the jagged hole that had once been the outer airlock door.

The machine gun was where he'd last seen it, the fractured mounting still determinedly locking it to the deck, its muzzle pointed up and off at a wild angle. There was no sign of the corporal's body. He'd expected as much. Everywhere, deck and bulkheads were scarred, dented and holed by the exploding ammunition. He noticed holes letting into the inner bulkheads had all been patched by the bots from the inside of the craft. He guessed, as with the inner airlock door, the bots had prioritised their repairs, concentrating only on filling holes that presented a risk to the most basic integrity of the vessel.

Stepping round the gun, he edged toward the red glow. Shell casings shifted underfoot and clinked at his passing, but his entire focus was on what lay ahead. He paused a pace from the outer hull and looked carefully through the hole, cautiously scanning beyond.

The pulsing red fuel burn and heavy black smoke emitting from the still struggling locust engines beneath him made it hard to focus. He struggled to see any details of the crater's sidewall, even though it was close. His helmet's light beam helped, and after a little delay, when he wondered if he had somehow positioned the craft incorrectly, he saw what he needed.

Time was running out. If the locusts kept racing their engines like that, they were going to blow, and soon. Another deep breath – it was years since he'd done any physical exercise even remotely like this, but needs must. He shuffled to the edge and peered out. Below was an inferno of firing engines. It seemed discipline had completely broken down, and the locust captains were each attempting to thrust up and free independently. Futile. Even if they coordinated their efforts perfectly, they could never generate enough force to overcome a gravity brake.

Directly in front of him, the crater wall was about five feet off. Close, but not as close as he wanted. Gingerly, he ran his left hand over the jagged edge of the doorframe, and finding a spot that he hoped would not slice his glove, he gripped tight, then leaned his whole body out into the void. His full weight supported by his left hand as his right stretched out ahead of him.

Fingers scrabbled and failed to make contact. A belching cloud of black oily smoke surged up and suddenly he couldn't see at all. Time and again, he swept his arm right to left against the crater wall, methodically feeling for what he knew was there, somewhere.

His left hand was beginning to ache as it acted as both support and hinge for his arcing body. Jamie was just reconciling himself to hauling back inside the airlock when a shift in the red and black emissions from below cast a different light, and there it was. Just beyond his reach.

He grimaced, realising he had a one-time-only ticket. Should he go for it now, or swing back into the airlock and rest before going in a few minutes? In a few minutes, the locust vessels could blow, and there would be no way out.

Eyes focused only on his goal, he used his left hand to pull himself back, flexed his knees several times then moved. His knees straightened, jumping out of the airlock as his left arm straightened, pushing out and directing his body. His right arm fully extended in front, fingers spread wide, he crossed the narrow gap before gravity began to drag him down.

His hand closed about the locust cable that was attached to the broken warbird above. He gripped hard and swung his left hand forward to grip too. Wrapping his legs around it, he was set tight, suspended above the raging inferno. He smiled to himself and looked up. He could see nothing but black smoke but knew what lay beyond. He raised one hand and pulled himself up, testing the friction between glove and cable.

Regularly buffeted by thruster blasts from below, and with a seemingly endless climb above him, Jamie settled into a rhythm and began to haul himself up. Hand over hand, he climbed, filtering out doubt and focusing on the climb and the future. That brought his thoughts to Steph and only her. Something changed inside, and he knew he needed to get out of this hell to be with her – that was all that mattered now.

Chapter 29

Earth

Major Coral was very happy. In a world of uncertainties, he understood his role and was delivering. Senator Longthorn had allocated him the use of an observer craft and pilot, and he'd spent his time in an almost constant circuit about the States, visiting the various regional hubs. His mission was proceeding as planned.

Longthorn drew long on his cigar. 'So, Major Coral, where are we?'

'Positive news, sir. Not perfect, but we're moving in the right direction.' Coral squinted slightly. Longthorn had a small array of lounge chairs placed on the parade square just within the sample craft's shadow. It was warm out, though a cooling breeze offered a pleasant atmosphere in the shade.

'Take a seat, major, get out of the sun and bring us up to speed.'

'Thank you, sir.' Coral stepped closer to the chairs and out of the sunlight, nodding politely toward Longthorn III who was also seated in the shade. 'Congressman.' Then he sat, upright, waiting for an invitation to speak.

Senator Longthorn drew again on his cigar and waved toward Coral. 'Well?'

'Sir, seems a similar mix wherever I go. The people – military and civilian – seem to fall into three roughly equal groups. One favours your perspective outright – the best way of supporting global recovery is to build the position here in the States first then leverage that as appropriate to help other parts of the world. The second think the brigadier has it about right and are happy to see the recovery project continue as is. There's a third group that either don't know or change their view depending on who's speaking to them.'

'I see. I'd hoped for a stronger demonstration of loyalty to the flag,' said Longthorn.

'Yes, sir. But you know there's a solid group who think like you,' said Coral.

General Pashman nodded enthusiastically. 'It's a good foundation, senator. A third are floating – I'm sure we'll swing them behind us soon enough, as your momentum grows.'

'Thank you, general, and let's be clear – I'm not looking for anything other than loyalty to our country. Nothing else,' said Longthorn.

Longthorn III held up his empty glass and waved it at a waitress who was sat a little way off, beside a refreshments trolly. She hurried forward to replenish his drink. 'It's hot today, major. Would you like a drink?' said Longthorn III.

'Thank you, sir, no. I've got a couple more meetings to attend.'

They all lapsed into silence as the waitress freshened Longthorn III's glass. Once she'd retired a little, the senator fixed Coral with a stern eye. 'You are being very careful, major?'

'Of course, sir. I'm following your advice to the letter. I never lead a conversation, just let it flow and note who expresses what views. I'm thinking most people view me as just a functionary going about his duties.'

'Good. I've learned, over a long career in politics, it pays to be careful. We mostly meet out here for a reason. I don't know what, if any, surveillance technology is installed in the sampler. I've no reason to think anyone wants to monitor me, but who knows what goes on behind the scenes?'

'No American would act against you senator! That would be a betrayal of the nation,' said Coral.

'Well, we'll see. Now tell me, major, how is the preparation going?'

'Perfectly, sir. Every time I note individuals who support your perspective, I offer gentle suggestions to their local leadership, guiding where those people's skills might best be placed. It's working. I'm steering your support to coalesce into cohesive clusters – civilian work groups, would-be pilots, engineers and military units. They don't realise it's happening, but it is.'

'Excellent. When the atmosphere is opened, I want to know the first groups sent to Primo for training and fitting of these bio-suits are all sympathetic to our aims.'

'Steady progress, sir. I could put forward a thousand names right now. Many more to come.'

'Thank you, major. And as ever, let's be careful to keep Colonel Jamison at arm's length. I'm not sure his heart's in the right place. Keep us posted.'

Major Coral stood and saluted. 'Thank you, sir.'

Chapter 30

Perseus Arm: Prenar b.

Ossie left the observer and hurried through the grass. It was much shorter here, close by the eastern river, where wild herds paused to graze while shifting between drinking spots along the bank. Just ahead, he could see Major Sarsen surrounded by a cluster of officers.

'Ossie, welcome. Glad you've joined us.' The major made brief introductions then fixed Ossie with a concerned stare. 'I hear your own team have been taking it hard at the other end of the line. A lot of losses.'

'That's right,' said Ossie. 'But you heard Jamie MacAulay made it out?'

'We did, and there are some pretty wild stories about what he's been up to.'

'Yes. Though knowing Jamie, I doubt there's any exaggeration. Seems they have the whole thing under control now. What's your position here?'

'Quieter, so far. We have four burrows stretching away in a rough line from here at the river toward Jamie's location. I've got soldiers guarding each. There are plenty more that we haven't reached yet.'

'Have you had any contact?'

'None. But our warbird has only hit each location once, so the locusts are likely still deep enough below to be undisturbed, or maybe think we're passing them by. You'll have seen as you came in to land, we have a crater just over there.' Sarsen pointed away toward a spot obscured by intervening bush.

'Without blowing a deeper hole, we can't be sure whether there is one or half-a-dozen vessels hiding below. We need to establish if the stack Jamie unearthed is the norm or a one-off,' said Ossie.

'Well, now the marines have their end under control, we'll need to find out what's hiding down here. But Ossie, we can't think why they were burrowing anyway. The locusts aren't a frightened bunch. We know they get stuck in when it comes to fighting. Have your teams come up with any reason yet?'

Ossie shook his head. 'No idea. It leaves them as sitting ducks. One guess is they assessed our warbirds far out-perform their combat vessels and decided to lure us down to places where the warbirds' advantage was reduced.'

Sarsen looked at him sharply. 'Well, that's working. We couldn't sustain our current rate of losses for long. The warbird losses are a huge price to pay for five of their combat vessels.'

'It's equally possible they didn't realise our detectors would locate them so deep beneath ground. But the truth is we just don't know why they have gone to ground here.'

Sarsen nodded. 'Well, we need to deal with them. Elsewhere about the planet there are still plenty of combat vessels flying about.'

'There are, but they are all being kept at a distance just now,' said Ossie. 'I know Colonel MacMillan has deployed flights of warbirds from the other Leviathans to ensure no locust reinforcements can get here from elsewhere on the planet. They're trying to get through, but our pilots are doing well. Gravity and the atmosphere constrain the locusts' manoeuvrability, while our gravdrives give us a superb advantage in the air.'

'The colonel said you have something new you want to test,' said Sarsen.

Ossie turned to check on the progress of technicians who were unloading kit from the observer. 'It's a laser weapon. Very loosely based on the warbird laser but scaled way back. To deliver enough power, we're using two small beams from two portable sources. The burning point is where the beams meet. We're going to need two mobile power sources. We're not sure how this will work in practice, but we do need two hoppers for power and as mounts for our lasers.'

'No problem,' said Sarsen, signing to one of his officers. The man hurried off to detail hoppers and drivers who were quick to put in an appearance, stopping at the heap of equipment stacked beside the observer. With their top hatches open, the drivers stood and leaned out to learn what was expected of them.

'Major Sarsen, I've got to get this rigged now,' said Ossie.

'Fine, go to it. Let me know when you're ready or if you need anything else. We know for sure heavy machine guns work wonders. It's a pity so few were transported up from Earth before it all went wrong. Our ones are already mounted in observer airlocks, ready to fire. We'd love more, but there you are.'

'I guess, heavy machine guns were low on the list of equipment General Dower and his planners expected to need at Primo,' said Ossie.

***

Ossie was happy the technicians had done as he asked, and now he was settled in the shotgun seat of one hopper, its driver still looking quizzically at the newly installed paraphernalia. He had seemed no clearer after Ossie had answered his questions, but the man was a veteran of the defence of Secundo and had learned to trust the science teams. Now he sat quietly waiting, confident that whatever the scientist had planned would deliver.

Sarsen had moved off with the bulk of his command. They were already concealed about the nearest blast crater, which sported fresh earth thrown up where the warbird's missile strike had opened it up.

'We're ready. Moving up to join you now,' said Ossie.

His hopper set off at a brisk pace, followed by the second with a technician overseeing operation of its duplicate equipment rig. In just a couple of minutes, they reached the location. Brushing through a cluster of bushes and low trees, they emerged at the edge of a clearing, perhaps two hundred paces wide. In the middle was the blast crater, a hole of quite modest depth.

'Hold it there, hoppers,' said Sarsen over the collar-phones.

Both hoppers stopped at once, maintaining their distance apart at twenty paces. From the longer grasses fringing the clearing, a figure rose – Sarsen made his way across to the hoppers, looked up and called to Ossie. 'I'm going to bring in the warbird now. It's detailed to blast this hole good and deep. Then we'll see what comes out.'

Ossie peered down and raised a thumb in acknowledgement. 'We're just about set.'

Turning away, Sarsen opened a comms channel, calling for action.

Either side of the clearing, the bush-line was suddenly broken as two observers raised above the green, their stern airlock doors open, with heavy black muzzles showing and shadowy figures crouched behind.

A moment later, a streak across the sky signed the arrival of a warbird missile. With unerring accuracy, it plunged into the existing shallow crater and exploded. The blast filled Sarsen's ears with noise and churned out a great plume of earth. The noise abated and dust settled as he hurried the few paces to his command point.

A small drone flew over the enlarged hole. Everything seemed quiet.

'The signal is still confused; we can't tell if it's one or more vessels.' Sevrine's voice sounded in Ossie and Sarsen's collar-phones simultaneously.

Sarsen called in another strike, then a third in rapid succession.

As the dust cleared, they saw the hole had become much wider, with most of the blast debris mounding around the edge to form a high raised lip.

The drone flew over, beaming back images that showed a deepened crater but still no sign of the target beneath.

'Just how deep did these guys dig?' said Sarsen, glancing up toward Ossie's hopper. He called in another strike, dropping to the ground as the missile came in.

'Hello, this is Sevrine. We're getting a much better scan signal now. I'm able to differentiate vessels. I can count four, but this burrow runs deeper than the previous one.'

'What does that mean?' said Sarsen.

'It's likely there are more than four vessels,' she replied.

'Okay, let me know as soon as you get a more detailed resolution.' Sarsen broke off as fresh drone footage began to come in. He studied the images displayed on his sleeve. 'Are you seeing this too, Ossie?'

'I am. Looks like you've opened the nest with that last missile. What now?'

'Let's wait a little – see what they do now we've uncovered them.

'Warbird, stand by, in case they come up firing missiles or try to make a run for it.'

'Wilco,' said the pilot. 'There's another flight of warbirds coming in; they'll stand off and catch anything that manages to break past me.'

'Good, and remember, under no circumstance fly over the crater or anywhere near groups of locusts on the ground. Some are armed with shoulder launchers. We've lost enough warbirds today.'

***

Nothing had moved about the crater in a quarter-hour, giving Ossie some extra time to refine the calibrations on his kit. The hopper driver gave up trying to understand the one audible side of a collar-phone discussion Ossie held with the technician in the second hopper. Rolling his eyes, the driver settled down to focus on the crater rim, letting the boffins get on with it.

'Driver,' said Ossie.

'Sir?'

'You understand, when my device is active, it will be drawing all the power from your hopper. You will not be able to move at all. The lasers are cross-calibrated based on our current position. Move, and we'll need to reset everything from scratch.'

'Yes, sir. I'll still have comms and peripheral circuits, won't I?'

'That's right, in theory. But this little machine we've built is very thirsty – we just don't know for certain. When the action starts, just assume you have no power.'

A sudden flash high over the crater signalled activity as the spy drone was blown from the sky.

'Stand by,' said Sarsen, his voice sounding in a hundred and more collar-phones. In silence, an extended line of fifty soldiers rose from the grass. Crouching unseen beside each was another soldier – each ready, waiting to pull the pin from a tendril grenade. 'We've got action. Get me another drone in the sky; we're blind right now.' He fell silent, as all eyes locked on the crater, then he opened another channel. 'Sevrine, are your scanners picking up anything more?'

'No movement, major. But we are getting in fresh readings on the crater since you last blasted it. Hold on, they're resolving for me now… Yes, here. Wow! Major Sarsen, it seems you have a group of twelve combat vessels set in two columns of six. Again, I confirm we've detected no movement by the vessels yet.'

'Okay, keep me posted if anything changes.' Sarsen closed the comms channel, glanced at his sergeant and then followed the man's pointing hand, signing where a newly launched drone was closing on the crater. 'There's twelve locust vessels down there, sergeant,' said Sarsen.

'That's a lot of locusts, sir.' The sergeant pursed his lips and shook his head.

'We faced more at Secundo the last time.'

'We did, sir, and we came out on top. And we've got the heavy machine guns this time. I heard talk that they really took the locusts apart earlier.'

'Yeah, you're spot on. I saw Major Browning's report. And we've got two heavy guns here. Better odds than at Secundo.'

'I'll say, sir. What about them?' The sergeant nodded back to the bush-line where the hoppers waited. 'Have the science bods got something up their sleeves?'

'They've got something, but they're a bit cagey – want to make sure it works before saying too much.'

'Approaching the crater lip now, sir,' said the technician flying the drone.

'Good, let's see what's happening,' said Sarsen. He and the sergeant turned their attention to the little scout drone, now just a black smudge approaching the crater. They looked down at a portable control unit set amid the long grass. Beside it was one technician piloting the drone, a second had control of the camera system.

As the drone cleared the crater lip, Sarsen caught his breath. The inner crater sides were covered in locusts. The foremost rank was just about at the lip. Sarsen opened a channel to all his command. 'This is it, everyone. You've got your orders. Stick with it. Do not allow yourselves to become isolated. Locusts are coming over the lip any moment.

'Observers, once they are clear of the crater, hit them with everything you've got. Let's thin them out fast.' He looked to his sergeant. 'Here we go again.'

'Yes, sir. With your permission, I'll get along to join the troops.'

'Carry on.' Sarsen looked down at the screen again. The more he looked, the worse things seemed. He'd calculated his men had the advantage of numbers. Now it seemed he'd been over-optimistic. There was a swarm coming up, so many. Then the screen went blank.

'Sorry, sir, we've lost the drone,' said the technician. Sarsen glanced up in time to see a little puff of smoke marking where the drone had hovered moments before.

'Get another one up, now. And feed the pictures through to me.' Sarsen waved a hand toward two soldiers who crouched close by. 'You two, cover these two technicians. Make sure they don't get surprised by a locust.' The soldiers acknowledged the order. Sarsen felt confident; he could see they both sported a number of tendril grenades, had sharp blades in their belts. Yes, the numbers had suddenly swung against them, but his soldiers were experienced locust fighters.

He stepped forward to join the line while tapping open a collar-phone channel. 'Hello, mortar section. I want you to start dropping mortars into the pit ASAP.' The mortar team had spent time lining up on their target, and almost at once, explosive thumps rolled across the clearing as Sarsen's mortars fired their first rounds. He looked toward the crater as the descending munitions hissed their incoming messages of death.

A moment later, explosive reports came from deep within the hole as the mortar shells detonated. He gave a grim smile and hurried on. *That would have hurt the locusts, for sure.*

A locust's antennae appeared above the crater rim, switching to and fro, attempting to sense what was ahead. Cautiously, the head rose, and big black eyes began scanning the surrounds. The observers were noted where they hovered just beyond the clearing, as were the many soldiers standing in the long grass around the clearing's edge and, beyond them, the two motionless hoppers.

Suddenly, the antennae twitched frantically, contorting as they tried to fix on an unfamiliar sound. The mortar team had fired a second volley. At such close quarters, their incoming whoosh began almost before the launch sound had faded.

The locust's head dropped from sight, quickly followed by more explosions deep inside the crater.

Everything was still for a moment, then there was a riot of movement. From their concealed spots beneath the crater rim, a first wave of locusts leaped up and over, landing on the flat beyond. Others rose to clamber across the rim and hurry to join the first landing wave. Both groups merged and, with a jump, moved swiftly into the clearing. They landed midway across and immediately sprung again.

'Observers, open fire,' said Sarsen as a further locust wave cleared the crater rim. 'They're closing fast; launch tendril grenades, prepare for contact!'

From either end of the clearing, heavy machine guns mounted in the hovering observers' airlocks burst into fire. The rat-tat-tat sounded from two directions to form a single wall of sound, punctuated by yet more mortar round explosions. Many locusts in the leading wave were peppered with heavy calibre rounds as they hurtled through the air. Their bodies seemed to perform acrobatic tricks as the heavy metal rounds punched through their outer shells, propelling them off in all directions.

The locust front line fared poorly, as yet more became entangled with flying tendril grenades that wrapped about their limbs, locking the grenades close to the hard casing of their bodies before exploding, blowing them apart.

The following line was already advancing toward the soldiers and another was forming at the crater rim. All the time the rat-tat-tat continued, cutting swathes through the locust ranks, but still, they massed and advanced.

'Bayonets ready,' shouted Sarsen. He stepped into the line, joining his soldiers as the second rank of soldiers rose from where they had been concealed in the long grass. Sarsen registered the bellowing voice of his sergeant, which echoed the order from further up the line. As the locusts closed, he had one moment to note a further wave of locusts cresting the cone. *How many are there? What's that? Oh no!*

Sarsen tapped his sleeve to call a warning to the observers, but before he could speak, a locust landed directly in front of him. He threw himself backward to avoid the lunge of its great stretching leg, the joints extending to achieve maximum reach. Sharp talons sliced at his body; he felt his body armour ripple and stretch as it was snagged, dragging him down. The locust held him trapped against the ground with one foot and loomed directly over him.

With a triumphant hiss it stooped, jaw opening, aiming direct for Sarsen's neck. He could do nothing but watch the monster's killing strike sweep in. Then a blurred image crossed above him, and the locust deflected, pulling its head up in anger. The solider beside him had dealt the locust a heavy blow to the skull with his rifle butt. Not enough to harm its exoskeleton, but just enough to distract it.

Sarsen remained pinned to the ground, and the soldier, still holding his rifle, stared up at the angry locust, which grabbed him with its short arm and pulled him toward the snapping mouth.

The soldier screamed an involuntary cry as the jaw began to close about his head. Then he was thrown to the ground as the locust suddenly clacked and hissed in distress, the sergeant's bulking figure atop it. His legs clamped about the locust's thorax and one arm about its neck, he clung on like a bronco rider. His other hand waved free, clutching the combat knife that had just swept across the locust's head. The severed antennae twitched and writhed on the ground beside Sarsen.

The sergeant jumped down from the distressed locust. Pulling out his pistol, he fired three rounds through its half-open carapace, and the locust fell, silent and dead.

'Come on, sir. Up!' shouted the sergeant, reaching his hand down and gripping Sarsen's, hauling his leader up.

Then he stooped to shake the recovering soldier by the arm and pointed to their left side where two men struggled with a locust. One, bayonet dropped, was clinging to its back, both arms wrapped about the neck – safe from the mouthparts but unable to hurt the locust in return. The second was trying to distract the locust while avoiding its flailing feet.

'Well done, soldier, good work. Now, pick up your bayonet and help those boys out. Get up there and cut those antennae.' The sergeant turned his attention back to Sarsen.

'Thank you, sergeant,' said Sarsen, scanning the field. There were hand-to-hand battles raging all about him. Beyond the scrimmage line, he could see yet another wave of locusts emerging from the pit. He took in all the locust bodies scattered in the space between. The machine guns seemed to be taking down huge numbers of locusts, but even so, the numbers reaching the conflict line were beginning to turn against him. Just so many locusts.

Then he remembered what had caught his eye a few seconds before, just as the locust had attacked him. A little team of locusts had emerged on the far side of the crater, away from the conflict zone. There they had mustered and were readying to use the weapons he'd glimpsed only moments before. Their target, the observers.

'Observer pilots, pull back. Pull back now!' He'd told the pilots to post spotters in the airlocks beside the machine-gun operators for just this eventuality. *What the hell had gone wrong?*

As he spoke, half-a-dozen telltale vapour trails raced up and over the clearing. One observer responded to his warning quickly and arced away. Its hull was hit by two missiles that destabilised it as the craft's arc continued up, then over and down, the observer plummeting into the ground. But Sarsen couldn't hear that crash over the noise of the second observer. Two missiles had plunged into the airlock. One continued into the accommodation before detonating, one exploded in the airlock. The observer burst open from within in a flowering of flame, smoke and debris.

Sarsen muttered a curse. The aircrews were all keen and brave but, as Jamie had said, just too inexperienced.

The noise of the exploding observers overlaid everything, and everywhere, soldiers and locusts alike could not help but glance to see what had happened. Sarsen knew he could not continue to hold the position. He saw yet another wave emerge over the crater rim – that lot would not suffer any losses before engaging. 'Everyone, close ranks as you can. We'll fall back as one. Now!'

The sergeant moved further along the line, his booming voice rallying the troops. The soldiers separated as best they could from the locusts. Mustering tightly together, as one, they stepped back and away from the enemy.

Sarsen looked to either hand. Half his command was still standing, others were ferrying wounded away to the rear. Perhaps fifty active soldiers in the line. More locusts, and still more approaching by the moment. 'Close up. Close up. Any with tendril grenades remaining, get them ready.'

He made a brief call to Colonel MacMillan for evacuation flights. He knew it was futile. Out in the open, men alone were no match for a locust swarm. Any rescue craft would be minutes away – minutes they didn't have. He needed more heavy machine guns and had none; they were lost with the observers. He considered diverting the warbird from its guard duty, but big picture, it had to cover the crater and prevent the locust combat vessels from getting airborne – right now, any breakout would be a disaster beyond measure.

Opening a channel, he played his only remaining card: the hoppers could come forward to physically support the retreat. He'd seen what a good hopper driver could do to a locust. It wouldn't be enough. If he had half-a-dozen hoppers, then maybe, but two… no chance. But at least they'd take some locusts with them and give some of the troops a fighting chance of escaping into the bush.

'Hello, hopper drivers. I want you to come forward now. Get out in front and kick some locusts. We'll keep in close and try to mop up those you wing while the wounded are escorted away.'

The hopper drivers acknowledged the order at once and readied to advance.

'Major Sarsen, Major Sarsen. Can you hear me?' said Ossie.

'Go ahead, Ossie, and where's your new weapon? If it works, we need it right now,' said Sarsen, while weighing the balance of his bayonet.

'I don't want the hoppers to move, major,' said Ossie.

'Sorry. Hoppers will advance,' said Sarsen.

'No, no, we've just focused our weapon. If we move, we'll have to start again – we don't have time to do that.'

'What do you mean?'

'We have fitted a pair of lasers. Steph suggested how the beams might be harmonised to hit targets.'

'Which means?'

'Each hopper has a laser. On their own, not enough to do significant damage. We've harmonised them to work together but that's set to our current relative locations. We believe we can hurt a locust with the beams – think stereo in light. I control both beams from here and—'

'What do you mean hurt?' said Sarsen curtly.

'Well, kill, I guess… we hope. But we can't change our position, or we'll need to reharmonise the two beams, and we need all the hoppers' power to run the system.'

'Fine, stay. We'll fall back to you. But whatever you've got there, Ossie, you've got one go, and we need it now.'

'We're ready when you are. But best you're behind us when we start. We're calibrated for getting through locust exoskeletons, so that won't be good for human flesh.'

Still steadily stepping back with the remains of his unit, Sarsen chanced a glance behind. The wounded were already beyond the hoppers which were now only twenty, perhaps thirty, paces off.

The locust line was matching them step for step; he sensed they wouldn't wait much longer. Opening a channel to the whole unit, he issued orders. Step by step they retreated, the locusts toying with them, frightening their prey before feasting – a cruel game. A feint forward, a rattling of carapaces and clacking mouths, still the men retreated steadily. The gap to the hoppers narrowing with every step.

Another wave of locusts joined the swarm, and suddenly silence fell – now they had overwhelming force. So many locusts, the time for toying with their prey was over. Now was the time for feasting.

'Keep pacing back! Grenadiers, stand by. Throw on my command. Then everyone run.'

A ripple of anticipation ran through the rank of retreating soldiers.

'Wait for it! Steady! On the officer's word only…' the sergeant's voice rolled across the field. Any wavering vanished, and in unison, the remains of Sarsen's company continued their measured pacing back, one step at a time.

Sarsen had been scanning the ranks of locusts. Their silence broke with a sharp hiss from a leader; the whole swarm picked it up, and the noise grew into a high-pitched whistle.

'Ready grenadiers…! And together, pins out and counting down now. Three, two, one, and throw your grenades NOW! Everyone, run!'

Sarsen turned and ran with his troops. With less than a dozen paces to pass the hoppers, they sprinted, energised like Olympic athletes. The longest two seconds on his life completed the countdown and a series of explosions rang out amid the locust ranks. So tight-packed, every blast a kill, but with so few grenades and so many locusts, he knew it would make no difference. The hissing had stopped with the grenade blasts, and without looking back, he knew they were following.

'Ossie, whatever you've got, it has to be now!' shouted Sarsen into his collar-phone.

'Just a moment, your men are nearly clear.'

'No time, use it now!'

Ossie had his helmet up; the black-eyed visor had been modified to mirror the warbird's laser aimer. Seen from inside the helmet, moving crosshairs displayed against the visor. Its bio-link meant the crosshairs moved with his eyes. Whatever his eyes lined up on was the target of the moment.

Running around and behind the two hoppers' legs were the soldiers. Following immediately behind them, a seething mass of locusts, like some medieval host charging into battle. One rank had jumped to get ahead of the fleeing humans.

Ossie pressed his sleeve to activate the lasers. From above him, where the kit had been rigged through the top viewing hatch, a fine white beam burred out. It was joined by a similar beam from the second hopper. Wherever Ossie looked, the two beams met and combined at point of touch to instantly burn to nothing whatever life form the beams encountered.

His eye had been drawn toward one of the leaping locusts. It was descending on a trajectory to land between and behind the two hoppers, just where Sarsen's men were heading to. Passing through Ossie's gaze took it through the beam, and it was sliced clean through. It landed in two parts, mouth still clacking, claws repeatedly clenching, dead.

Ossie recognised the power of the new weapon at once, and his eye swept along the front rank of locusts. They fell as though hay to the scythe. He ran his eye back and many of the second row fell. Behind them, the tightly bunched ranks were still pushing forward, and Ossie continued to sweep back and forth. If his eye could see them, they died.

'We're running low on power, sir,' said the driver. 'At this rate, we'll be flat in a minute, no more.'

'Same here,' said the other hopper driver.

Ossie let his eyes range once more along what remained of the locust line. Everywhere were heaps of dismembered bodies. A wicked smell of burning locust filled the air. He couldn't count them but sensed it was well over a hundred. The rearmost locust ranks had stopped trying to advance as they struggled to understand what they faced.

'Ossie, don't stop man! Hit them while you can. Get them all,' said Sarsen into Ossie's collar-phone.

Ossie touched his sleeve and reactivated the laser beams. They burred out across the field, following his gaze as it swept once more along the line. Everywhere, locusts died. As he ran his eye across the rearmost ranks, the surviving locusts turned to escape. Some ran, some jumped and leaped for the crater's rim. It didn't matter how they moved, they couldn't outrun Ossie's gaze.

'Power's running down, ten seconds, nine, eight… we're done,' said the driver as the beam cut out and the hopper's power displays died.

'No power here either,' said the second hopper driver.

But it didn't matter, the locusts had fled or were dead. Ossie opened his helmet and took in the wide view of the field. Countless dead locusts scattered all the way back to the crater lip.

'You nailed it, sir,' said the driver. 'That sorted them.' He reached over and clapped Ossie on the shoulder. Ossie nodded, a wistful smile on his face. It had worked way better than he could ever have imagined. The grinning driver was too ecstatic to register Ossie's pain. The scientist had never killed anything before.

Ossie climbed down from the hopper to cheers from the soldiers who quickly gathered around. Sarsen slapped him on the back.

'Great work! I knew you science bods would come up with something, but my, you played that one down. It's a killer!'

Chapter 31

Perseus Arm: HA-1 over Prenar b.

Everyone who gathered on the bridge of MacMillan's flagship Leviathan shared the same feelings. Devastation at the loss of so many people and jubilation at the effectiveness of the new portable laser. It was a game-changer.

Majors Sarsen and Browning, reinforced by companies from the other Leviathans, had worked methodically across the plain between the two rivers. One burrow after another had been cleared. Scores of combat vessels had been destroyed and countless locusts.

The many locust vessels that had not burrowed beneath the ground had been scattered about the planet. As they picked up more and more distress signals from the buried locusts, those scattered vessels had hurried back to help. Arriving in ones and twos, they were easily destroyed in short order by the patrolling warbirds.

As the number of incoming vessels had grown, MacMillan committed the fleet's last warbird reserves. They marshalled into a big wing that cut through the incoming locust vessels, burning them from the sky. The warbirds' greater manoeuvrability and gravity control reinforced their advantage as the inrushing locusts struggled between the twin constraints of gravity and planetary atmosphere.

They were swept aside at every turn.

'I still don't understand why they split their forces and buried half, so they were unable to engage fully. Had they all been active, it would have been a very different battle,' said MacMillan.

Ossie raised his hand. 'If we may, colonel?'

MacMillan nodded and Ossie stepped forward, Sevrine with him.

He looked about the group. 'We've been thinking through events. It was Steph who first identified the presence of queens, their importance in the reproductive cycle and, perhaps most importantly, the willingness of locusts to sacrifice themselves for the queen. We know the queen is key to the egg stage. But what about the full life cycle? What about the other developmental stages? Back on Pardamax, we saw how eggs are laid in clutches, each one placed in its own little cone. Nothing like a honeycomb, more like a steep-sided cell. We know locusts feed on living flesh. So, once placed in the cell, the living food source could not escape up those steep sides when the egg hatched into a larva and began to feed. With other insectoid species, as the larva feeds, it grows and eventually forms a protective shell, a pupa or chrysalis, within which it seals itself. There it undergoes a gradual transformation, or metamorphosis, until one day, a finished insect emerges, ready for life.'

'Where are you taking us with this Ossie?' said MacMillan.

Sevrine rested a hand on Ossie's arm. 'Let me, please.'

Ossie shrugged.

She looked about the group. 'At Pardamax, we came across evidence of the early reproductive stage, a feeding queen laying eggs, those eggs protected and tended by worker locusts. When the eggs hatched into larvae, they were contained in cone-like cells and fed live food. You all know that—'

'Sevrine, what does that have to do with the locusts' behaviour down on Prenar b.? Why are they digging in?' said Jamie.

She raised a hand, one finger up. 'Eggs laid'—a second finger rose—'larvae hatched'—a third finger—'chrysalis formed.' Her hands came together, palms up, as she gave a theatrical shrug. 'But where are all those chrysalides? There was no sign of them on Pardamax. They must have been moved.

'Pardamax was eaten out, nothing other than the smallest animals surviving. It would take centuries – millennia – for large animals to evolve again. Had the locusts emerged after their metamorphosis there, they would have starved. What's different here on Prenar b. is we're seeing virtually no significant consumption of animal stocks. The locusts that have not buried themselves on the plain have dispersed about the planet to feed, just grazing and thinning herds rather than massacring everything. The locusts are treating this planet differently to the others—' she broke off as MacMillan raised his hand, interrupting.

'Sevrine, Ossie, again, please, both of you get to the point,' said the colonel.

Ossie jabbed his hand at the viewscreen where Prenar b. loomed large. 'We think… believe what's happening down there is a stage of the locust reproductive cycle. All those combat vessels buried deep beneath ground with their locust crews; they're not hiding from us – they're burying the next generation of locusts, the chrysalides. Once the burial is complete, the rest of the fleet will move on to feast elsewhere, leaving this planet as a pristine nursery ready for the next generation's emergence. They're planting another new locust swarm to plague the galaxy.

'When the locusts eventually burst out of their pupae – in one, ten, a hundred, a thousand years' time, we don't know – they will be contained, safe and deep below ground. Presumably, the accompanying adult locusts were to hibernate below ground with them until that emergence. Then they'd wake to act as protectors, teachers and trainers for the new swarm.' Ossie looked about him, ready to field questions. None came.

'I can see your logic,' said Jamie. 'Does this mean we can effectively destroy all the locusts?'

Ossie shook his head. 'I don't think so. The swarm at Pardamax had eaten the planet bare. We know, when it left there, at least three queens had emerged. Presumably, when they split from there, it was with the intention of generating several new swarms. We destroyed one when they attacked Primo. We're on top of this one now, thanks to your warbirds and the soldiers with the new lasers. It will take a little time to eliminate them, but here, our technological advantage is absolute.

'There's still the cone and its swarm in the Pelesius System, and I expect you'll now have a similar edge there when we attack. But that's not an end to it. The locusts don't swarm and move on. We've seen they divide up and swarm. That's a practice seen on Earth too. Sevrine and I believe the swarm we first encountered at Pardamax would long ago have been part of a swarm that itself divided, far away, who knows where in the galaxy.'

'You mean there could be more locusts elsewhere?' said Jamie.

'We think it's almost certain. But they could be anywhere, working along the spiral arms. It's such a big place to get lost in – we may never find them,' said Ossie.

'Well, that's a problem for another crew another day,' said MacMillan. 'Right now, I want all our effort focused on destroying the locusts here, along with every one of their vessels. If we miss a few locusts, I don't want them mobile. At the very least, we can ensure they're trapped here. There's a lot of work to do before we're finished here, plenty more burrows to clear. It'll take some time, so let's get on and finish the job. Meanwhile, Jamie, you and I need to be thinking about how we deal with Pelesius next.'

Chapter 32

Earth

Celine half-turned in her seat, twisting away from the room full of people, and whispered into her collar-phone. 'Repeat that please.' She listened intently before firing a series of whispered questions. Each answer prompted another hushed and yet more urgent question in response.

Brigadier Smith-Brown was stood beside her, busy delivering a closing speech to the roomful of delegates, wishing his international visitors a safe flight back to their countries at the conclusion of the first pan-national recovery meeting. It had been positive. Everywhere needed more, and yet most interim leaders understood the limits of the current recovery project. Even Congressman Longthorn III, attending in his grandfather's stead, though sullen, had managed not to sound a dissenting voice.

The brigadier paused at the gentle tug on his sleeve and looked down toward Celine. His eyebrow arched slightly, asking a silent question.

She stood and pressed close to his ear. 'Brigadier, we're picking up a signal!'

Smith-Brown's renowned self-control betrayed nothing to the watching audience.

'Ladies, gentlemen, please – wait one moment.' The brigadier's hand was raised, his voice carried across the room, calm as ever, giving no indication of the reason for the delay. The delegates dutifully waited, watching him with passing interest, wondering what new obstruction might have arisen.

Turning from the crowd, he asked Celine to expand.

'First hint of it was about twenty minutes ago. Very faint. Sparks thought it was just a natural anomaly at first. But he's been monitoring it, trying to clean it up. The signal is broken and diffused by the debris field, but in spite of that, he's decided it's too consistent. It has to be a message.'

'How can that be? I thought you'd calculated it would be some time yet before our snowplough had cleared enough debris to get a signal out.'

'I did. But this is a signal coming in to us.'

'But the distortion will be the same in each direction, surely?'

'Yes. There's only one logical answer. Somebody, it can only be Primo, has marshalled a second fleet of samplers and is deflecting away debris from above. Even as we're working our way up, they're working down to us, broadcasting a constant signal as they come. It will dramatically reduce the time it takes to clear the atmosphere.'

'How much time?'

'I can't say yet. But hopefully, we will be able to establish proper communications very soon. And brigadier, it means we can be confident Primo saw off the locusts.'

The brigadier allowed himself a slight smile then suddenly frowned. 'Unless it's the locusts…'

'No, it can't be. They don't have the bio-suits needed to control anything, much less a fleet of samplers working in close order. It's Primo, for sure.'

Smith-Brown nodded. Pursed his lips for a moment. 'Are you quite sure there can be no other explanation for the signal?'

Celine nodded, her eyes sparkling with excitement. That sparkle, perhaps more than the nod, convinced the brigadier of her confidence in the signal's meaning.

He turned to face the waiting audience.

'Delegates, thank you for your patience. It gives me the greatest pleasure to relay Celine's report that the communications officer has picked up a signal. It appears Primo has more samplers working to clear the atmosphere down toward us. Our work at clearing—'

His words vanished in a roar of cheering as the delegates erupted in joy at the first piece of truly good news any had received beyond their own personal survival. The tumult continued for several minutes, and the brigadier did nothing to curtail it while Celine continued to whisper further detail. Eventually, though, he was obliged to call for order.

Looking round the room, he could see there were a hundred questions waiting to be asked. Every one of them would ultimately boil down to the same thing.

How long?

'I know what you want to hear. I'm afraid it's too early to say when we will break through the atmosphere. But it's going to happen, and far sooner than we'd ever imagined. Thanks to those on Primo who've been attacking the problem from above, and particular thanks to Celine and her team down here, who have worked tirelessly for us to clear the debris from below.'

The delegates rose as one to cheer Celine, and she could do nothing more than smile.

'That is all I can report today, but be assured,' the brigadier, continued with a raised voice, 'we will keep you all informed. As soon as we have more news, it will be shared. The plans we made today may need to be revised in the light of developments, but I know everyone will be happy to reconvene to that end. Now, for the second time, thank you all for attending. Everyone, have safe journeys back and get ready. When the atmosphere reopens, things are going to change fast, and I sincerely hope, that will be very soon.'

Chapter 33

Perseus Arm: Pelesius System

Standing far off, under Captain Stewart's cautious command, HB-3 had been maintaining a careful watch over the locusts at Pelesius d.

During the day of the cone's destruction, the curve of the planet's atmosphere had highlighted scores of combat vessels rising at random from the planet to flit aimlessly around like wasps about a broken nest before dropping back down, only to be replaced by other equally lost locusts.

On the second day, the aimless buzzing of the combat vessels was steadily replaced by increasingly coordinated action, with vessels assembling into flight formations of ever larger scale.

Stewart looked up from the navigation LPA toward Joe Li, his chief scientist. As a child, Li had moved with his parents to Britain from Hong Kong. He didn't recall much of the city of his birth. He just thought of himself as British – a British Hongkonger. 'What should we make of this change in behaviour, Joe? Looks to me like they're getting organised.'

'It does, captain. They must be pulling themselves together after the loss of the cone.'

'How do you think they'll cope?' said Stewart.

'Given time, I expect they'll build a new one. To us, they always seem focused on killing and eating, but for them to have achieved their level of knowledge and technology, they must invest effort in other things, liked shipbuilding, from time to time.' Joe paused, looked thoughtful. 'And who knows, perhaps reaching a new planet is the trigger for rearing a new queen? A new generation.'

'How would they create a queen?'

'I don't know. Some insect colonies influence the creation of new queens by the way they feed and care for larvae, selecting some to develop into queens. But we determined that the larval stage of their current reproduction cycle is past. So it can't be that. Perhaps there were already some proto-queens among the pupae they transported.'

'Would one be ready to emerge already?' said Stewart.

'We've been monitoring their communications, using the translation system Steph's team developed back at Primo. After yesterday's woe and jabbering, it's all gone quiet and business-like. Whatever's happening down on the surface is not being discussed by the vessels mounting patrols above the atmosphere.'

'Okay, Joe, keep your team on it. As soon as there's a breakthrough, let me know.' Stewart stepped across the navigation room to the bridge doorway, pulled back the deadlight curtain and leaned his head in. 'I'm going to my cabin now. Maintain this distance and call me if anything changes out there.'

'Very good, sir,' said the first officer.

Chapter 34

Earth

Major Coral's most recent message had shown his true worth and Senator Longthorn was delighted. He rose from his lounge chair and strode toward the observer that had just landed on the parade square beside the great sampler. Longthorn III matched his grandfather step for step. Neither man spoke, every effort focused on closing the distance fast.

The observer access door slid open to reveal Coral lending an arm to assist a frail and stooping man onto the tarmac.

'There he is!' called Longthorn, pointing toward the visitor who was unkempt and dressed in a set of military overalls at least two sizes too big. 'Man of the moment. Good to see you, senator! Welcome aboard.' They embraced like old friends. Then Longthorn took a step back, carefully masking his repulsion at the smell of unwashed humanity. 'Senator Al Petraeus, my old friend and colleague! Thank the Lord! Wonderful that you made it. You know my grandson, of course. Who'd have thought it? We three, I think, are the extent of America's surviving lawmakers. Welcome to the hub; everything spins through here.'

A soldier hurried from beneath the sampler's shadow pushing a wheelchair, and the ageing senator slumped into it. The man was little more than sixty, but arthritis had been an early visitor and cruelly wreaked its damage throughout his joints.

'Longthorn, what in God's name has happened?' said Petraeus. 'Thank God your search squads found me. I've spent I don't know how long alone at my ranch surrounded by dead people. It's been hell, Longthorn. How in damnation did all this happen? What happened? Where did you get all…' The senator waved his arm toward the sampler, let it fall and just shook his head, uncomprehending.

'Come on over here. Let's get you a drink – you look like you could do with one.' Longthorn set off toward the chairs, signing for the soldier to push Senator Petraeus.

The group reached the furniture, and Longthorn beckoned forward a waiter. 'Drinks! My usual, Senator Petraeus takes the same.

'Soldier, you can go.

'Now Al, you can put your hardships behind you. You're safe. Here, everyone will be attending to your needs, or I'll know the reason why. You have a cabin on the sampler, close to mine, and I've had a young woman volunteer to look after you.' He waved toward the waiter's station where a fresh-faced young nurse, herself only recently rescued, waited to be called forward. 'Once we've had a drink, she'll get you on board and take care of everything for you. You can get cleaned up. The doctor's booked to visit you in your cabin. I've allocated him to dedicated duties in the hub. We need to make sure everyone here at the centre is kept fit and well to support the recovery everywhere else.'

Senator Petraeus looked stunned. Less than six hours ago, he had been struggling to make it through the day. Wife dead, daughter dead, grandchildren dead. House staff dead, ranch hands dead – everyone dead. He couldn't bury any of them. He'd moved out of the house, the environment inside having become too oppressive, instead settling into a shed and living off tinned foods foraged from the kitchen larder.

That had ended when the house caught fire, cremating everything within. A kind of blessing, burning away the smell of dead human, but he'd been reduced to scrabbling in the dirt for greens and roots to eat. When the soldiers had found him, he was close to the end.

Petraeus eyed the glass of Bourbon then brought it to his lips. His cheeks drew in, responding to the spirit's fire. He swallowed and gasped. The waiter stepped forward to refill the glass.

'Just leave the bottle. The senator will take it to his cabin,' said Longthorn. The waiter stepped away to stand beside Petraeus' newly appointed carer.

The senators talked for several minutes, sharing personal losses. Then, after the broadest brush explanation, Longthorn moved matters along. 'Al, I'm sorry for your losses. It's tough but we've all lost. I'll not lie to you, everything's a mess and we're working flat out to restore order, getting the country back under control. I'll get you fully up to speed later. For now, just know things are starting to move in the right direction at last. I can see you're beat; we need to get you on board the sampler.

'Your girl will help with anything you need, get you cleaned up, get you some food, clean clothes, deal with anything else you want. The doctor will check you over, get you the drugs you need, no problem. Once you're rested and comfortable, we can talk about how we three sort this country out.'

He raised a hand and beckoned the nurse forward. 'Here she is. Becca, take good care of Senator Petraeus – he's important to America, to all of us.'

'Yes, sir,' said Becca, gripping the wheelchair's push handles. Senator Petraeus was fast asleep.

For a few moments, the two Longthorns watched as Becca wheeled Petraeus off toward the sampler. As they made the ramp, Longthorn III turned to his grandfather. 'What next, sir?'

'What next? You watch him like a hawk. I don't want him left alone with the likes of Colonel Jamison. Al Petraeus is sickly, which makes him vulnerable; we need him comfortable and seeing the world through our eyes. So, your every effort is needed to keep him well and on side. Luckily, he's a party man. If he knows which way we're heading, he'll fall in line. Let's just keep him close.'

'I'm on it. But why are we making such a fuss over him? He's sick and just about done.'

'Because, grandson, Al Petraeus is our key to control.'

'He is?'

'Oh, yes. Trust me. Right now, that British brigadier is keeping us from full control of the recovery project because of what he asserts is his existing command structure; he reports directly to General Dower, who has asserted his command is now independent of any civilian input. But believe me, control of the recovery project is small fry. Which is why we've not been rocking the boat. We want control of Primo – that's where our and America's interests lie. To do that we have to get around General Dower.'

'What's the plan?'

'Six hours ago, it was complicated; now, it just got simple. I know Dower, one senator's voice would not be enough to sway him. He'd cite my self-interest and ignore my orders.'

'He's a dog!'

'Oh, worse than that, he's a conscientious prig. But it does appear his last order from the secretary of defense gave him direct control of Primo over my head. I can't change that alone. But two senators…'

'Of course. And with me representing the House, we are as true a voice of American democracy as there is.'

'Exactly. With Petraeus in tow, we can legitimately transfer control from Dower. And he's too much the honest man, too much a go-by-the-book man, to resist.'

Longthorn smiled, drained his glass and beckoned the waiter back.

Chapter 35

Perseus Arm: HB-3 at Pelesius d.

The first officer stood in the bridge doorway. He looked ahead to the viewscreen while listening for Joe Li's commentary from where the scientist was stooped over the navigation LPA. Li peered deep inside while his hand tweaked at sleeve settings to shift scale and focus. For many days, the locusts had settled into a predictable behaviour pattern. That had suddenly changed.

'There is definitely something happening in the atmosphere. Several vessels have just dropped from their orbits – uncontrolled descents. One exploded for sure. Can you see anything on the screen?' said Li.

The first officer shook his head. 'Nothing, we're too far off.'

'What have we got Number One?' said Captain Stewart as he hurried to join his first officer.

'Science is detecting disturbances in the atmosphere, looks like vessels are struggling to stay airborne. But we're too far off for any detailed visuals,' said the first officer, waving his hand up toward the screen.

Stewart nodded, pursing his lips as he searched the screen for detail. Frustrated, he turned back into the navigation room. 'Joe, what are you seeing?'

Li looked up from the LPA. 'It's fascinating, captain. See – it looks as though some combat vessels are trying to leave the planet, get into space. But something is stopping them.'

'What?'

'I've no idea. But a lot of them are going down. Something big is happening.'

Stewart looked to his first officer. 'Number One! Move us in fast. We need closer visual on this, need to know what's going on.'

'Moving ahead now, sir.'

Its previous discreet stance abandoned, the Leviathan raced to close on Pelesius d., hurrying to understand what was happening. Still orbiting about the planet were perhaps fifty combat vessels, untouched by whatever was unfolding below. As the Leviathan closed sufficiently to gain clear sight of events, it was evident that, whatever *it* was, it was still happening.

Joe Li instinctively raised a hand and swept it across his head of close-cropped hair, muttering to himself as he tried to rationalise events.

Captain Stewart pointed to the screen. 'Look, here comes another.' The whole bridge crew focused on the distant image of a combat vessel rising fast through the atmosphere. It was racing to join the flotilla of vessels stationed over the planet. Making good speed, it was clearing the atmosphere when it just stopped, all power lost. It hung in space for a few moments then began to fall back into the atmosphere.

'What?' said Stewart as a burning red cape of fire formed about the vessel, marking its uncontrolled re-entry to the atmosphere.

'There's another,' said the watchkeeper, her arm pointing to the far side of the screen where a vessel had been climbing out of the atmosphere only to stall and plunge back down.

'They can't all just be running out of fuel,' said Joe. 'It makes no sense. They must be fighting between themselves.'

Stewart wasn't so sure. He looked to his first officer. 'Stand the crew to, Number One. For whatever reason, the locusts seem to be in some sort of self-destructive mode. That's good, but with fifty vessels in formation over there, we need to be alert and ready for anything at a moment's notice. Watch them like a hawk.'

'Very good, sir. Shall I launch the warbirds as a screen?'

'No, keep them in the hangar, ready to launch.' Stewart only had two warbirds on board; he wanted to keep his force together unless really necessary. 'The locusts must have seen us, but they are treating us as a sideshow. Whatever else is happening – right now, we don't matter.

'Joe, are we close enough for your lot to do a surface scan? Get me some info from somewhere.'

'Already on it, captain. We are picking up disruptions that are likely explosions. There may well be fighting going on at the surface, certainly something is sustaining damage.'

'And what's downing those vessels trying to escape?'

'We can't tell. They just seem to lose power and drop away.'

'Okay, keep your team on it,' said Stewart. 'Number One, hold our position here. Any closer and we'll be within missile range. That locust flotilla may not be interested in us right now but better safe than sorry.'

'Yes, sir,' replied the first officer.

Stewart's collar-phone signalled a call from the comms control room. 'Yes, Sparks, what have you got?'

'Sir,' said Sparks, 'first time we've ever encountered this – a real debate among the locust ranks. Our translation isn't perfect, but it seems there's an argument raging among the flotilla of combat vessels. Seems some thought it best to stay up, others want to get down to the surface and help rescue the queen.'

'But rescue the queen from who? Is it a rebellion?' said Stewart.

'Sir, they're going in now,' said the first officer. All eyes on the bridge turned to watch the whole locust flotilla tilt and dive into the atmosphere as one. The Leviathan was alone in space.

'I'm guessing they've decided whose side they're on,' said Joe.

'Fair dues to them. They never do anything by halves,' said Sparks, who had appeared at the bridge doorway.

'Yes, with a bit of luck they'll wipe themselves out,' said Stewart. 'Okay Number One, move us in closer now. Establish a very high orbit; keep a close eye for anything coming up from the planet.'

***

'Captain Stewart, we've got a change here. Can you return to the bridge?' said the second officer. Now midway through his watch, things on the surface had been quieter for some time, but the quiet had adopted a strange aspect.

'What have we got?' said Stewart, hurrying onto the bridge.

'We're still all quiet out there, sir – no vessels coming up from the atmosphere.'

'And?'

'Sparks has reported a change in comms. All communication from the planet has just gone. Quietened down then simply petered out, ended, radio silence.'

'We need to know what's happened down there,' said Stewart, as he turned to stare up at the viewscreen and the calm, seemingly untroubled planet. 'Call the crew back to stations; we need to get to the bottom of this right now. There's something not right here, for sure.'

'I've been running more of their transmissions through the translator,' said Joe Li, joining the bridge team. 'It's truly weird. There's been a conflict down there, we know, but it sounds like even the locusts didn't understand what was happening.'

'That may be a good sign.'

'Yes, sir, perhaps. But Sparks is pretty concerned…'

'Captain, it's crazy,' said Sparks, joining them on the bridge. 'There are definitely no signals coming up from the planet. Nothing. And that can't be. We know there were several hundred combat vessels shed from the cone. Not to mention individual locusts making calls. It's all gone silent. Like there's nothing there at all.'

'Impossible! There must be something.'

'I've checked and checked again. Just radio silence.'

'He's right,' said Li, while taking a collar-phone message from his team. 'I'll tell you what our scans are saying: there are downed and wrecked locust vessels everywhere. Whatever happened down there, it's as though they fought to the last locust, literally.'

'What triggered this?'

Joe shrugged, then half-turned away to take a further call from his science team. 'Are you sure…? Okay, we'll see what to make of it.' He closed the call and turned back to the captain. 'There doesn't appear to be any technology in use down there at all. But some things are moving about… big things that we can't identify. Mostly in the water – life of some sort. They're… they're… insubstantial, like shadows, coming and going. We think perhaps they vanish when diving deep to feed then surface for air.'

'Locust-related?'

'Not based on our knowledge of locusts, no. Whatever they are, their movements are uncoordinated, quite random, natural behaviours. Seemingly benign, part of the planet's natural fauna going about its business. Probably quite oblivious to the destruction that's just unfolded.'

Captain Stewart again gazed into the viewscreen. Everyone followed his gaze, and a long moment of silence prevailed. 'Right. We need to understand what happened down there. We need to know if it was an act of self-destruction – some of their previous behaviours tell us they could be single-minded enough for that. Or did the locusts come unstuck against something else? Something dangerous. Something more dangerous than locusts?'

There was a slight stir among the bridge crew. *More dangerous?*

'I want an observer down to the surface and a warbird flying shotgun. They are to keep a channel open with Sparks in the comms control room at all times. Let's get a sense of what happened to the locusts and, if not self-inflicted, what might have done it.'

Chapter 36

Perseus Arm: Pelesius d.

Like all of HB-3's crew, Zac Peres had followed the earlier events with puzzlement. Yes, it seemed the locusts were spent, but why and how? Unanswered questions demanded extra care. Guiding his warbird in a cautious descent, he kept his eyes on the sky around and below. Meanwhile, turned in her bucket seat, co-pilot Stacey watched in the LPA for any signs of unwanted company. The only moving signal was the observer that was following in directly astern of them.

They broke through the cloud layer at about five thousand feet. Directly below was a broad yellow streak of coastal sand. To their right, blue sea, smooth and calm, reaching out to the horizon. To their left, the sand gave way to steep, reed-covered dunes, behind which was a plain, greened by wild grasses and stands of hardy trees, all shaped and bent away from the coast and what must have been the prevailing wind. Today the air was still.

Zac glanced toward Stacey. 'We'll follow the coastline to where the first locust signal is showing. Beyond that, there's a bigger cluster. The scans show they're all inactive. No life signs showing so it should be quiet, but who knows? Let's find out. I'll need to focus on flying; you take control of the laser. If anything at all even hints at a threat from the surface, laser it first, ask questions later. Just burn it.'

He set the warbird into a gentle turn, aligning with the coastline while continuing their steady descent. 'Hello, observer. Stay well astern of me. Once we're over the locust vessel, we'll do a circuit, check for any nasties, then stand watch while you go in and check it out properly.'

The warbird continued toward its destination. With the sun shining behind them, they flew along the beach-line. On one side, Zac could see inland to where small groups of animals stood amid the grasses. Unconcerned by the craft passing overhead, some ate contentedly while others moved slowly toward whatever new greenery attracted them. Flocks of birds cruised beneath the craft, patrolling the beach-line. As every wave broke and retreated from the beach to the sea, birds swooped down to collect fresh food from the wetted sand. Just off the coast, Zac spotted numerous large shadows swimming beneath the waters. This was a bountiful planet.

***

'All quiet everywhere,' said Lieutenant Beth Surtees, the observer's pilot. She looked up from the LPA set at the back of the observer's bridge. 'The first target anomaly is coming up – it should be a locust combat vessel. We will get a visual pretty soon.' She stepped forward, dividing her attention between the viewscreen and data refreshing on her sleeve display.

'There it is,' said Lieutenant Bach, the ground team leader, while pointing up toward the viewscreen.

'I see it too,' said Beth. Then she paused to answer a collar-phone call from the warbird. 'Hello, Zac. Yes, we see it... Okay, I'll put the observer down about fifty paces from the vessel. The lieutenant and his team are ready to go now. Stand by, we're going in to land.'

'We'll head to the airlock,' said Bach.

Beth watched him and his squad leave the bridge then she turned her focus to landing the observer. In the back of her mind was the pleasure every human experiences when a new relationship begins to take shape. She and Zac had been spending a lot of time together. She felt especially reassured that it was him flying shotgun over her observer and its landing party.

***

The airlock door slid open to reveal the nearby dead hulk of a locust vessel. Already, a little line of sand was pressing up against its seaward side. Soon enough, it would be claimed by the planet, buried forever beneath the sand.

'What do you think?' said Bach to the sergeant standing beside him in the airlock.

'Nothing moving, sir.'

'It's completely dead. No residual energy consumption of any sort and no life signs in the area,' said Hazel, the scientist detailed to the team. She wafted a little scanner about. 'Nothing.'

'Those are tough vessels; I wonder what could have stopped it like that,' said the sergeant.

'I guess we'd better go see,' said Bach. He waved two soldiers forward, and they darted ahead, scouting for any signs of danger. Leaving two soldiers at the heavy machine gun in the airlock, Bach led Hazel and the sergeant out toward the downed locust attack vessel. Two more soldiers brought up the rear.

Ahead, both the scouts waved almost simultaneously. Bach picked up the pace and quickly reached the nearest scout who stood over a body. Weapon at the ready, he glanced about searching for whatever could have inflicted such damage.

Bach took in the scene then waved the sergeant and one soldier on toward the second scout. 'See what he's got over there.'

As the sergeant departed, Bach stepped close to the locust body and knelt beside it. He reached out and pressed the palm of his hand hard against the locust's shell, which was covered in a mosaic pattern of cracks. It gave beneath the pressure of his hand. As he released the pressure, the broken shell eased partially back into place.

'What's happed here?' said Hazel.

'That bad boy's been crushed. God knows by what – locust shells are tough as hell.'

'And that?' said Hazel, pointing gingerly toward the locust's head.

The top was missing, as though chopped off.

'And that is nasty,' said Bach, shuffling round to the head. 'Come see.'

She crouched beside him and immediately struggled to contain her retch reflex.

'Head bitten open and life drained out from the top. You'll need to record this for your science teams. Whatever did this is an expert killer.'

Hazel had regained her composure and began recording the find. 'It may be some cannibalistic ritual, but if so, it's extremely inefficient. The feeding component is insignificant, and it's certainly not the way we know the locusts like to eat. We've never come across evidence of cannibalism before.'

'Look at the head. It's been opened cleanly like a machete on a coconut. That's not the locust way,' said Bach. He looked up and acknowledged his sergeant's shout. 'Come on, let's see what they've got.'

Joining the sergeant, they were faced with an almost identical scene. A dead locust: crushed so its exoskeleton cracked like chainmail, head opened by a single clean chop or cut… or bite.

'What do you think, sergeant?' said Bach.

'I see locust footprints here and there, but for the most part, the sand seems rolled smooth. Could be some sort of local weather phenomenon, maybe?'

'You're right. Same with the other victim – only locust footprints. Looks as though only locusts were involved. But how did they do that shell-crushing business? We need to know how that works.' Bach looked toward the nearby vessel, where several more bodies were scattered about the open stern hatch that let into the cargo bay. He turned toward the observer, raised a hand then pointed toward the locust vessel. 'We're going forward now. You'll have seen what we found from our bodycam transmissions; looks like more of the same ahead.'

His collar-phone crackled with an acknowledgement from Beth Surtees on the observer.

Then, as Bach turned back to the locust vessel, his collar-phone opened again. 'Hello, Bach. Warbird here. FYI, we've spotted a bunch more locusts scattered at random about the sands. I confirm, all are down.'

Lieutenant Bach raised a hand and waved an acknowledgement toward the circling warbird. 'Roger that, Zac. We'll double-check them once we've finished here.'

The locusts scattered about the entrance to the vessel were all clearly dead, and all had died in exactly the same way. Crushed exoskeleton, bitten head resulting in what seemed a certain kill every time. The team could see more bodies inside the hold. Evidence gathered, they circled around the vessel. Reaching the front, they spotted the nose cone's inset heavy glazing panes that ordinarily offered the bridge deck some limited external view. The glass was broken, holes punched through from the outside to give direct access to the bridge from without.

Circuit complete, Bach again stood at the stern entrance to the cargo bay. 'Right, let's get it done. You two soldiers, stay on guard here. Everyone else, on me.'

As they made their way forward through the smooth-sided cargo bay, they passed several more dead locusts. A cursory glance was enough to confirm cause of death. Already, they had resorted to simply counting bodies. At the forward end of the cargo bay was the great winch used to haul nets filled with live prey into the vessel. Set in the deckhead was the hatch they knew let into the locusts' living quarters.

'Come on,' said Bach, and the sergeant joined him to push at the hatch, which quickly swung up and away. The sergeant linked his hands to offer Bach a stirrup boost and the lieutenant heaved himself up. Quickly swinging his legs into the upper passage, he jumped to his feet. There was no threat here. Everywhere were dead locusts – every death the same. He bent down to offer the sergeant a hand.

The team searched the vessel but found nothing alive and no evidence as to the killers.

On reaching the cockpit, Hazel knelt down and began measuring the wounds that split every locust skull so precisely. Her growing suspicions were quickly confirmed. 'Lieutenant Bach, this doesn't add up,' she said.

'Hazel, nothing adds up. What bit are you talking about?'

'See,' she said. Having unfolded a measuring scale, she had set it against a locust's jaw that yawned wide in a lost death scream. 'There's no doubt a locust jaw is strong enough to bite through locust shell, including the skull. But look at the size of the head wound…' She turned the measuring rod, moving it against the split skull. 'That wound is far too big to have been inflicted by a locust jaw.'

Bach knelt beside her. 'Are you certain?'

'For sure, the locusts have a big bite, but it's just not physically possible for their jaws to open that wide.'

'And we're sure it's a bite? Not some ritual weapon the locusts might use against one another?'

Hazel gave him a blank look. 'Honestly? I can't be certain of anything. I don't know how the locust shells have been crushed; I don't know how their heads are opened or what with, by bite or mechanically. I do know it's not locust jaw on locust head.'

Bach tutted to himself. 'Sorry. We're all grasping at straws.'

He stood and stepped to the shattered remains of what had been a glass viewing port, inches thick. Outside was the perfect peace of a beach, washed by gentle waves and caressed under a warming sun. Inside, a butcher's shambles. Leaning on the port's rim, he considered the glass, designed to cope with the immense pressures of flight and space vacuum. *What had punched through that? What could?*

He opened a channel. 'Hello, all stations. Be advised, this is likely not locust-on-locust, so there may be something else out there. Something nasty. We're done with this vessel, moving on now.'

As he made to move away from the port, something caught his eye. 'Hazel, what's this?'

She joined him and produced tweezers to poke at a sliver of something that was caught on the jagged glass edge. 'I don't know.' She produced a magnifier and studied it closely. 'It's very fine, sheer, gossamer like, but'—she tugged gently, trying to remove the sample from where it was caught on the broken glass—'incredibly strong.' It came loose and she presented it to Bach. 'It's not part of the glass port.'

'No, which means it's a foreign body. Likely scraped off whatever punched through this glass to get at the crew inside. What is it?'

'I can't say – strong like metal, soft and flowing as silk. And I think there's the faintest of patterns, see.' She held it up to the shaft of sunlight that was now pushing thought the broken port. It shimmered the slightest shade of violet then lapsed to bland sheer. 'We'll need to get it up to the Leviathan and put it through a mass spectrometer as soon as possible.'

Chapter 37

Earth

'Hearing you clear as a bell, general,' said the brigadier. He beamed across a comms workstation to Celine whose expression offered nothing but smiles. Sat between them was Sparks, quietly tutting and tweaking at controls, seeking out the best possible signal. At last, the debris field was depleted sufficiently for good communication – almost safe for space traffic.

'Great. You're coming through clear too. A short time delay, but we'd expect that. How are things?' General Dower's voice played out through the room, reassuring everyone things were coming back together.

'The virus' impact was every bit as bad as Steph had feared. Mass mortality everywhere. There are survivors, and we've made a start on rescue and restoration, but it's a mammoth task,' said the brigadier.

'Okay. What are your priorities?'

'Our rescue model is effective, but we are just too small-scale. We need lots more observer pilots, more staff able to populate and operate our equipment on the regional hubs. The solar storm fried every electrical circuit, active or passive, everywhere. Now we need Primo to start manufacturing electrical products for distribution – torches, heaters, radios, everything. But be sure they are produced for manual operation – no bio-suit constraints.'

'Right, I'm on that. We'll start to marshal our resources, focus everything on your needs. I understand it will take a few days more to ensure the atmosphere is safe for craft to get down to you. As soon as we can, you'll get everything we've got.'

'Thank you, general. I should say the best way to expand will be to get some survivors up to you, fit them with bio-suits and train them so they can get back down here to contribute. Right now, we're just scratching the surface of this problem. If you gave me every person you have at Primo, it wouldn't begin to be enough.'

'Agreed, we can start that process as soon as the atmosphere's open. As long as you have candidates, we can ferry them up here in the craft used to bring down kit. Get a rota going.'

'There's no shortage of recruits here, general.'

'Good. It's been a pleasure to speak with you again, and I'm looking forward to seeing you face-to-face soon. Now I'll hand this line over to admin – let's get a detailed spec of exactly what's needed. From that, Steph will sort out print manufacture and whatever else. I'll make sure we have a convoy ready to come in as soon as the atmosphere is given the all-clear.'

'General! Hold on one. There's something else.'

'Go on.'

'We've turned up some survivors you'll know.'

'Excellent, who are they?'

'Senator Longthorn and his grandson, Congressman Longthorn III. Another senator, Al Petraeus, and General Pashman, vice chair of the Joint Chiefs.'

There was a time delay considerably longer than merited by the distance between them.

'I see. Please pass my greetings on. But both Longthorns survived? What are the odds on that?'

'Celine's already commented on it. Slim to none, she reckons. But they made it. We found the Longthorns and General Pashman holed up in a backwoods bunker.'

'Okay, interesting. What is Longthorn up to?'

'All good here, no problem at all. At first, he tried to assert global control of our rescue. I pushed that back. He's settled himself in as head of American rescue and restoration. It seems to be working out.'

'Let me think on it. There may be some difficulties ahead with Longthorn. But right now, let's focus all our efforts on readying for the atmosphere's opening. Two weeks is the target.

'Meantime, let's you and I schedule daily talks to get us all up to speed everywhere… Get ourselves in order ahead of the atmosphere opening.'

***

Senator Longthorn stepped through the opening door and beamed a smile toward his fellow senator. 'Great news, Al, I've just heard that a full signal is getting through to the Primo Base. It won't be long before craft can get through safely. Then the recovery can really begin.'

Petraeus nodded an acknowledgement. His infirmities and the shock of losing all his family before his eyes had extinguished much of what remained of his enthusiasm for life.

Longthorn waved toward the door, directing the young nurse out. She hesitated for just a moment. Then, with a tweak at the blanket resting over the senator's knees and a gentle hand of reassurance on his forearm, she obediently left.

As soon as she'd gone, Longthorn leaned across to his fellow senator. 'Won't be long now, Al. I know it's tough for you, but I'm going to need you to be strong for America. We both agree on the need for proper control of Primo, to make sure it doesn't fall under the control of undesirables. You and I together can do it, for sure.' Longthorn sat beside his colleague.

Petraeus looked up. 'I think things are going as well as they might.'

'Al, Al, Al… think how much faster we can get the recovery going if the resources are directed properly. That's a political task, not something for a soldier, especially not Dower.'

'I'm still struggling to understand what you have against the man. Strikes me he's done as well as possible under difficult circumstances.'

'As well as a soldier might with people obliged to follow his orders. But he lacks the vision, the flair for leading the civilian population. If you and I don't step up, it will fall to Dower to lead. Do we really want to build our recovery out of a military dictatorship? Come on, Al, you know it's what you and I have spent a lifetime guarding against.'

'Okay, Longthorn, okay. I know. We've been over the situation often enough. But I'm tired – tired of life, tired of living. Just let me be.'

'You, me and my grandson are all that remains of the democratically elected leadership of our country. If we don't stand for democracy, who does? It's our duty to the people to step forward, no matter the personal pain.'

'I've told you already, Longthorn, I'll vote with you. I'm a loyal party member, always have been. But for now, please, let it lie.'

'Good man. I just wanted to share the news with you, keep you in the loop. We're a team, after all. For now, just leave me to keep the wheels turning; you concentrate on getting your strength back.'

Chapter 38

Perseus Arm: Pelesius d.

As the sun dropped to the watery horizon, the ground team was readying to wrap for the day.

Lieutenant Bach guided them between two rows of wrecked vessels. It was clear from blast marks beneath their wing thrusters that several had attempted to take off, without success. Many of the other vessels they'd inspected had been airborne and simply dropped from the sky, coming down to explosive ends. They, just like all the dozens of others the team had inspected through the day, contained only dead locusts. The day's body count was high, very high.

'Hello, observer, we're done here,' said Bach into his collar-phone. 'It'll be dark shortly. We'll be with you in five.'

'Roger that,' said Beth. 'It's been a long day.'

She watched the ground team approaching. Bigger now than this morning. Having decided at lunchtime there was no locust threat remaining, the soldiers manning the airlock's heavy machine gun had been drafted in to help with the fieldwork. Everyone in the team was ready for a break.

Beth looked out toward the sea and the low setting sun then back to the team making its way across the beach to join her. Each person threw a long shadow across the sand and up against the dune that rose beyond them. She watched the shadows advance, each exactly matching their caster's movements. She smiled; the day was nearly over. She reached her hand to open a collar-phone call to Zac who still flew cover above, but suddenly puzzled, she didn't open the channel.

Suddenly on guard, she focused entirely on the viewscreen, and made a different call. 'Lieutenant Bach, it's probably nothing, maybe just an optical anomaly, but look to your right. Is there something moving on the dune, where your shadows cast their longest?'

She saw the line of soldiers stop. They all looked across to the dune and their giant shadows. Bach took two or three steps toward the dune.

'Beth, what am I looking for?'

'I'm not sure what I saw, like something moving through or with your shadows. I can't see anything now.'

'Me neither. There's nothing there and no prints in the sand, just natural wind-formed rippling.'

'Okay, you guys hurry back. Let's all get back to the Leviathan.'

'We're all good for that,' said Bach, stepping back into line and waving the team forward.

Beth watched their progress and saw no further suspicious movements. As the party neared, she turned and left the bridge.

Reaching the stern, she noted the airlock was open. The machine-gun crew had not closed it when they left earlier to join the rest of the outward-bound team. Sand had carried into the passageway and a bot was busy clearing it away. *Damned squaddies. Surely, common sense says close the airlock doors when on a sandy beach – surely?*

The landing party appeared at the airlock entrance and funnelled aboard.

'It's a mess out there, a complete slaughter,' said Bach.

'What's your take on it?' said Beth.

Bach paused beside Beth, keeping to the side as he waved his team into the observer. 'Keep on moving, everyone in.' He turned his attention to Beth. 'We started out thinking this was all locust-on-locust. The more I see, the more I'm certain that's not it. All the wounds on the bodies are consistent, and we've never seen locusts inflict such wounds.' He shrugged. 'But then we've never seen a locust-on-locust conflict. Perhaps this is how they fight among each other.'

'You think?' said Beth as she slid shut the outer airlock door.

'Well, there are only locust bodies out there, but I can't help feeling we weren't looking at a battlefield. They all died the same way, and it's not nice. It was more like a slaughterhouse.' Bach followed Beth into the passageway and closed the inner airlock door behind him. 'I'll be glad to get back to the Leviathan – this is a beautiful planet, but something about it gives me the creeps.'

'Probably all the dead locusts. Though knowing what we do, that's more likely a cause for celebration. You get something to drink while I get us airborne. Captain Stewart and the science team are keen for a full briefing as soon as we get up there.' She left Bach at the canteen entrance and headed directly to the bridge.

'Hello, warbird, Beth here. Zac, I've got the landing party safely on board and we are good to go.'

'Hello, observer. Great. You take the lead, and we'll follow you up.'

Chapter 39

Perseus Arm: HB-3 at Pelesius d.

The observer flew into the wide Leviathan hangar and touched down gently beside a second observer. Beth immediately began to power down systems as the landing party gave a spontaneous cheer. She grinned to herself. Today had not been the best of days for any of the team. Through the viewscreen, she saw the warbird had landed toward the aft end of the hangar beside the Leviathan's second warbird and the pilots' standby mess.

The hangar door closed and the atmosphere within began to fill. She watched the readings display on her sleeve. As soon as it reported safe, she looked back at the team gathered around the back of the bridge. 'Okay, we're good to go!'

As they stepped onto the deck, Zac and his co-pilot crossed from the warbird to join them. 'Captain Stewart's waiting,' said Zac.

'So we hear,' said Bach. 'Let's get up there.'

Bach looked toward Hazel. 'All set?'

She nodded and they set off, leaving the hangar still and quiet.

A little while passed, then very slightly, at the stern of the observer, the access light within the open airlock began to ripple and shimmer. A strange apparition appeared to glide out and away from the observer. Within a few moments, the disturbance had vanished, and once again, all was still in the hangar.

***

Captain Stewart was flanked by chief scientist Joe Li, Major Darrow, the Leviathan's military contingent commander, and the Leviathan's first officer as he welcomed the landing party to the navigation room behind the bridge. At once, an enthusiastic discussion erupted as the group tried to understand how the locust threat had been destroyed.

'There is no sign of any other forces on the planet. It must have been locust-on-locust,' said Joe Li.

'You'd think,' said Bach. 'But I'm telling you, there are no locust-type wounds. I'm not sure the deaths are down to the locusts at all.'

'I spent the whole day flying over the area – there was nothing other than wrecked locust technology,' said Zac.

'Come on, people,' said Stewart, 'let's focus. We were right here over the planet when the massacre happened. If there were others involved, surely we would have seen something. Joe, are you sure your people didn't detect any anomalous signals?'

Joe gave a brisk shake of his head. 'None, nothing at all… It's always remotely possible that a broadcast at some extreme frequency range might have been missed – but I think not.'

'If the killing was by something other than the locusts themselves, where did the perpetrators go?' said Beth.

'And where did they come from? Other than locusts, nothing's gone down or left the planet while we've been in orbit,' said the first officer.

'So, if there's nothing on the surface and nothing has left the planet, the killings must have been locust-on-locust. There's no other option,' said Major Darrow.

'Yes, that's logical,' said Bach. 'But it doesn't feel right.'

'What about the material we found in the locust cockpit?' said Hazel. 'It's weird and definitely not locust.' She pulled it from her sample bag and held it out between her outstretched hands. 'It's pretty well transparent. We found it where it had caught on the broken glass of a cockpit window.'

Joe reached out and stroked it. In response, the material wafted away and the air around Hazel's hands seemed to ripple as it moved.

'It's really strong stuff,' said Hazel. Her hands moved a little apart as she tried to stretch out the near-invisible material. Her face strained and her arms quivered slightly as she struggled with the substance.

'Let's get it tested now,' said Joe.

'Sir,' said the first officer, who had moved aside to take a call from his second officer on the bridge. 'Something odd's been detected in the hangar area. Several unauthorised life signs.'

'Unauthorised?' said Stewart.

'Well, unrecognised too. There are seven life signs in the main hangar area. Two are the standby warbird crew in their crew mess. Five are gathered at the other end of the hangar, near the entrance into the central passageway.'

'We didn't bring anything up with us,' said Beth.

'Sound the alarm Number One. Have the hangar guard seal it off immediately. I want a full armed response unit down there right now. And tell the crew to lock down in the mess,' said Stewart. He turned to Darrow and Bach. 'Gentlemen, you might want to get down there.'

'Yes, sir,' said Darrow and Bach in unison. They saluted and together hurried from the navigation room.

'Come on,' said Stewart, leading the rest onto the bridge. 'Get me visual of the hangar. What's in there?'

'That's just it, sir. There's nothing there,' said the first officer.

'If the sensors say there are bodies, they must be there. Get the hangar picture feed onto the main viewscreen – let's have a closer look ourselves.' Stewart stopped in the middle of the bridge and looked up at the great screen as a feed from the hangar appeared. The observer rested where it had landed, close to the hangar access door. Beyond it, the second observer, and at the far end were the two warbirds. Nothing moved.

'You see, sir, all's quiet,' said the first officer.

'Could there be a fault in the scanner, Joe?' said Stewart.

'It's not something we've experienced before, but I guess any piece of equipment might malfunction sometime.'

'The armed response squad is assembled and ready to go in, sir,' said the first officer.

'Let's go for it,' said Stewart.

The first officer gave the order, and everyone on the bridge watched the hangar picture feed. For just a moment, nothing happened, then the hangar access door slid open to reveal a line of four soldiers. On Bach's order, they darted inside. Fanning out into an arc, weapons raised as they ran, each scanning their allotted area. After ten paces they paused, knelt and maintained a watch.

Four more soldiers appeared at the hangar access and sprinted forward to kneel in the gaps between the first rank of soldiers. Behind them, four more had stepped forward to stand just inside the access door, which slid shut behind them.

'We're in, sir,' reported Lieutenant Bach.

'I see that, lieutenant. We have you on the screen. Commence search,' said Stewart.

They watched the soldiers spread out and conduct a thorough search. Finding nothing, they searched the observers and both warbirds before reaching the pilots' mess and rest quarters at the far end of the hangar. They searched that too, in spite of the crew's assurances that nobody else was there.

'Hello, sir. There's nothing here. False alarm.' The lieutenant's voice sounded in Captain Stewart's collar-phone.

'Thank you, lieutenant. You can stand your people down,' said Stewart. He looked at Joe. 'So, faulty equipment it is.'

Joe Li looked less than convinced. 'Well, I guess there's a first time for everything. With your permission, captain, I'd like to get on with an analysis of that material the landing party brought aboard. It might shed some light.'

Stewart nodded, and Joe hurried away, closely followed by Hazel.

'Number One, detail another expedition team. I'd like to continue our hunt for answers as soon as the sun rises on our search area.'

'Very good, sir,' said the first officer as the captain left the bridge.

***

Joe Li alternated his gaze between the console in front of him, where the strange material rested, and the data results feeding into his sleeve. He didn't quite understand what he was seeing.

'This is odd,' he said.

'Yes,' said Hazel. 'It's a contradiction. In fact, a whole bunch of contradictions. It's not synthetic, so not the product of a manufacturing process. Yet it includes the components of glass: sand, soda, lime, some traces of several rare minerals and some other natural bio-components. In particular, something very like rubber. Rubber's a natural tree sap, isn't it?' said Hazel.

'Yes, a very specialised tree. But this is no tree.' Joe lifted the artefact from the console and looked at it intently, holding it up to the light. 'It's very light, virtually weightless and transparent too –

fascinating.' He gently closed his hand about the material and it scrunched up without resistance; he opened his hand and the material returned to its original form. 'Fine and malleable – more like silk. I've no idea what it is. Could it be a wrapper or container?'

Hazel shook her head. 'I don't think so. I found it jammed in the shattered edges of the locust vessel's viewing port. There's no need for wrappers or containers there.'

'Mmmm,' said Joe. 'It reminds me a bit of shed snakeskin. But with sand and lime, it couldn't be that. I'll go report to the captain now. Then let's sleep on it. Hopefully tomorrow's search can unearth more information.'

Chapter 40

Perseus Arm: HB-3 at Pelesius d.

With no signs of any threat, the second day's search of the locust killing fields employed two observers and two ground teams to speed up the whole process. They had made great progress working through the wrecked remains of the locust vessels. Nowhere had they encountered any survivors. All the dead had died similar brutal deaths. Ultimately, an absence of any surviving locusts indicated it had not been a locust-on-locust affair. Something else had likely killed the locusts, but no more clues as to what that might be had been found.

Captain Stewart acknowledged his first officer's report that darkness would shortly be falling on the second day of their search. 'Call them up now, Number One. I think we've done enough. Whatever did the locusts in, it's not there now. But where is it? What is it? Has Science got any more for us?'

As though on cue, Joe Li joined them on the bridge. 'Sorry, captain. It's a complete mystery.'

'Next trip down, we'll broaden our search. I want to see what might be lurking beyond.'

'Okay, captain, but every scan has indicated there are no signs of technology or developed activity anywhere, Still picking up occasional big shadowy signals, but in the waters. We're thinking big sea creatures appearing in scans as they surface then vanishing as they deep dive. Perhaps the equivalent of Earth's whales. Whatever they are, there's no technology involved, just raw nature,' said Joe. 'Pre the locusts' arrival, this planet was pristine, its fauna and flora living and interacting with one another quite naturally. My team's consensus is this is a prime planet for human settlement one day.'

'Except there's something here that can destroy a whole locust fleet in short order. Could they do the same to us?' Stewart looked out toward the planet. 'What the hell is out there, Joe?'

'The observers and warbird escort are approaching, sir,' said the first officer.

'Get them in, please.'

They watched the three craft close on the Leviathan then disappear into the gaping landing bay. A side screen displayed an internal hangar view and the berthing craft. Then the hangar door swung shut and all was still as the crews waited for the atmosphere to fill.

'By the way, sir. That detector fault, reporting unrecognised life forms, it's still on the blink and spreading. A while back we registered several in the central zone then the count in the hanger zeroed out – we're thinking it may be an intermittent fault,' said the first officer.

'Why haven't the bots fixed it yet? They're normally quick off the mark with repairs.'

'No idea, sir. I believe Science was trying to push them.'

'That's right,' said Joe. 'My people have sent two prompts, but the bots must consider it low priority.'

'Well stay on it. At least we know it's a fault. I want a debrief with the leaders of the landing teams – let's say in thirty minutes in the navigation room. Meantime, if you need me, I'll be in my cabin.'

***

'I can't believe you've never been inside a warbird before,' said Zac, as he led Beth across the hangar deck to his warbird. He opened the craft's stern airlock.

'I'm not so keen on fighting. I've never needed to get aboard one before.'

'Well, come aboard… the tech is awesome.'

They both knew her sudden interest in warbirds had nothing to do with design and technology. She was thinking exactly what Zac was thinking – this was the perfect venue to secure a little private space and time. Turning back to the outer airlock, he hesitated. Something, a shimmer of light, caught his eye. He peered across to the far side of the hangar: there was nothing there. He swiped the outer airlock shut behind them and began the short, guided tour.

***

Captain Stewart stood on the gallery that traced around and above the length of the central passageway on his and every Leviathan. This was the moment he loved most in the day. Of course, on a Leviathan in space, there was no day and night, and it operated on a 'four hours on, eight off' watch system. At any one time, well under half the crew worked the watches, the majority serving on a notional dayshift. For them, the day shift had ended, evening meals had been eaten, and now most people had a little time to themselves to socialise. And the central passageway was a social magnet, a public place to gather and relax – the village green.

Spread at random along the gallery were various crew members walking alone or in twos or threes while others jogged. Amid them all, a slightly larger group of off-duty soldiers moved as one; the sound of perhaps a dozen pairs of feet running together in ordered rhythm carried back to him. He smiled, sipped from his coffee mug and looked down to where other less energetic crew members went about their business on the fore and aft travelators. Others stood about and talked or sat at seat clusters that would, here and there, pop up from the deck like little street cafés.

'Hello, captain. Are you free?' The sound of the third officer's voice came through the collar-phones.

'What's up?'

'It's those false life-form readings, sir. I'm just a bit uncomfortable – they're spreading.'

'What do you mean, spreading?'

'There's more of them. Seems the number registering went up some time after the observers berthed.'

'Well, the hangar's been searched; we know it's a system fault. Maybe call Joe Li and have him prompt his bots again to get it fixed. Keep me posted.'

'Thank you, sir. I'll get on to Science now.'

Stewart glanced aft toward the hangar entrances. Armed guards were on the doors, as per fleet standing orders. Everything was quiet. With a sigh, he drew himself away from his own leisure thoughts. The third officer had sounded concerned. *He'd better get up to the bridge and lend some moral support.*

***

Stewart stepped quietly from behind the deadlight curtain onto the bridge. The third officer had been speaking with his watchman but broke off at once to attend to the captain.

'Sir, all quiet up here. I spoke with Joe Li. He said he'd do the life detector repair himself. He's working on it right now.'

'That's good. I got the feeling you were unhappy with it.'

'Well… everything else works; it's just odd to have something not functioning.'

'I'm sure Science will get it fixed directly…' Stewart broke away to accept an incoming collar-phone call. 'Captain here, go ahead.'

'Captain, it's Joe Li, where are you?'

There was uncharacteristic concern in his chief scientist's voice.

'I'm on the bridge, what's up?'

'I'll come up to the bridge now. There's something really weird happening. Give me one minute.'

The captain had scarcely had time to let the third officer know something was afoot before Joe Li rushed onto the bridge.

'Well, what's the issue?' said Stewart.

'Captain, I've been working on the detector the bots failed to repair.'

'So I understand. What's the concern?'

'Well, that's just it. The bots haven't repaired the fault because there isn't one.'

The captain looked at him sharply. 'And that means?'

'If there's no fault, there must be something in the hangar.'

'But we searched, there's nothing there.'

'Nothing we could see, captain. I think we have to assume there is something there.'

'Eleven things there, sir,' said the third officer. 'The number rose after the observers returned. Could something be hitching a lift up on our own craft?'

The captain was quiet for a moment, then he issued orders to the third officer. 'Call Major Darrow, the first officer and the chief engineer. I want them all up here right now, but quietly. If we have intruders, let's not let them know we know.'

'Yes, sir,' said the third officer. He stroked his sleeve and summoned the senior officers to the bridge.

'Joe, are the anomalies confined to the hangar?'

'I'm reviewing the alert count record now,' he said, while staring intently at data displaying on his sleeve. 'Unfortunately, over the past twenty-four hours we've been disregarding these particular readouts as errors. There were originally five readings in the hangar. About twelve hours ago, that number dropped to zero, and I'm afraid those five dispersed into the wider ship. Nobody thought too much about it, just an expanding error. The number was still five, which we'd taken as the total error count.'

'Where are they now?'

'I'm just checking. But don't forget the number has risen in the hangar. I think the third officer must be right. They hitched a lift up to us on the observers.'

'Joe. I need to know now – where have they spread to?'

'I'm trying to call up the information now.'

The deadlight curtain flipped aside, and the first officer hurried in followed by Major Darrow and the chief engineer.

The captain beckoned them directly to him. 'We may have a problem… Correction. We have a problem. The anomalous life-form readings we attributed to system error… There is no system error.'

Darrow paled. 'We have intruders aboard, sir?'

'That is a distinct possibility, yes.'

'But my soldiers scoured the hangar. They found nothing.'

Joe was frantically tapping his sleeve as he turned to the viewscreen. 'Watch this, I know why. See. This video recording is from yesterday, while your soldiers searched the hangar.' He jabbed a finger toward the screen.

They all watched what they had seen play out the day before. The hangar door slid open, two squads of four soldiers hurried into the hangar. A third squad entered but stayed beside the closing door to mount a guard. The soldiers conducted a rapid sweep.

Joe tapped his sleeve to stop the replay. 'There, see it?'

'No. What am I looking at?' said Stewart.

'Against the far wall. It's a shimmer, a gleam in the light as the soldiers pass, nothing more.' He played it again, and this time they all saw what he saw. It was something and it was nothing.

'What is that?' said Darrow, taking a step toward the screen. 'My soldiers have just walked right past it!'

Joe was almost shaking as he tried to explain. 'That material we found on the first day aboard the locust vessel. It's been analysed.

Natural but weird… I'd actually say unnatural for humans. Its components include organic matter but also non-biologicals – sand, soda, lime.'

'Come on, Joe! What is it?' said Stewart.

'The artefact we found could have been a skin scrape from something as it squeezed in through the damaged vessel's cockpit port. It's transparent. Sand, soda, lime – they make glass, that's transparent. I think, whatever it is, it's transparent. Sort of glass-like.'

'That's not natural!' said the chief engineer.

'Not Earth natural,' said Joe.

'It means we have almost invisible beings on board, and they are likely what did for the locusts,' said Stewart. 'So where are they?'

'I have that info for you now, sir,' said Joe. Consulting his sleeve, he began to read out the data. 'There are eleven life forms in the hangar: two standby warbird crew in the mess, five unidentified near the internal hangar access door that leads into the central passageway, two more are immediately behind a warbird, which shows two humans on board – I understand they are the warbird pilot Zac Peres and the observer pilot Beth Surtees.'

'What the hell are they doing there? Number One, have them contacted and warned. They are not to exit the warbird for any reason, period. Warn the standby crew too,' said Stewart, cutting over Joe, whom he then nodded toward. 'Carry on, man. Quick now.'

'Five, which is likely the five who got aboard during that first observer trip, have got out of the hangar. I'm guessing they've just slipped out as and when they could during our routine coming and going.'

'And where are they? What are they doing?' said Darrow, who had just completed a discreet call to Lieutenant Bach. The soldiers would be mustering right now without any fuss. In a few minutes, Darrow would hunt the intruders down.

Joe shook his head and looked up from his sleeve, nervousness writ large across his face. 'I think these are intelligent,' he said. 'Very intelligent.'

'Of course they're intelligent – they took down a whole locust fleet like it was nothing. Where are they now?' said Stewart.

Joe grimaced. 'In strategic positions spread out along the central passageway. One just beside the port hangar access, one at the starboard hangar access. One each outside the Gravdrive and Folddrive Power Units.'

'Hell,' said the chief engineer, touching his sleeve to open a collar-phone channel to the engine room.

'And one's at the foot of the stairway leading up here,' said Joe with an exaggerated point toward the deadlight curtain.

'What the hell's going on?' said the first officer.

Darrow had drawn his pistol and directed it toward the deadlight curtain while the third officer opened a cabinet and pulled out two more sidearms. He proffered one to the watchman and both men stepped beside the major. Darrow glanced briefly to either side, nodded to the two men and gestured forward with his hand. 'On me,' he said, and stepped cautiously toward the deadlight drape, leading them through into the navigation room. He pointed to the stairwell access door. 'There's one of those things doing something at the foot of the stair. I don't know what, but odds are it will eventually make its way up here. If… when that door opens, fire and keep firing. I'll be back.' He left the two men on guard and turned to rejoin the captain on the bridge.

'I think they may be trying to bring us down,' said Stewart, acknowledging Darrow's return with a crisp nod. 'That's exactly what they did to the locusts.'

'But why haven't they acted yet?' said Joe.

'God knows, and thank Him for that delay too. There may yet be time to save us,' said Stewart. 'What I can say is they have positioned themselves close beside the power units and our armed guards. That must be for a pre-emptive strike against us when they are ready.'

'Lieutenant Bach has the duty platoon armed and ready in the barrack section, sir. The other two platoons are called to duty, but it will take a little while before they are ready because I have them reporting for duty via the service passages rather than through the central passageway – don't want to be seen to be panicking. That might trigger the attack before we're set. How do you want First Platoon to deploy?' said Darrow.

'Tell Lieutenant Bach to stand by a little longer, I'm not ready yet. And Joe, what can you tell us about these things?'

'I'm working on it. They are transparent, invisible in our visible light range, but we saw those glimmers, so not entirely invisible. Perhaps they will be visible at higher or lower frequencies. I've had an idea, just hold on,' said Joe, as he opened a comms channel to Hazel who was standing by in the science labs.

Stewart looked to his first officer. 'Let's start by minimising risk of harm. Get a message to all those who are not in the central passageway that it's off limits to all, as of now. Have people stand by wherever they are for further orders. Then, discreetly, start to summon people out of the concourse. Let's get as many out of harm's way as we can before it kicks off. But carefully. Don't show our hand.'

'Yes, sir. In what order should I call people away?'

'No individual priority, everyone's valuable. Try getting those closest to the things away first. Start with them.' He pointed to a group who sat drinking at a cluster of pop-up chairs close to the hangar entrance.

'Sir,' said Major Darrow. 'The hangar guards are due to be relieved now. What should I do?'

'Have Lieutenant Bach send out the relief squad, business as usual. Brief the soldiers he's sending out, so they know what we know. Have the current guard remain in place too. That will double our boots on the ground.'

'Right, and Bach will still have twenty-plus men ready for action. The other platoons are still assembling; they're not ready yet,' said Darrow.

'Thank you, major. When it starts, Lieutenant Bach is to split First Platoon's efforts. He must reinforce the hangar doors – let's not let any more of these things out of there. And he's to reinforce the guards on the power units and engine room.

'Once the other platoons are ready, they will provide any support as required in the light of events.'

Major Darrow frowned. 'Yes, sir. Meantime, I could try to slip past the thing out there, get to the troops.'

'No, major. For the time being, I think you need to command your troops from here.'

***

Lieutenant Bach peered cautiously out into the central passageway. The relief guards were making their way to their appointed destinations. Moving as normally as possible, they were trying not to give any signs of alarm. He had briefed the in-situ guards by collar-phone that there was a problem and they would need to remain at their posts.

Stepping back into the military assembly chamber, he looked at his remaining force. A sergeant, three corporals and twenty soldiers watched him intently. Some had been on the surface with him and knew what these creatures could do. Others, probably the lucky ones, only had barrack-room hearsay to go on. Deeper into the room, he could see the other two platoons slowly shaping up, as troops filed in from the service passageways.

'Right! Listen up, First Platoon. I want four squads, each comprising one NCO and five soldiers. These are your tasks: get ready, you move hard and fast on my word…'

***

Captain Stewart's eyes were fixed on the viewscreen displaying the central passageway. The numbers of off-duty staff there had slowly thinned as his first officer called people away. The relief guards had arrived, and the old guard were casually lingering for a conversation with their reliefs, doubling their strength on the ground, though that couldn't be sustained for long – it would start looking very suspicious, very soon.

'Come on Science, what have you got for me?' said Stewart.

Joe's frustration was clear to see on his face. 'I really need to be down in the labs with my team, steering them. I can't do much from up here.'

A voice sounded abruptly in his collar-phone. 'Hello, Joe? Hazel here. I think we might have something, maybe.'

'I'm feeding your call through to the rest of the bridge crew, Hazel. Go ahead now. What have you got?'

'To confirm, the guys have managed to implement your instruction and disabled the hangar door. The ones in the hangar will not be able to join those already in the central passageway.

'We've been testing the sample based on what you noticed about the light spectrum earlier. You're right. Though it's not readily visible in white light, it stands out like a beacon in the ultraviolet range—'

'Yes!' said Joe. 'We have them!' He looked to the captain. 'We have something here. Hello, Hazel. Good work. Now, I have no idea how long before this kicks off. It can't be long. I need you to do two things very quickly. One, get the team to revisit the ship's light settings. There is a setting that switches to include UV light, no idea why – it's always set to off. Get them to modify the settings so we can emit UV on my word. Two, and this is very tricky, so I need you to do it personally. You need to work on the crew helmet visor settings. I want them adjusted to allow crew to see ultraviolet imagery.'

'I don't know how.'

'You'll need to use my master workstation and the LPA next to it. I'll talk you through the steps as you do it.' Joe ended the call.

'What exactly does this mean?' said the captain.

'We can't see ultraviolet light, but if we can play about with the helmet visor settings, the visor will detect it and convert it into visible light… well, not really converted, just processed by the helmet so the visor display shows the viewer a visible proxy of the UV – likely as a shade of regular violet. It's all smoke and mirrors really, but it means we will be able to see what we're fighting,' said Joe.

'That's halfway to winning,' said Major Darrow. 'How long?'

Joe shrugged. 'We're working on it. As soon as is humanly possible.'

Captain Stewart stared at the viewscreen and its display of the central passageway. 'Why aren't they attacking? If they move against us now, we have little chance. What's holding them back?'

'Let's just hope they continue to hesitate,' said the first officer.

'Are they hesitating? I don't think so. Everything they've done so far seems to have been patient and planned. I think they're waiting for something specific. But what? Why risk losing their advantage?' said Major Darrow.

'Perhaps they are waiting for the newly arrived whatever-they-are to get out of the hangar too,' said Stewart.

***

Looking into the bridge viewscreen, Captain Stewart could see there were now just a few dozen crew members relaxing in the central passageway, their presence serving to allay any suspicions on the part of the stationary intruders. Those remaining crew members' locations were sufficiently distant that they would be able to dive into side cabins and be safely out of reach in just moments. Each person had been briefed by collar-phone and was bravely sitting out the threat.

Stewart felt the strain of waiting. He thought of the two men covering the navigation room doorway with their pistols as they waited for whatever presently lurked at the foot of the stair. Sweating palms and nervous trigger fingers. Everyone was waiting.

Then word came: at last, tech was ready. It had taken far longer than she'd hoped, but under Joe's guidance, Hazel had done it. Beneath her closed helmet, her visor was now enabled to display a visible proxy for UV: she could see what had been invisible.

Chapter 41

Perseus Arm: HB-3 at Pelesius d.

Lieutenant Bach and the soldiers at the muster point had their helmets up. Each held their personal weapon close, knew they were about to run toward danger, and hoped they had the tools to deal with whatever was out there. Their collar-phones opened on an all-crew channel.

It was Joe Li. 'Listen up, everyone. Your helmet visors have been programmed to enable you to see ultraviolet. Lighting throughout the vessel has been programmed to expand its wavelength range to include ultraviolet. We believe these intruders are visible in those wavelengths, so while you saw nothing before, now you should see something… Something violet. Maybe still a bit transparent, like glass or plastic, but certainly violet.'

Captain Stewart's voice replaced the scientist's. 'On my countdown of three, Science will implement the lighting change. We have to assume they will notice it at once and respond. So, on three, those still sitting in the central aisle are to immediately break for their designated places of cover. Those elsewhere are to lock their doors and wait in place until the military have done their job. Lieutenant Bach, you and your squads have each been detailed what to do. You will implement your tasks. Stand by.' Stewart looked about the bridge.

Major Darrow moved to the deadlight curtain, ready to join the men guarding the stairwell access door at the rear of the navigation room, should it be necessary.

Stewart looked to Joe who gave a curt nod to confirm everything was ready. 'Attention, crew,' said Stewart. 'May God bless you all, and good luck. Helmets up in three, two, one. Now!'

On the captain's word, Joe touched his sleeve to activate the emission of ultraviolet light through the general lighting system.

Knowing there was a brutal killer just at the foot of the bridge stairwell, it took all Stewart's self-control to keep looking into the viewscreen, to follow and oversee events in the central passageway. The ultraviolet light kicked in and his stomach knotted at what it revealed.

***

Bach led the soldiers into the central passageway, gesticulating as he ran, pointing the squads off to their allocated duties. In their various groups, they sprinted toward danger. As they left, the second and third platoons filed forward ready to move on Bach's command.

All locations were crucial but none more so than the hangar. If the initial intruders got that open and allowed in those presently locked on the other side, the job would treble in complexity.

For perhaps the first dozen steps, the soldiers were unclear what they were running toward. They saw several vivid violet tubes, like thick rolls of carpet, but partially transparent, like glass, violet glass, lying shimmering along the sides of the central passageway.

The shapes seemed to suddenly realise they were visible and broke into action. No longer prone tubes, they began to move, flexing and rising in silent surprise at their unmasking. Glinting in the wash of ultraviolet light, the vague shapes consolidated.

'Open fire!' shouted Bach into his collar-phone.

The sound of running boots was lost beneath a blast of gunfire, as everywhere, sprinting soldiers fired at their rapidly closing targets.

'Second Platoon, Third Platoon, stand ready.' Bach waved them into formations while watching events ahead of him. Among the scattering of violet shapes, two near the hangar access doors stood out, now less than twenty paces ahead of his charging fighters. Each beast was nearer three times as long as a man's height and thick like an oil barrel. The shapes seemed to flinch at the impact from so many bullets but were not downed. Instead, they arched their backs, heads raised, presenting like cobras ready to strike.

All the soldiers were running flat out, screaming self-encouragement into their helmets and firing, firing, firing.

'Second Platoon, forward!' Bach shouted, waving them into supporting action. As they sprinted away, Bach formed up the Third Platoon, his eyes always on the action. He suddenly felt sick at what he saw when the First Platoon soldiers tried to engage. *Christ, what the hell are these things?*

The violet shapes elongated to five, six times their original length, their girth narrowing accordingly, towering high above the attacking soldiers. Bach could see the iridescent violet bodies quiver under the fusillade of fire, seeming to dent where rounds struck home, then restoring to shape almost at once. The soft suppleness of the bodies was in direct contrast to the heads which crystallised into shape. A broad hood formed immediately behind a gaping mouth that glistened with shards of violet death.

A hooded mouth swept down and struck. A cruel mouth, every bit as sharp and hard as the torso was smooth and flexible. The two soldiers mounting guard at the hangar entrance died immediately, decapitated. The First Platoon reinforcements arrived as the killing bites were delivered, but they could do nothing to assist. For just a moment, they hesitated, stunned; that moment killed them.

What had appeared a single tail opened into four strands, each with grasping little digits that clawed and gripped. The multiple tail strands whipped round to sweep away the legs of the standing soldiers. One strand coiled about a fighter's legs. A second strand captured another soldier about the waist and held him struggling. A third slithered around a man's chest, holding the soldier immobilised and off the ground.

Working independently, the serpent's tail strands constricted to crush the first soldier's ribcage completely, his desperate cry still on his lips as the serpent's head swept round and dispatched him with a single bite to the head. Then it turned its attention to the next struggling victim… and the next.

As the Second Platoon reinforcements closed in, the serpents reared up, preparing to strike.

'Fall back, fall back,' said Bach into every surviving soldier's collar-phone. He turned to Third Platoon and pointed up the side stair leading to the gallery. Get up there, try grenades from above, everything you've got. The platoon sprinted for the stair.

Bach turned his attention back to the serpents. They had all killed with a uniform and scary efficiency. He could tell, now they had started, they were not finished. Most of Second Platoon made it back to him. None of First Platoon, nor the guard detail, had survived.

'Sergeant, get some men into the muster room, there are two heavy machine guns stowed there. Break them out. That should make a hole in them. Quick as you like now.'

'Yes, sir,' said the sergeant, who signalled half-a-dozen soldiers to follow him back into the unit's base.

'Hello, Lieutenant Bach, Major Darrow here. We saw that engagement. It looks like their bodies are bulletproof. Have you anything there to hit them with?'

'Sir, we're readying heavy machine guns now. Two or three minutes, I guess.'

'Doubt you've got that, lieutenant. They're coming for you now.'

'I see them, sir.' Bach broke off and waved the remnants of Second Platoon into the muster room. A quick glance along the passageway assured him the civilians had fled as planned. Third Platoon had made it safely up to the gallery, and there were no surviving soldiers out anywhere on the open deck. He stepped inside, and the door slid shut behind him. It was immediately struck by a violent blow that made him flinch.

He surveyed the door, stepped forward and ran his hand over the dent. Then he reeled back in shock as another blow hammered the door and enlarged the dent.

***

'Lock down everything! Seal every door!' Captain Stewart's voice boomed across the bridge and sounded in every collar-phone aboard.

'Major Darrow, I want something to hit these serpents with, now!'

'Bach's breaking out the heavy machine guns, sir. Ready imminently.'

'Right, and anything else that might hurt them.'

'The best we've got would be the RPGs. But they might damage the integrity of the craft.'

Captain Stewart jabbed a hand toward the viewscreen. 'I'll take some collateral damage the bots can fix later. Right now, we can't let them get a free run.' On the viewscreen, they could see the serpents drawing back their heads and sweeping them forward to break open doorways.

'Captain, that one's trying to batter open the Gravdrive Power Unit. There's another going for the Folddrive Unit,' said the first officer.

'I see them, Number One.'

A series of flashes and black smoke signed the detonation of grenades around the serpents.

'Look! Our people are up in the gallery,' said Li.

A sense of elation swept among the bridge crew as grenades continued to rain down on the serpents. They squirmed and reeled amid the blasts and shrapnel, their violet bodies writhing on the deck, appearing then vanishing within the swirl of smoke. Another shower of grenades dropped from above to explode among the invaders.

'It's looking good, sir,' said the first officer to Captain Stewart.

'It is, Number One, it is,' said Stewart, touching his sleeve. 'Three Platoon, another grenade shower, really blow them away!'

They watched as more grenades rained down. One of the violet serpents lay still, its head blown from its body when a grenade had fallen fortuitously into its upturned mouth.

Stewart smiled grimly, 'That's the way.'

As a fourth volley of grenades dropped, one of the serpents rose up directly from the deck. Carrying its cruel head high, it arced over the safety rail and slid onto the gallery.

'Oh, hell, no,' said Joe Li. 'Those grenades are little more than an inconvenience to those things.'

'You're right,' said Stewart. He opened a collar-phone channel. 'Three Platoon, fall back, get away from them. Find cover wherever you can. Fall back now!'

The bridge crew watched in horror as events on the balcony played out. The soldiers nearest the violet hell-bringer were dead almost before they could register the risk. Caught, crushed then decapitated, their fight ended. Others had managed to dodge the initial attack and were hurrying for the stairway down to the central passageway and their muster room.

They never made it. Violet death was sliding up the stairway to meet them while the original attacking serpent, having dispatched all the soldiers caught in the initial attack, was now sliding along the gallery, quickly closing on the retreating troops. In desperation, the trapped soldiers fired. There was no sign their bullets caused any harm or even slowed the slithering killers.

'Lieutenant Bach. I need those heavy machine guns in action now!' Stewart watched on helplessly as the slaughter continued.

'Sir,' said the first officer, 'they're almost into the power units. Both the folddrive and gravdrive access doors are buckling. The engine room is sound. But if they put the power units offline, the engine room has no power anyway.'

'We're coming out now, sir,' reported Lieutenant Bach.

'Good, I can see you're all clear. The thing battering your door has moved on,' said Stewart, staring anxiously into the viewscreen.

Stewart and the whole bridge team looked on as the battered muster room doors slid back and teams of soldiers struggled out with two heavy machine guns. They set them down on the deck, allowing the heavy tri-legs to settle flat to provide maximum stability. Ammunition belts were locked into position and the gunners took aim. One pointed directly along the central passageway to where a serpent had raised its body high off the deck and was swinging its rock-hard head into the buckling hangar door. A second aimed at the serpent still sliding up the balcony stair and killing as it went.

'Open fire!' called Bach. The guns roared. At first the serpent battering the hangar access door reacted as it had done to the previous light arms fire, ignoring it. Then the high velocity impact of the heavy metal began to tell. The thick violet body quivered under the concerted fire.

'One spot. Stay on one spot,' said Bach to the gunners. 'You're hurting them.'

The serpent had dropped to the floor. Its body had stretched and was now nearly thirty feet long and perhaps only a foot wide. The gunner was aiming at a single spot about the midpoint in its body. Bach watched the body flex and squirm under the torrent of fire, the fusillade so strong the serpent could not propel itself forward to attack the gunner. He felt a sudden sense of elation and stroked his sleeve to open a channel to the bridge.

'Hello, bridge. Are you seeing this?' said Bach.

***

'Major Darrow! We've got a winner here,' said Stewart.

'Thank God,' said Darrow as he and the rest of the bridge crew followed the action in the viewscreen. There they could see the heavy rounds having a devastating effect on the serpent. The rounds punched into the writhing violet tube and out the other side, the spent ammunition casings smashing into the craft's deck and bulkheads. The firing continued remorselessly, first to perforate then slice apart the tube. The serpent was cut in two, its body parts falling to the ground.

The bridge crew gave a spontaneous cheer and Major Barrow fired a swift collar-phone message to Bach. 'Keep those guns firing – you're cutting them to pieces.'

Stewart rested his hand on Major Darrow's arm. We should move one of the guns. Divert its fire to the drive units before they break in.'

Darrow nodded and issued an order to Bach. They watched as Bach redirected one of the guns toward the serpent that continued to assault the Folddrive Power Unit door. Everyone felt a degree of relief as its body began to respond to the stream of bullets powering into its body.

'We're getting on top of them,' said Darrow. 'I think it's turning our way, sir.'

'I think you have it, major. Good work by your men down there. Number One, find out what's happening in the hangar.'

'Just ended a conversation with the warbird, sir. Lieutenants Peres and Surtees are safe and locked into the warbird. The standby crew safe in the messroom. The life forms are still showing in the hangar, but they are making no attempt to break into the warbird.'

'Make sure they all keep inside under all circumstances,' said Stewart as he turned suddenly in response to the first officer's gasp. 'What's up?'

'Look, captain. Disaster!' The first officer raised his hand and pointed toward the viewscreen.

The two severed snake parts outside the hangar entrance were moving, slowly but decisively. 'It was dead! What's happening? Science, what's going on?'

Joe Li was engaged in a frantic collar-phone discussion with his team. He looked across to the captain and shook his head. 'Sorry, captain, it's not good, not good at all.'

'What exactly is happening?' said Stewart, watching the two half-snake bodies wriggle on the deck, with every passing moment their movements becoming more structured. One truncated part, the front end, raised its head from the deck and began to survey the scene.

'I think it's some form of regeneration. We see that in certain worm species on Earth.' Joe Li faced the captain with horror in his eyes. 'And… I don't know how to kill them. They're impervious to everything we've got.'

Stewart stared in despair at the viewscreen. The serpent head section was moving away from the hangar door, now hurrying toward the gunners.

Major Darrow slapped his forearm and shouted into his collar-phone. 'Bach! Look out, it's nearly on you!'

'One's inside the Folddrive Power Unit, captain' said the first officer. 'Seems to be attacking the power infrastructure. We can't stop it.' He generated a split screen, and they saw a number of dead crew and soldiers, all with crushed bodies, and heads bitten away. A serpent was at the base of the unit, pulling itself up to full height; it repeatedly crashed its heavy head against the drive's power control unit.

'They're taking out our power. What's going on?' Stewart spun to his chief scientist.

Joe Li looked aghast. 'The folddrive is inoperable, captain. My team are working flat out, but we've got nothing to stop these creatures with.'

An alarm sounded throughout the craft. 'What is it, Number One?' said Stewart.

'The gravdrive's down too, sir. We're functioning on buffered power only.'

'How long have we got?'

'Four, five minutes at best. Not enough.'

'Not enough to do anything. Options, team? What can we do?'

Li looked ashen, frozen in horror. He was unable to drag his eyes from the viewscreen as the cut serpent reached the machine-gun team in the central passageway. The soldiers stood no chance; the killer serpent swirled its truncated body about, knocking them over like skittles. Then, with frightening speed, the glistening head rose and fell, every descent followed by a vicious killing bite.

Li finally looked away from the screen, unable to watch as Lieutenant Bach struggled to his feet, last man standing, square beneath the monster. Bach pulled the pin from a grenade and, gripping it fast, thrust his fist high into the air. The brutally hard and sharp mouth dropped, engulfing the soldier's arm and head. The jaws closed in a killing bite and, a moment later, blew apart as the grenade detonated. Head destroyed, the snake's body collapsed permanently onto what remained of the dead lieutenant.

'The drives are down! We're losing everything! What's happening?' The chief engineer's voice sounded in Stewart's collar.

Before Stewart could reply, the second officer's voice carried from the navigation room. 'Orbit decay, captain, we're going down fast, sir. I think we're already dropping out of control.'

'Chief, the serpents are unstoppable. Our soldiers are all dead. The drive units have been destroyed, no chance of any restoration.'

'What are you telling me, captain?'

'We're going to crash into the atmosphere, any minute. I must advise abandon ship now.'

'How the hell do we do that?'

'There are lifepod escape shoots throughout the vessel; some crew might reach them. Others should make for the hangars; there are shuttles there.'

'And a slew of monsters in between. What chance of making it?' The chief's voice was gravel dry.

'Little to none, but we have a full crew on board. Maybe some will. See to yourself and your team, chief. I'm giving the order now,' said Stewart.

The captain looked about the bridge, but just as he prepared to speak, a banging sounded against the navigation room access door.

'It's here, sir! Trying to get in now,' shouted the watchman stationed to guard the door. 'The door's giving.'

Stewart ordered abandon ship. He remained still, staring at the viewscreen. He watched as doorways slid open, and his crew hurried from accommodation, tech rooms, the medical centre, everywhere. Some ran for nearby lifepod shoots, many ran for the hangars and the salvation of the observers. He flinched visibly as a young nurse running for all she was worth was encircled by a snake. Her arms rose in despair as one of the tail coils gripped her and carried her toward its mouth. Throughout the central passageway and beyond, the scene was repeated countless times.

He saw a lucky few make it to lifepods and thanked God for their salvation. Others continued to run for the hangars. Suddenly the light changed, the main lighting lost and with it the ultraviolet. The emergency white lights kicked straight in, but the attackers had vanished from sight. The only signs of their presence were crew members bodies' contorting within unseen coils and bites from invisible teeth dealing death with every second.

'The door's giving; it'll be here at any moment!' called the watchman.

'Leave it. Too late now. Come through to the bridge, both of you,' said Stewart, turning to his bridge team. 'Get into the lifepods now, all of you. Save yourselves.'

The second officer left the LPA and followed the guards through from the navigation room. 'Orbit's lost, captain. We're already grazing the atmosphere. We're starting to burn up now.'

'Okay. Get in a pod and flee while you can.'

A final crash from beyond the deadlight curtain confirmed a serpent was in. Stewart looked up at the now dead viewscreen, glanced about the bridge of his pride and joy; smoke was wafting from some unseen burning, accumulating as the ventilation failed. He turned toward the navigation room; it was over for him. His collar-phone sparked.

'Captain, what are your orders?' said Zac from the cabin of his warbird. 'What shall we do?'

Stewart paused; he'd forgotten about the warbird in the hangar. He gave a grim smile to himself. 'Lieutenant, can you launch?'

'No, sir. I don't think there's any power to open the hangar airlock.'

'Activate your laser, burn it open and save yourselves. God speed you both…' Stewart watched the deadlight curtain ruffle and strain, rising and billowing as though driven by a strong wind. The air was still; there was no wind.

'Sir, captain, please repeat.' But there was no more for Zac to hear. The channel had gone dead.

***

Zac looked to Beth, and she gave a shiver.

'Everyone's lost,' he said. 'The captain's told me to laser open the hull and escape immediately.' He reached for the power controls as Beth looked on, stunned into silence.

'Wait,' she said. 'There are two crew in the pilots' mess; we can't leave them.'

Zac sucked on his tooth. 'I don't think we've got time, the Leviathan's going down.'

'Please, Zac, we must try.'

He nodded, activated the power system and the warbird began its warm-up. Less than a minute, and they would be ready. Opening a channel to the messroom, he registered the relief in the voices of the standby crew. 'We're coming over for you now. Helmets up, I'm not sure we have atmospheric integrity in the hangar anymore. I'll bring our stern airlock as close as I can to the mess door. When I give the word, open your door and run. No second chances, move on my word. And move fast, we know these serpent things are somewhere in the hangar.'

The standby crew overcame the terror of the moment and responded exactly as Zac had ordered. Once on board, they closed the airlock behind them and hurried forward to join their rescuers in the cockpit. There they huddled down beside the mini LPA. 'What now?' said the rescued pilot.

'This,' said Zac, powering up the laser. The warbird's viewscreen darkened to shade their eyes as burning light burst out like a white-hot rod, carving a hole in the Leviathan's hull. Zac guided the beam, widening the hole until he was content the warbird would pass through comfortably. As he killed the beam, they all gasped in horror. Beyond the hole and far below, but perceptibly closer than their last sighting, was the planet. Outside, flitting past the hole in the hull flashed streaks of orange and white and blue as parts of the Leviathan heated and burned away against the atmosphere.

'Now or never,' said Zac. 'Hold tight, here we go.' The slightest of touches to the joystick got the warbird airborne. He deftly aligned with the hull breach and pushed ahead, edging the warbird safe and clear through the gap. They exited the falling wreck, and Zac immediately powered them up and away. He established a safe orbit above the crashing hulk and all four watched in stunned silence.

'What actually happened?' asked the relief pilot.

'We've no more idea than you two; we've been locked down in this warbird, just heard pretty well the same collar-phone broadcasts as you. And then the captain's ordering me to abandon. Seems those dodgy life form readings weren't dodgy, after all. God knows what they turned out to be though. I'm going to try and connect with the Leviathan's data system before it burns away completely, see if we can learn anything. Then we'll decide what to do.'

'I don't want to land down there, ever,' said Beth. 'Whatever did for the Leviathan lives down there. In a little warbird, we'd never stand a chance.'

'Agreed,' said Zac, while continuing to link with the Leviathan's data system. 'It's on emergency power, so access and transfer are slow. And don't worry, we can survive for weeks in here until the squadron arrives. It'll be cosy though.'

Boom! Boom! The whole warbird rocked from the impact of violent blows.

'What the hell is that?' said Zac, turning in his seat. 'There's something very wrong back there.' He triggered a video feed from the passageway and could see nothing. The ship rocked again.

'What is it, Zac? Some system failure?' said the relief pilot.

'No idea, but it's not good. Something is going wrong in our Gravdrive Power Unit. I'll need to go back and check it out. First, though, I'm going to break orbit, fire away from the planet. If we lose power, I'd rather be adrift in space than burn in that atmosphere. Or face what's below.'

'Too right,' said Beth. Then she gasped and clutched Zac's wrist. 'Zac, look, beneath the Leviathan, there are objects glowing in the atmosphere. They're not lifepods, are they?'

All four looked out through the viewscreen. Below them, the Leviathan was glowing brighter as it cut into the atmosphere. They all knew its high-velocity, uncontrolled descent meant only one outcome. Further below it, scores of tiny artefacts displayed similar burning but much, much brighter – the Leviathan's lifepods.

'They are, God rest all those souls. At their launch velocity above the atmosphere, nothing can save them. They're hitting the atmosphere too hard. They'll burn, explode, or any that make it through will be moving so fast the occupants will be crushed on impact – no gravity dampener could cope with the speed of descent, even if it were still functioning after that heat and burn.'

There was a still moment as the four of them processed what it meant. 'We're all that's left,' said Beth. 'From a full Leviathan, just four of us.'

A further round of booming from the gravdrive unit prompted Zac into action. He pulled the warbird's head up and powered out of orbit, heading directly toward the clear space of the system's outer reaches.

'We'll be out of the planet's gravity pull in no time. Now I'm going back to find out what's causing that trouble with the gravdrive unit. We're losing power fast.'

'I'll come with you,' said the relief pilot.

Beth and the relief co-pilot watched the two men stand and shuffle to the cockpit door. They swiped it open and moved cautiously into the passageway. The storage space access door, that let into the power unit, was gone. Smashed in. Further booms echoed from within.

'Right, I'm going in,' said Zac. He hesitated and called out. 'Everyone, helmets up and gloves on. Just in case.' As he flicked up his own helmet, he glanced back into the cockpit and saw Beth doing the same. Turning to the access way, he puzzled. A bot was also trying to get in but seemed to be bouncing off nothing, unable to gain access.

He closed on the doorway and found his body pressed against a nothing that blocked his way. It flexed and moved in time with the banging from within. Zac pressed his hands against it, then his shoulder: quite immovable.

Beth's voice sounded in the collar-phone. 'It's one of them, isn't it? It got in when we picked up the relief crew.'

Zac didn't answer. He knew she was right. Drawing his pistol, he turned his head to look at the reserve pilot. 'We've got to try,' he said. The domed helmet nodded, and the reserve pilot pulled his pistol. The two men stood tight together and aimed at the hatch. They could see nothing, but knew the intruder's transparent body filled the space. Suddenly power failed, emergency lighting kicked in at once. The banging stopped.

'Fire everything you've got,' said Zac.

They emptied their pistols in a frantic discharge, immediately reloading as they felt the nothing in front of them begin to move. As the serpent withdrew from the power unit, its body forced the pilots back into the cabin. Reloaded, they began to fire again. Beth and the co-pilot stretched their arms forward and added fire from their own pistols.

All four were being pressed further into the cockpit. Then the head, unseen, and now clear of the power unit, slid into the cockpit joining the tail that was pressing the team back. There was a violet glint as rounds crashed off the head's super-hard teeth. The artificial gravity collapsed as the buffered power levels began to drop. They were suddenly weightless.

'Zac!' called Beth. 'Zac!' A forlorn cry. The tail unfurled its four fronds, which swept through the cabin, each wrapping around a body. The coils contracted to constrain and squeeze all resistance from the team members. The relief pilot went first. The tail frond swept him toward unseen teeth, which bit without mercy – the cabin filled with blood.

Zac, a frond wrapped around his waist, could feel himself being drawn toward death. He couldn't stop it. But his free hand swept across his sleeve and the suit sent a signal. He gambled there was enough residual buffered power left to execute his order. As the serpent's mouth closed about his head, he felt a sudden strange surge and knew he'd guessed right. Then he died.

At the stern of the warbird, the inner and outer airlock doors had opened simultaneously in response to Zac's command. The outside vacuum sucked, an irresistible vortex, and the serpent was at once dragged through the passageway, out of the airlock and into space. Its tail strands still held all four crew, two dead.

In open space, the unseen head continued killing. With two bites, Beth and the relief co-pilot died instantly.

The stuttering end of the warbird's power buffer supported its forward momentum just enough to carry it away into open space. Gradually it left the serpent and its prey behind as the violent airlock ejection proved enough to propel the monster back into the grasp of the planet's gravity to steadily pull the monster in and down.

The Pelesius System fell silent as the dead.

Chapter 42

Earth

Walking slowly across the parade ground, Longthorn considered the small sample craft that waited to carry them to Primo. It was similar to, but far smaller than, the one that had been their base for so many weeks.

To Longthorn's left was his grandson. To his right was Senator Petraeus, his wheelchair guided by his personal nurse. Behind them followed Major Coral and two score of hand-picked candidates. They were an eclectic mix – soldiers, pilots and scientists, experts in a variety of subjects. The common threads: they all bought into Longthorn's perspective; they were all Americans.

From the earliest days of his involvement, the senator had ensured that rescue efforts had focused on two types of location: military bases and the environs of the major American universities. He had decided that muscle and minds were equally important. If he was to achieve his aim, he needed to have as many fit, capable people as possible recruited. People who were supportive of him, who would feel a debt of gratitude to him personally.

The product of his plan would be a host of strong bodies and bright minds eager to help apply the new technology, to help humanity recover along the path he considered most appropriate. From his deep and growing pool of supporters, the phalanx behind him were the first to fly. They, like him, would soon be introduced to Primo, fitted with their bio-suits and trained in the new technology. Then they would be returning to Earth to operate yet more recovery equipment. From this moment, recovery and everything else would see exponential growth.

The sampler's access door slid open to reveal the pilot, who stepped forward to greet the approaching party.

'Senator Longthorn, Senator Petraeus, Congressman Longthorn, and General Pashman, sir, welcome and please come aboard.'

Longthorn led the group on, noting with approval a slight mid-West drawl in the pilot's voice. 'Thank you, pilot. Where to?'

'Straight along the passageway, then up, senator. Keep going. I'll be with you in one moment.' The pilot allowed the whole party to funnel by him then he closed the airlock doors and hurried past the line of regular passengers who were being shown into the canteen by his crewmate.

Once the VIPs were safe on the bridge deck, the pilot began to program a course for Primo into the navigation LPA. Longthorn watched with interest. 'I see you're very comfortable with the new technology, pilot. Was it easy to master?'

'No real problem, sir. Just needed a change of mindset. Once you've got over that, the learning is easy. Easier than our Earth-based technologies.'

'Good to hear. We're going to need to train a lot more pilots… a lot for every job.'

'So General Dower was explaining to us all the other day. Thank God you have people ready to learn. Reckon I'll be ferrying folk up and back for the foreseeable.

'Now sir, perhaps you'd all like to focus on the viewscreen? It's worth it. First time leaving the atmosphere for deep space is a real experience, not to be missed.'

'Lead on pilot. The sooner we reach Primo the better.'

Chapter 43

Base Primo

The open promenade at Primo Main Base offered access to viewing ports that let onto the Grand Canal, and to the docking hangars where some of the crewed craft would berth. There were normally a few people to be seen here, dotting from one task to another about the base, and others relaxing and watching the comings and goings of assorted craft passing by the viewing ports. Today there was quite a crowd waiting in anticipation.

General Dower recalled there had been several occasions where he'd stood with the crowds to wave off squadrons of Leviathans as they travelled out into the galaxy. On every expedition, they'd lost craft and crew to conflict, inexperience or plain bad luck. That was always in the back of his mind. Today was different – for the first time, the crowd was here to welcome an incoming craft loaded with new people.

The newly arrived sample craft's airlock access door slid open, and General Dower stepped forward. As the Primo crowd clapped and cheered, Senator Longthorn emerged, smart and well-tailored. Beside him was a man, smaller in frame, with a face as drawn in pain as Longthorn's was beaming in pleasure. Senator Petraeus sat quietly in his wheelchair, pushed forward by his young nurse. Behind them came Longthorn III, General Pashman and Major Coral.

Dower saluted the visitors then extended a hand of welcome to Longthorn. A series of introductions followed as the enthusiastic crowd maintained their applause. The newly arrived VIPs were guided ahead by Dower, a security detail ensuring joy did not spill over into bumping and jostling. The dignitaries moved away, and a new round of cheering erupted as the first intake of Earth survivors emerged through the airlock. Once kitted out with suits and put through their induction, it was they and the many more who were to follow who would do the heavy lifting in Earth's ongoing rescue and recovery.

Every new soul was welcome, and the greetings were warm and enthusiastic.

***

Dower stood beside his desk as Longthorn's party, Major Coral included, made themselves comfortable. Longthorn waved the nurse out of the office as the general moved forward to offer coffee or something stronger. Dower couldn't help wondering what a major was doing in such a high-level meeting, but it was clear Longthorn was in no hurry to explain.

'Well, general, first impressions of Base Primo are every bit as impressive as we'd been led to expect, more even,' said Longthorn. 'We're truly grateful to you and your staff here and under Brigadier Smith-Brown down on Earth. We recognise absolutely that, but for you all, we'd be finished.'

General Dower nodded. 'It's our job and we're doing it, senator. Hopefully, with a steady flow of recruits, we'll be able to boost the rescue efforts fast.'

'That's exactly the kind of talk I like to hear, general. Action, make it work!'

The door opened and Steph hurried in. The three ambulant visitors stood to greet her as General Dower made introductions to all.

'I'm sorry I wasn't here when you arrived,' said Steph. 'I've been refining the program for mass production of the electronic kit needed on Earth. Once the volunteers get back to Earth, they'll all have collar-phones for local comms, but what we also need is a portable comms system for general use by people without bio-suits. We'll get them distributed everywhere, a sort of network.'

'Sounds impressive,' said Longthorn. 'And may I say, I have been impressed by so many reports of your work and ability.'

'Thank you, senator, we're all just doing our best.'

'Well, that I do know. Now perhaps you and the general can bring us up to speed. How we reached this point, what you're doing and where.'

'Where to start!' said Steph.

'I believe the beginning's as good a spot as any.'

General Dower cleared his throat. 'Senator Longthorn, Senator Petraeus, there's a lot to tell, and we're delighted to share. Perhaps you'd like some food first? And I wondered, why did you all come up on the first people transport? Where do you see your role in the recovery process?' He looked from Longthorn to General Pashman – the man was vice chair of the Joint Chiefs and, as such, in ordinary times would outrank him.

'Let me put your mind at rest, general. While it's true I and my colleagues here represent the surviving leadership of US government and General Pashman is undoubtedly the surviving senior commander of our armed forces, we are here only to learn of events and understand how Primo might help us back on Earth so we can all pull together for the common good.

'We politicians intend to spend some time here at Primo to properly understand the facility. Unfortunately, General Pashman will need to return to Earth as soon as you have equipped him with one of the fancy suits we've all heard so much about. Likewise, Major Coral must return to Earth. But I know they'll both want to return here so they can fully appreciate what you have at your disposal.'

Dower nodded. He could not push for more clarity, but somehow, the assurance lacked substance, particularly in the light of his discussions with Brigadier Smith-Brown. The Englishman had made clear his concerns over Longthorn's motives.

'Well, senator, I've allocated each of you a cabin, so accommodation is no problem. Perhaps it would be best if we eat, give you a sketch outline of events first, then get you all fitted for suits before a much more detailed account.'

'I'm good with that, general. Let's get started, shall we?' Longthorn leaned back and beamed a smile about the office.

Steph leaned forward slightly. 'Really, I need to get back to the manufacturing process – there's so much to do. Please excuse me, but if I may, perhaps later Senator Petraeus will allow me to take him to the sickbay? I can't be certain, but perhaps our advanced tech could help him. It would be worth a try.'

Chapter 44

Base Primo

Steph left Senator Petraeus' bedside and crossed the sickbay to join the attending medical team who clustered beside an LPA. During the first few days, some had been unconvinced by her suggestions, but acknowledging she, more than any, best understood the advanced technology that filled the medical bay, they had gone along with her proposal. One or two of the senior medics had also pointed to her success in using the technology to save the general's daughter and her co-pilot.

That set of skills had been passed on, and now several of the doctors were familiar and happy with the equipment and techniques used for trauma care. Another breakthrough in the use and application of Weeman's medical technology, this time for the treatment of chronic conditions, would be welcomed. Though some of the medics were cautious about using the senator for what amounted to a medical trial.

Steph had tried to assure them it wasn't guesswork – she had it. Now they all recognised she did indeed have it.

'I can see real improvements in the data,' said Steph quietly, ensuring the senator could not hear her words. 'Let me recap the procedures we've applied so far. Then the next steps with the machine too. I think you'll be able to handle this without me from here on. There is perceptible regeneration around his joints already. Another week or so and he could be strong enough to get out and about on his own. Hopefully you'll progress him to complete independence pretty quickly.'

She guided the medics through the machine's next sequences and settings and then, pointing into the LPA, showed them where she'd placed detailed instructions. Steph straightened up and smiled. 'Another week using this kit and you'll be the experts teaching me. Check out my expansion notes too. You should be able to develop applications well beyond the senator's problems. Now, you know where I am if you need me, otherwise just keep me posted.'

The doctors thanked her and eagerly turned back to the LPA, delving into the knowledge like children exploring a box of toffees. She stepped away and returned to the senator's bedside to take her leave.

'It's looking good, senator. Better than we could ever have imagined. I'm sure there's a good deal more the doctors will be able to do, given a little time.'

Petraeus smiled and reached out his hand to grip Steph's. 'They're doing a good job, and I'm feeling so, so much better. But nobody's fooling me. I know it's your doing; you're the smart one, not those doctors. Look at this.' He kicked up his legs beneath the sheet, flexing his knees and straightening. 'That's your doing. I believe you when you say there's more improvement to come, but let me tell you, the pain's gone, and I've already got back movement I'd lost years ago. You, *you* have given me back my life. No… more than that, you have given me a new life!'

Steph smiled, extracting her hand from the senator's and stepping back a little. 'It's a team effort, senator, everyone plays their part. I'm pleased you're getting better, very pleased. But I've got to go now; the medics have got your care in hand.'

'You say it the way you want, young lady. But I'm not stupid – I know I owe it all to you. You saved me. Anytime, anywhere, you say the word and Senator Al Petraeus is your man. Whatever you want, you got it.'

Steph raised her hand and waved a casual acknowledgement back to the senator as she walked out of the sickbay. The door slid closed behind her, and the senator was left smiling contentedly at nothing.

***

Fay took a series of tentative steps across General Dower's living space. Her mother, Gail Dower, forbidden by her daughter from interfering, looked on anxiously, ready to provide the unwanted support at a moment's notice.

'It's no good, Mom. I'm going to do it myself. And I'm doing it now.' Fay reached the far end of the room and turned about, preparing to retrace her steps.

'The doctors said you're not to stress your body or over-exert yourself. And that's just what you're doing.'

'I'm getting better. I want to get back to the warbirds. They'll never let me be a pilot again if I can't get about freely.'

'It'll come, honey. Just not all at once.'

'Well, I can't wait. I need to get better.' She began the return journey, one small but determined step at a time. 'Nothing's gonna beat me, nothing!' Halfway across, she paused, wavered – it wasn't as easy as she'd envisaged.

The accommodation door slid open, and Lily Dower entered, followed by Steph.

'Hey! What are you doing?' called Lily, hurrying across to her sister. 'Fay, I was there when the doctors released you from sickbay this morning. You know what they said!

'Mom, Fay's to do short pace walking exercises only, four times a day, and with one of us supporting her. There's a whole list of sitting exercises she can do.'

'That's not what she told me,' said Gail, while taking Fay's other arm to help Lily guide her back to the lounge seating.

Steph rolled her eyes at Fay's predictable determination and sat herself down as the others settled Fay into a seat. Then Gail stooped to kiss Steph before taking a seat too.

'She won't listen to me,' said Gail.

'She never has,' said Lily; 'it's always her way.'

'Hey, I'm here you know,' said Fay.

'Oh, we know,' said Gail.

Steph looked at the two sisters; they had both become her firm friends over the months, but they were very different. Paul and Gail Dower's daughters were good souls but with very different motivations. The younger, Lily, was academically brilliant, exceptionally so. A key member of Steph's team, her smart thinking and analytical mind had helped them all out on numerous occasions. Meanwhile, Fay… Fay was Fay. Clever, but more than that, she was an athlete, a fighter and, most of all, brave. In her single warbird, she had faced off against the whole locust attack formation. A Valley of Death charge that had bought Primo vital time to evacuate Main Base into the Deep and seen her warbird hammered in the process. She had survived, just, and only because of Steph's medical tech. Now, after months in sickbay, she was out and starting to fight a whole new and very personal war.

'You've got to take it easy, Fay,' said Steph. 'I know it's frustrating, but little by little is the only way.'

Fay scowled at her. 'I know, but it's just so maddening. My mind says go, my body says yes, but it's just not strong enough.'

'Tell you what, let me look at your bio-suit settings. Maybe it can be adjusted, stiffened somehow, to give you more support. We've never had to do that before but let's try. It would be good for you now, and I'm sure there will be plenty of others who might benefit in the future.'

'You can do that?'

'I don't know, maybe. Let me look into it.'

'Great. Thanks. When?'

'Fay, she'll do it when she can,' said Gail. 'Now, Steph, what's the news with the senator?'

'I think he's going to be fine, seems a lot better already. In fact, he seems convinced he's in my debt.'

'That could be useful one day.'

'What do you mean?'

'I get the feeling the general is uncomfortable with these newcomers. He's a bit uneasy.'

'Mom? What do you mean?' said Lily. 'He seems his normal self to me.'

'Oh forget I said anything. I'm sure I'm overreacting. Your father will be annoyed if he thinks we're gossiping. Everything's fine.'

Lily, Fay and Steph all looked at Gail – she'd closed down the conversation, but could trouble be brewing?

Steph shrugged it off. Senator Petraeus seemed sound and grateful. She couldn't imagine him doing anything to disrupt the general's work or life here on Primo.

Chapter 45

Base Primo

Longthorn was very pleased. Coral's planning and coordination ensured there were ten of his people coming up for induction for each person nominated by Smith-Brown. He looked across at General Dower who was standing in front of the desk.

Every day, a craft docked and delivered a hundred new recruits for a ten-day induction course. Every day, it left carrying a hundred freshly inducted staff back to Earth. There they would continue their initial training on the technology and flying observer craft. Craft that were being delivered to Earth with equal regularity, some having been salvaged from the holds of long-retired samplers waiting their turn in the scrap line. Others were being manufactured by Steph's team when they had time between producing the powered tools and kit needed for recovery.

The senator felt sure everything was going his way.

'General, I understand your concern about equity, and believe me, I share it absolutely. But what can I do? Stateside is well organised and generating far more candidates than the other core countries, to say nothing of the outlying countries that Smith-Brown is pushing to open up.'

'Well, senator, I think it may be time to introduce some positive discrimination. Make sure our allied countries and others have people being trained up to help the recovery.'

'Agreed,' said Longthorn, banging a fist into his palm. 'Agreed, but let's not slow the process for now. We're bringing forward more people ready and willing to be trained every day. Primo has the capacity to process them, so let's do it. Yes, when the Brits or the Aussies or anyone else start to bring forward candidates in larger numbers, we can accommodate them, allocate a bigger proportion of places.

'Meanwhile, let's not cut off our noses to spite our faces. Not inducting all these ready and willing American volunteers will leave training places unfilled up here and undermine social cohesion in our country. Come on, general, you're an American too! You know what's good for America is good for everyone.'

It had been a while coming, but Dower sensed it: a change in Longthorn's tone. *Was this the start of things?*

'Yes, senator, I am an American and proud of it. But this is an international project, run jointly with the UK, and we invited many allies on board too. Our president made that agreement and, together with the secretary of defense, bound me to it. I'm not happy with any process that does not recognise those establishing principles.'

'General, general, relax! I'm not questioning the history nor asking you to do anything other than follow the established order, while it stands. All I am asking is, since there's a shortage of foreign candidates for training and a surfeit of Americans, let's train the Americans – for everyone's benefit.'

Dower nodded. Deep down, he felt something was not right, but the senator's request was both fair and logical. 'Agreed, senator, but I'm going to have to speak with the brigadier. Recruitment may be slow out at the edges where it's all rescue, but there should be plenty of survivor Brits coming forward.'

'Yes, well… Perhaps the brigadier is not quite as efficient as you'd judged.'

'No, senator. Smith-Brown is solid. It's likely he's been so busy organising the international relief, his home country may have attracted slightly less of his attention than your team has been able to devote to the States.'

'As you say, general. But if you suspect the brigadier is spreading himself too thin, perhaps we should refocus his area of responsibility. I'm sure we could appoint somebody else to global command while he focuses on just the UK or perhaps all of Europe…' Longthorn looked across the office toward Longthorn III.

'A great suggestion, senator,' said Longthorn III. 'You know, general, perhaps the brigadier would welcome such a move, and I think we have just the person in mind to take over wider management down there.'

General Dower stiffened. 'Thank you, gentlemen, your thoughts are appreciated, but I will make no changes without careful consideration and certainly not without consulting the brigadier, who is the UK's senior officer on the project and, as such, the project's second in command. Meanwhile, we must maintain the flow of new inductees and keep up the training schemes at all costs. Since it is primarily American candidates coming forward to complete induction and training, I agree we must push them through. We'll need to do more to enhance the mix of candidates, but for now we continue to train those who present.'

As the door slid shut on the general, Longthorn scowled. 'That man completely lacks vision. How the president and secretary of defense thought he was the man for the job here at Primo is beyond me.'

'You've said it all along, sir,' said Longthorn III. 'We've been letting him rule the roost like he was the elected representative; surely it's time to play your hand now?'

'Soon, I think, very soon,' said Longthorn. 'We have more than enough trained people to ensure things carry on smoothly no matter what that dolt Dower does. Let's arrange to get General Pashman back up from Earth, and meanwhile, I'll have a long talk with Senator Petraeus.'

'Will he be a problem, do you think?'

'He was so grateful for the signs of recovery to his health from the new tech, I thought we were losing him for a little while. But he's a good man, knows about leadership and control, the importance of the party standing together. Now he's had time to get used to the idea of his recovery, he's coming back into line.

'Starting from now, we'll shake things up a bit. I'm going to press for some advanced training for staff who have already been inducted, get them back up here learning more and putting their new skills into practice here as well as down on Earth. Spread the work burden and responsibility wider. I want you to get in touch with Major Coral, have him line up our best and most supportive to commence extended Primo training. I want our people coming back up here for advanced training from now.'

'How will you get General Dower to clear that?'

'Why wouldn't he? It's for the common good, enhancing skills and capacities, and there's plenty of spare accommodation. I want our people familiar with the detail of every aspect of Primo. And I want it now!'

Longthorn III looked appreciatively at his grandfather. 'Yes, sir. I'll get in touch with Pashman and Coral at once. They'll be pleased we're moving at last.'

'Good, thank you. I know it's been frustrating for you. But you be sure to remember: timing is everything. Timing and being right. Now get moving, I'm going to call round on Petraeus.'

Chapter 46

Perseus Arm: Pelesius System

'What the hell's happened?' said MacMillan.

'There's nothing here,' said Jamie.

Each man stood on their own Leviathan's bridge, looking out onto the same scene. After long weeks spent clearing the locusts from Prenar b., they had all travelled to Pelesius eager to finish the job. Of all the scenarios they had war-gamed ahead of arrival, this one had never been considered.

Both squadrons had left the Fold on the edge of the Pelesius System and searched – the scanners had picked up nothing. Even at the point far away from the planet, where HB-3 should have been maintaining a distant watch, there was just empty space. MacMillan called out, and Sevrine hurried from the navigation room LPA to join him.

She shook her head – still nothing. 'Sparks says his comms unit is picking up no signals at all. It's like a ghost system. I must speak to Ossie, see what we can come up with.'

'Yes, whatever you can. We need to know where the locusts are and where our Leviathan has gone,' said the colonel, turning back to the viewscreen. 'And we need to know now!'

He stroked his sleeve, reopening a comms channel. 'Hello, Jamie, I think we should get in for a closer look at the planet. Both squadrons will advance and have their warbirds ready for immediate launch.

'I want you to take Bravo into orbit above the planet and find out what's going on down there. I'll hold Alpha Squadron off a distance, ready to support you in case of any surprises.'

'Will do, colonel,' said Jamie. 'But this just doesn't make sense. HB-3 could be passing through a planetary shadow or behind one of the moons dotted about the system's planets, but it must have picked up our signals by now. Why is it not declaring itself?'

***

The two Leviathans of Bravo Squadron dropped into orbit above Pelesius d., while far above them were Colonel MacMillan and Alpha Squadron's three Leviathans. Jamie looked across to where Captain Wills gazed deep into the viewscreen.

'Captain Wills, we need to put boots on the ground, a reconnaissance mission. Never mind the missing Leviathan, there should be a swarm of stranded attack vessels. Where have they gone? Just no live signals of any sort, but the surface scans have thrown up some possible target anomalies that need to be checked out.

'I'll pilot the recon team down myself. In my absence, you have the squadron command. You know what to do. If push comes to shove, saving the Leviathans and their crews is more important than saving my team on the ground. Am I clear?'

Wills nodded. 'Good luck, sir.'

Jamie moved swiftly from the bridge, down several decks to the central passageway and onto the aft moving travellator which quickly carried him back through the heart of the Leviathan. He stepped off at the hangar entrances, acknowledged the armed guard at the hangar door and hurried in.

At the far end was a single warbird, C2. It would be flying shotgun with his expedition today. Nearer to hand were two observers, newly transferred from other Leviathans. Assembled beside each was a squad of marines waiting to board. As Jamie approached, his old friend stepped forward to greet him.

'All set Baz?' said Jamie.

'We are, but it's weird. What the hell's happened here?'

'I don't know, but let's go find out… On me,' said Jamie, working his way through the resting marines to reach the observer's stern entrance. He swiped it open and stepped into the airlock. There he wove past the heavy machine gun, now a standard fixture across every observer in the expedition. Baz and the marines followed him in. Others filed into the second observer, led by Lieutenant Grieves.

'Listen up!' said Jamie. His voice transmitted to everyone aboard the observers and their escorting warbird. 'We're going in now. Our job today is to find out what's happened to HB-3. Anything else, including fighting locusts, is secondary.

'The scans are returning no active surface signals, no comms of any sort; the planet is silent. But there are echoes bouncing back to us from what may be concentrations of metallic constructions – Science speculates these could be spacecraft debris – ours or locust, we just don't know. We will be going down to where we've located the greatest concentration of these echoes. Just be ready for whatever we find.'

Without further ado, Jamie powered up the observer. It lifted a couple of feet off the deck and hovered. The other observer mirrored his move as did the warbird.

'Open the hangar please,' he said into his collar-phone.

The hangar door swept open, and Jamie was looking out into black space. He nudged the observer forward, and as it left the hangar, Pelesius d. appeared below. The sphere was all swirls and billows of white where weather systems worked their way about the atmosphere.

'Hello, Jamie. We've got something,' Colonel MacMillan's voice sounded in Jamie's collar-phone. 'Our long-range scanners have just picked up a passive echo. No active signal but analysis suggests it could be manufactured. Possibly one of our craft – dead. It's been caught in the orbit of the outer gas giant. Science is plotting its movement, and projects it's in a decaying orbit. If we move now, we could well get there before it goes down.'

'What do you propose?' said Jamie.

'I'd like you to abort your mission and get over to that signal, whatever it is. Top speed and you could save it. If it's one of ours, it might hold vital information as to where HB-3 is. I will remain on station here with the Leviathans to complete further detailed scanning. HB-1 will move to join you in support of the recovery.'

***

'It's certainly a warbird… and I can read its sign! HB-3:C2. Confirmed. It's from the missing Leviathan,' reported the pilot of the escorting warbird. It had approached first to ensure there were no nasty surprises.

Then Jamie had the warbird and second observer stand off as he closed the distance and began a careful analysis.

'Confirmed status. It's dead, a hulk. No life signs. Seems the crew abandoned her.' He began to fly a circuit round the warbird, which was in a gentle descent toward the gas giant. 'I see the stern airlock is open as though they left it in a real hurry. Weird.'

'Hello, Jamie. MacMillan here. Science is estimating two hours before it goes into terminal descent. Can you save it?'

'Maybe. We have no cables or salvage kit here. And I wouldn't want to put anyone aboard that bird until we've got it away from the planet's pull. I'm thinking I will close in and nudge it away. Keep pushing it out into deeper space. Out there, with some careful piloting, a Leviathan could manoeuvre into a position where its salvage arm could catch the bird. Then Science can fill its boots.'

'Be careful, Jamie. Don't damage your observer. You could end up going down too.' MacMillan's voice was matter-of-fact, but Jamie knew the senior man was worried more for him than the observer.

'No problem. I have a second observer here and a warbird. If anything goes wrong, and we have to abandon the attempt, between them they'll be able to pick us up. But right now, let's remain positive.'

The stricken warbird was travelling on a steady course, nose-first in a gentle inward arc toward its destruction. Jamie brought his craft alongside the warbird, exactly matching its direction and speed. This close precision flying was, in another life, good enough for a royal fly-past. Today, he just hoped it would be good enough to salvage the warbird.

Happy with the two crafts' relative positions, Jamie stood rigid, staring into the observer's viewscreen, and began to nudge very slowly toward the warbird. With the gentlest of touches to his sleeve controls he tweaked the observer's wing position so the gap continued to narrow bit by bit, until the warbird was just above the observer's wing. He kept closing the distance so the two craft were almost touching. The warbird raced on in gravity's pull, just an arm's length above the wing of the observer.

Very cautiously, Jamie shifted position again, raising the observer slightly. He stopped progress as a bump reverberated through the observer. Holding his breath, he switched his attention between viewscreen and sleeve data feed. He allowed himself the slightest of smiles. The warbird had not bounced; it was sitting on the observer's wing. He reported the success.

'We can see,' responded the pilots of the escorting warbird and second observer. 'Great manoeuvring.'

Now the moment of truth. Jamie edged closer to the warbird. A dull grating sounded throughout the observer as the warbird ground over the observer's wing. The noise stopped with a resounding clunk. The warbird's stubby port wing was pressed against the observer's starboard fuselage, and its whole weight rested completely on the observer's wing.

Jamie raised the observer's nose just a couple of degrees and waited. There was more noise as the warbird found resistance to its steady forward motion and it pressed into the observer's wing, resisting the tiny change of course. Once again Jamie held his breath, waiting and praying the warbird's course would bend to his will. The noise eased as the craft found it easier to adjust course and settle on the wing than break the observer's wing in pursuit of its original course.

With a smile, Jamie again reported the success. He knew now he could deflect the warbird into space. Little by little, he continued to change course. Eventually he carried the warbird away from the gas giant, in the crook of the observer's wing. To the acclaim of the accompanying craft, he shepherded the warbird far into space and away from gravity's influence. He dropped away from the bird, leaving it to drift. Now it was down to the salvage crew on HB-1. He'd done his bit.

Chapter 47

Perseus Arm: Pelesius System

Colonel MacMillan looked quietly about his office. In silence, the five Leviathan captains, five chief scientists and Jamie waited for his decision.

Ossie and Sevrine had led the scientific analysis of the warbird. Bit by bit, they had teased out the story from the hulk's memory store. The team had struggled to overcome its shock and then horror over events leading to the loss of HB-3 and all its crew. They couldn't answer all the questions their findings generated, but what they did know was enough to produce a unanimous recommendation for the colonel.

'It is clear,' said MacMillan, carefully choosing his words, 'there are some things in space that, even with our best scientific minds, we simply don't understand. Maybe we can't ever understand. Things that defy our science, defy our understanding of nature. There is something on Pelesius d. that broke an entire locust fleet as though they were so many fortune cookies. It brought down our Leviathan as easily as a kite on a string.

'Science says they have no answer for us today. Sevrine thinks, in time, maybe. But right now, down on Pelesius d., Science believes there is a life form that defies our understanding. It is aggressive in defence of its planet and seems to have an aversion to generated power. Irrational to us, but they moved with patience and with ruthless coordinated efficiency to destroy all the power sources they could detect.

'Doubtless, with time and analysis, we'll work out what's down there and how we might handle it. But today, it is clear from the data analysis, that nobody, whether on board or in a lifepod, could have survived the uncontrolled atmospheric entry. I will not risk another craft or crewmember on that planet. I am placing Pelesius d., indeed the whole Pelesius System, in indefinite quarantine.'

He looked about the office. Many kept their eyes firmly on the conference table. His officers and scientists agreed, though abandoning the lost Leviathan hurt.

'Furthermore, and on a happier note, whatever lives down on that planet did our job for us. The second locust swarm is destroyed completely. Our mission is complete.' He stood. 'Return to your Leviathans and make ready. In two hours, we set course for the nearest folding point and then on to Secundo where we will allow the crews a break, regroup and repair as required. From there, we return to Primo, mission accomplished.'

Chapter 48

Base Primo

Steph stepped smartly across the Main Base concourse. Recent days had brought her and all her science team members a new sense of enthusiasm. After standing alone for so long and having lost so many friends in the attrition of the past year, there was real joy at the influx of Earth survivor inductees. Particularly now so many of those early inductees were being channelled back up to Primo to build on their initial training. With more advanced training on Primo's core systems and facilities, they could make a greater contribution, more quickly. This innovation was welcome burden-sharing.

In quieter moments, Steph did worry they were depleting the Earth rescue teams. But everything was working just fine. They were managing to turn around a steady stream of inductees to more than replace the influx of people coming for advanced training – people who would likely provide a huge boost to Earth's recovery once they returned with the enhanced skillsets. She allowed herself an indulgent smile. Right now, the only thing that could improve things was Jamie's return. And he was almost home.

A homing buoy, previously received from Colonel MacMillan's Leviathan, had delivered news of events in the Perseus Arm and of Jamie's survival. The Hunter squadrons had returned to Secundo where they had paused for repairs, to reorganise crew and take a short break before heading back to Primo. Today's radio message from MacMillan confirmed they had exited the Fold and would be at Primo in under two hours.

Over the long weeks apart, Steph had missed Jamie more than ever, but he would be back at any moment, and right now, that was the only news that mattered. She stepped into the general's office. Her smile broadened further as she saw Brigadier Smith-Brown and Celine. 'When did you two arrive? I had no idea you were coming!'

She hugged them both, fighting back tears of joy. It seemed so long ago that her two friends had become isolated on Earth.

'We didn't know either,' said Celine. 'General Pashman turned up at our base in the UK and said General Dower needed him and us at Primo at once. Top secret, no comms. And here we are!'

'So, where is General Pashman? More to the point'—she turned to General Dower—'why didn't you tell me about this meeting. I thought we had no secrets.'

The enthusiasm stemming from her gushing welcome cut short as she caught the general's eye. He seemed perturbed. Steph took a half-step back from Celine. Her one hand still gently pressed against the small of the brigadier's back, her other holding Celine's. 'What's going on, general?'

'I'm not sure, but I'm sure as hell going to find out. I didn't call a confidential meeting, nor did I recall anyone from Earth: not Celine, not the brigadier, not General Pashman – no one.' The general stopped talking as a call opened in his collar-phone. As he listened, his face darkened, and the call ended with him uttering a single word, 'Okay.'

'What is it?' said Steph.

'I've been asked to join Senator Longthorn, now. There's been something brewing for a while – now we'll see.' The general stood, pulled himself up straight, forced a curt smile and made for the door.

The others made to follow him. He paused, held out a hand to stop them. 'Sorry, whatever's on the senator's mind, he made it clear this was a private meeting.'

***

The general entered Longthorn's workroom where what seemed an interview panel was assembled to one side of the worktable. A single empty chair rested on the other side. As the door slid shut behind him, Dower reviewed those arrayed before him. Longthorn, Petraeus, Longthorn III, Pashman and, to the far left, Major Coral, now sporting the silver eagles of a full colonel.

'General Dower, thank you for joining us so promptly,' said Longthorn.

'I understood you wanted a private meeting with me,' said the general, carefully masking the suspicion that was growing in his mind. 'What's this all about senator? I came as a courtesy to you, but it seems I've been summoned to something of a tribunal. I'm not used to being summoned to anything on my own base. What's going on?'

'Come, come, general, you're among countrymen. Please sit, let's talk.'

'I won't sit, senator. To do so would suggest acquiescence with whatever scheme you seem to have going here. Let me be clear. I have command of Primo and all its assets and staff. Why have you brought Brigadier Smith-Brown up on fabricated orders. I cannot accept such behaviour.'

'General! A lot has changed since you were put in full command of Primo and associated activities. I must say, on reflection, we are content that your posting was a temporary political decision in the face of extreme threat. A moment when the political establishment was unable to look beyond the immediate crisis when framing your orders. In truth, we all know every posting is ultimately temporary – nothing lasts forever.'

'There was nothing temporary about it, senator. My appointment was permanent and an indisputable decision, made by the president with the full support of General Troy, chair of the Joint Chiefs, and confirmed directly by the secretary of defense. Senator, the position is unequivocal, and I see no need for this discussion today.'

'Yes, I wouldn't think to challenge those events, general. However, times change, things move on. We'—he swept an arm back and forth over the table—'are acutely aware of the good works you have done, and the effort you put in across a range of affairs. However, you have overlooked something very important.'

'I don't think so, senator. Indeed, I think this meeting is drawing to its natural close.'

Longthorn suddenly fixed Dower with a piercing stare. 'On the contrary, general, it's only just begun. You were appointed by the political leadership of our great country. You will have noticed all those involved in your appointment are now dead. Indeed, I and my colleagues here are the only legitimately elected surviving members of that government – the government elected to govern in this term of office. A government whose mandate is still current and inviolate. You believe in democracy, general, you are sworn to serve and defend the country's constitution, am I right?'

Dower had half-turned to take his leave. He stopped himself and turned back to face the senator. 'What exactly are you driving at?'

'You, general, are a servant of the state. Your first and last responsibility is always the defence of your country while following the will of the people as expressed by their elected political representatives. You fit in a chain of command, you exercise power that ultimately lies in the political gift of the nation's leadership, do you deny that? Or are you seeking to install yourself as a dictator?'

'Senator, I have served my country my whole life and always will. I command Primo and all its aspects under an official order, as a duly appointed commander, not some strongman dictator.'

'Therein lies the confusion, general. You acknowledge the chain of command; you draw your strength and position directly from it. Yet you also ignore it when you choose.'

'You are talking nonsense, senator. I have never once in my career ignored the chain of command – never will, so help me.'

'General, we are delighted to hear your unwavering commitment to the chain of command, which is exactly what we'd expect of an American officer. As I say, all those who appointed you are dead, you cannot dispute that. I, Senator Petraeus and Representative Longthorn are the only legitimate surviving elected members of the United States government, in the current electoral term. It follows, unarguably, that we are the surviving political leaders of our country, and that position will prevail until such time as a properly constituted election can be held. Can you question our legitimacy?'

Dower was silent. He knew what Longthorn said was true but also that Longthorn was not the man he would like to see holding such power.

'I think as a loyal servant of our country you do recognise the accuracy of my observations. General, we three politicians sitting here are the full representation of both houses. Today we are the legitimate government of the country – your country. You must acknowledge that.'

Dower remained silent, knowing exactly where Longthorn's argument was going, wanting to reject it, but also deep down knowing the senator's case was logically correct – he needed time to think: *Could he legitimately challenge the senator, would that be mutiny?*

'One further point, general. Beyond the unassailable legitimacy of our political leadership, you know General Pashman's role as the permanent vice chairman of the Joint Chiefs of Staff. Following the sad loss of General Troy to the virus, General Pashman is empowered, and expected, to step up to assume full control pending the appointment of a new permanent chair by the nation's political leaders.

'I want you to know, as of now, in our capacity as civil leaders, we have asked General Pashman to accept his permanent appointment to that role. It follows, irrespective of your feelings about the political leadership, that General Pashman is your direct senior commander in the military chain of command. Since his own rescue, you know his efforts have been focused on ensuring the recovery plan in the States has been as efficient as it could be. And I know we're all grateful to him for those efforts.' There was a murmured chorus of agreement along the table, and Longthorn III gently clapped his hands, quickly mirrored by Senator Petraeus.

Longthorn nodded in support of the acclaim. 'I am sure, general, you will recognise the correctness of my assertions. You cannot do anything other than accept General Pashman as your direct superior. And you should know, General Pashman accepts this political panel's legitimacy absolutely.'

'What's this all about, senator?' said Dower, managing to control and mask his fury completely.

'We understand this will be difficult for you, general. But I know you, above all men, will do your duty. You may want a little time to consider your position, to think carefully how you might proceed.'

Dower looked Longthorn in the eye. 'You have not yet said what your intention is. Nor have you addressed the British control component. I cannot allow you or anyone to ride roughshod over the core and binding agreement reached between our president and the British for management of the project.'

Longthorn III leaned forward. 'I'm not sure you are in a position to negotiate this, general. We all recognise you've done the best job you could, holding things together in the absence of civil political direction and oversight. But now, happily, with the ordered convening of our country's surviving political and military leaders today, the chain of command and control is restored.'

'But what about the British?'

Longthorn turned his head swiftly to his right and raised a hand to cut off Longthorn III who was about to respond. He turned back to General Dower. 'General, I am a reasonable man, we're all reasonable men. It is truly a tragedy that the UK, like everywhere else, took such a hard hit from the virus. We have waited as long as we could in the hope that some of the British political leaders might be found alive, to join us in this enterprise of recovery. Sadly, to date, that has not happened. But we all live in hope. Let me assure you, as the UK search and recovery continues, we will welcome any surviving elected member of parliament to this table.

'And in days to come, in better times, I'm sure Britain, like America, will want to hold fresh elections. You can be certain I for one will welcome that fresh mandate and the British political leadership will be invited to take its rightful place at the table.'

'And for now?' said Dower.

Senator Petraeus touched Longthorn's arm and then spoke for the first time. 'General, we cannot wait in limbo when so much needs to be done. This must not be a military dictatorship. Anything with an American root should always be as it ever was: a civil administration supported and protected by a loyal military. In the absence of any available elected British representation, we, the remaining members of the joint American–British civil leadership panel, must act in the common interest of both parties. There is no other way.

'We three surviving political leaders are by default the political leadership of your country and, as a direct consequence, are your political leaders. You should know, after much thought and discussion, we have concluded that, pending elections that might be held when order and civil structure are fully restored, we have agreed unanimously that Senator Longthorn will assume the leading role. Until a new president can be elected, he is your ultimate commander in chief.'

Longthorn nodded sagely. 'Thank you, senator, wise words and an accurate summary of the situation. That Britain cannot take its joint equal seat at the table is tragic, but as Senator Petraeus says, we must act for the good of all, including the British, and act now for the sake of humanity. And you, more than anyone, know your duty and place, general. You are sworn to defend the constitution of the United States, whose duly elected civilian leadership is presently the only extant authority that can assure a fair and sustainable future for humanity's survivors.

'You know your duty and your oath. We are the elected leadership of your country, and General Pashman is your direct commander. You have sworn an inviolate oath to serve and protect your country and constitution. We expect you to honour your binding commitment. Is that clear?'

Dower thought hard. He felt almost certain that Longthorn's play, though logically argued and compelling to those bound by their word, lacked sincerity. He knew, too, that he had sworn an oath, serious and binding. To be faithful to his oath and to the constitution of the United States, he had to recognise the elected political leadership of his country. Yet it all felt so wrong, so against the spirit of everything they had worked for in the past year. He needed to think, needed time, remained silent.

Longthorn gave a tight dry smile. 'Well, general, I mentioned previously that you might need a short break to consider your position. Shall we reconvene in one hour to conclude our business?'

Dower tilted his head slightly to one side, listening to a collar-phone message. He signed off the call and looked Longthorn in the eye. 'Colonel MacMillan is bringing the Hunter squadrons in. They will be berthing in fifteen minutes.'

Longthorn stood. 'That's opportune. What better day to welcome back our returning heroes than the day civilian rule is restored? We shall reconvene in one hour.'

Dower left the room, he was not surprised to see a small squad of guards nearby – following the sabotage attempts in Primo's early days he had ordered constant guard patrols. He was surprised, however, to realise he did not recognise any of the soldiers. He decided they must be some of Earth's survivors being cycled back up to Primo for advanced training.

Opening a collar-phone channel, he called Steph and the brigadier hoping to get them up to speed before the Leviathans berthed. As he turned into the main concourse, crowds were beginning to build. Once again, he noted the patrolling guards were not his long-time Primo people. Here, too, the guards were fresh up from Earth.

Looking through the hurrying crowd, Dower spotted his wife and daughter Lily, each supporting Fay by the arm. He waved them on. They weren't alone – Steph and Celine were following his family, and Smith-Brown paced steadily behind them all.

'Stick close,' said Dower as they joined him. He turned to press through the crowd, which gave way to their leader, and he reached the viewing port that had been reserved for the leadership group.

'Here they come,' called Lily. 'See, HA-1! That's the colonel's Leviathan; he's coming in first.'

'Which is next?' said Steph, craning to see.

'It's HA-2; they must be coming in by squadron.'

Colonel MacMillan's Leviathan manoeuvred into its hangar as the others continued past and began to enter their own berths.

Steph turned to the general. 'It's great that they're home. Jamie and the colonel should be offboard pretty soon. By the way, what did the senator want?'

The general shook his head. 'Never mind for now. Let's get the crews off and celebrate the moment.'

She looked at him. The general had avoided answering her question – that was not like him.

There was a sudden hustle and stir behind them as some of the crowd, which had settled into position to welcome back the crews, were jostled and manoeuvred aside by a security squad. From amid the hustle, Longthorn, Petraeus and Longthorn III emerged, closely followed by General Pashman and Colonel Coral.

'My congratulations, General Dower, you've selected an excellent spot to greet our heroes,' said Longthorn, sidling with his group into the prime position. 'And good day to you, ma'am. This is an auspicious day.'

Gail Dower smiled politely. 'It is, senator, so many good friends and colleagues returning safe. Though the sad loss of a Leviathan is a high price to pay for our victory. So many dear souls lost.'

'You are so right, ma'am. A loss that is very hard to bear…' The senator's voice trailed off beneath a sudden burst of cheering as the airlock opened and the crew of HA-1 emerged into the concourse, led by Colonel MacMillan.

The colonel knew where Dower and the leadership team would be standing, and he angled through the crowd to join them. Many Primo people clapped him on the back, one or two women leaned forward and kissed him. Further back, the emerging crew were lost in the melee of friends and well-wishers.

Dower grasped MacMillan's hand, welcoming his friend back, then quickly ceded ground to his wife and daughters' hugs, expressing their high affection and esteem for the colonel. Steph and the brigadier joined in the warm welcome, and then Celine, MacMillan's chief scientist on the first Perseus expedition, hugged him with warm affection.

MacMillan sensed there were others at the viewing port who expected some engagement and he turned toward them. Longthorn reached out a hand of congratulation as General Dower made introductions.

After a brief round of polite small talk and a pause for photographs, Longthorn and his party made to take their leave. As though on an afterthought, the senator turned back. 'General, we'll look forward to seeing you as arranged, I think around half an hour, isn't it? Perhaps the rest of your group should stand by to join us. I think the Englishman, MacAulay, too.'

'He's Scottish, not English,' said Steph.

Longthorn nodded absently then turned to rejoin his party and left the thronged concourse.

***

General Dower, his wife and daughters, Lily and the now more mobile Fay took seats in his office. Seated too were the brigadier, Colonel MacMillan and Celine. All were engaged in an animated discussion which broke off as the office door slid open to admit Steph together with Jamie. Once again, a round of warm and affectionate greetings and 'welcome homes' were exchanged, soon superseded by the tension in the air.

Jamie sensed it at once and looked expectantly toward the general. 'What's going on?' he said.

'Sit, sit. It's great to have you back, but this is a difficult moment,' said Dower.

The latecomers settled, and General Dower quickly outlined the problem.

'That's not right, surely? Longthorn can't just take control on his own say-so. He can't be a self-appointed leader. It's not right! It's not politics; it's nothing but a damned coup!' said Jamie. 'Surely, general, you won't allow him to get away with it?'

All eyes turned to Dower, and he looked about the room, meeting the eyes of his colleagues one by one, each of whom had become firm friends, bonded together in the face of common adversity.

Dower took a sip of water, his throat suddenly dry. 'I think we are facing a real problem. I am bound by my commissioning oath to uphold and protect the United States and its constitution. That naturally includes ensuring and recognising that those elected to civil political office hold the ultimate leadership position and, consequently, are empowered to direct my actions.'

'No way!' said Jamie. 'I remember Longthorn's machinations before the virus; he is totally untrustworthy.'

Dower maintained a deadpan face. 'And yet he is the senior surviving elected political leader, the man the other surviving politicians have agreed should now be the leader pending elections.'

'What? Some sort of acting president? General, you know he can't be trusted.'

'What I do know, Jamie, is he's the senior surviving American politician. All my working life, I have been bound by my oath. I've seen good leaders and I've seen bad. I have never challenged any of their rights to govern and lead. He has the support of General Pashman, who is, in any event, my superior officer. And he has just been confirmed as the new chair of the Joint Chiefs. The chain of command is clear.'

'What I don't get,' said Celine, 'among all the hundreds of millions of American deaths, how come Longthorn, his grandson and General Pashman all ended up safe together in a remote rural bunker?'

'I understand the Longthorns were inspecting it with General Pashman when it all went pear-shaped,' said Dower.

'But why there? Why just then? You know what I think? I think they were running from the nuclear exchanges and got lucky by dodging the virus too. They left the people to die and hid away from the action,' said Celine, getting the bit between her teeth.

'Steady, Celine,' said the brigadier. 'The general has to balance his own thoughts and beliefs against the legal demands of his oath and national constitution. This is not an emotional decision for him.'

'To hell with that!' said Steph. 'The general can't believe that Longthorn will do a better job than our team has done from the beginning. Nobody could believe it!'

'That's not the question. The question is: where does the legitimate power lie?' said MacMillan.

Jamie laid a restraining hand on Steph's arm. 'Surely, general, never mind the American leadership position, there is meant to be equal British leadership representation. Your politicians can't just shunt us out of the picture.'

'You're right, and Senator Longthorn has acknowledged that. But he argues no surviving British MPs have been found.'

'Okay, but who needs members of parliament? In their absence, I nominate Steph to represent Britain's equal leadership interest,' Jamie's voice was calm but firm.

'Jamie, I'm sorry. I for one would welcome that. Longthorn had clearly anticipated such a proposal. They have made clear that since political leadership is a product of democracy, whoever represents Britain's interests must be elected, just as the American representatives are – and you know, I can't see a way to argue against that.'

Brigadier Smith-Brown leaned forward. 'I am the second in command of this entire operation, yet not a word has been said to me. It feels as though something is being stolen out from under us and there seems no legitimate objection or barrier we can present.'

The general nodded and noted Colonel MacMillan and everyone else were in sympathy with his British counterpart. 'I'm sorry, I don't know how else to respond,' said Dower.

'I'll tell you how we respond. We march round to his office and arrest him and his little cabal,' said Fay, her voice betraying a building rage. 'Come on, let's go right now, get it done!' She stood up, leaning heavily on her sister's shoulder for support.

The senior officers looked at her as one, all were shaking their heads. The general waved his daughter down. 'American or British, we've all sworn our various oaths of allegiance. We can't break our word without good cause. How do you think our people would react if I ordered the arrest of elected politicians? Remember, most of Primo's population are civilians.'

'They'd back you. That's how they'd react. You led them; you saved them when everything looked lost.'

'Yes, and I'm a soldier sworn to uphold a civilian constitution and law. Could I ask my American troops to march down the concourse against our surviving elected politicians and the chairman of the Joint Chiefs of Staff? Would they even be prepared to do so? I couldn't compel them.'

'You don't have to. Jamie has a company of British marine commandos on his Leviathan – they could do it for you. None of them swore to uphold our constitution!' said Fay.

'Fay!' The general banged his fist on the table. 'Sit down and shut up. You are preaching sedition. If I don't arrest you, likely Colonel MacMillan will feel obliged to.'

MacMillan stared intently at his clasped hands.

The brigadier looked toward Fay. 'Fay, I admire your fire, and what's happening sticks in my craw, as I suspect it does everyone in this room, including the general. You have to know Jamie could no more lead the commandos against the politicians than I. First, we're all within a chain of command that leads directly to General Dower – he decides for us all, it is the way. Second, and more importantly, were Jamie to lead such a move, your father would have to order the American servicepeople on Primo to resist. We'd be in a civil war in minutes. Bonds of friendship built this past year wrecked, as troops with divided loyalties start shooting one another. This is an impossible situation.'

Fay looked at the brigadier for a long moment then nodded and slipped back into her chair. Lily pressed her hand against Fay's forearm and squeezed silent support.

'What can you do, Paul?' said Gail Dower 'And where does it leave us all?'

Everyone fell silent, waiting for his judgement as Dower stared at a blank spot on the far side of his office, thinking intently.

The contemplation was broken by a collar-phone call.

'General Dower? It's Colonel Coral speaking. Senator Longthorn is expecting you in five minutes. He's asked you to confirm you will have some key personnel standing by to join the meeting as required.'

'Who exactly?' said General Dower.

'Much of your original leadership team. The brigadier, Colonel MacMillan, Jamie MacAulay, Celine Gold and Steph Simpson.'

'Very well, on our way.'

Gail reached out a worried hand to touch her husband as he stood. 'What's to happen?'

'I hope Longthorn intends to be reasonable. Perhaps his plan is to genuinely reassert civilian oversight and let us get on with it pretty much as before. That I could live with.'

'Do you think that's what he plans?' she said with hope in her voice.

The general gave a dry smile. 'I don't know.' He led the summoned out of the office. They all noticed what the general had seen before. Today the guard detail were all newcomers – and there were more of them than usual. It seemed all the old hands had been given time off to celebrate with their friends from the returning Hunter squadrons.

Chapter 49

Base Primo

Dower had protested at the plans Longthorn put to him. He felt they were divisive and would risk slowing the recovery while underutilising experienced people. General Pashman immediately put him in his place, and he fell silent as Longthorn completed the outline of their plan – it was illogical; it was madness. He felt cheated by Longthorn and his cronies, and there was nothing he could do. So he stood impassively as they completed the outline of their blueprint for the future.

Longthorn leaned back in his chair. 'Well, general, that's what we will do. How do you feel about your role?'

'Senator, I find it hard to believe you think the proposal is an improvement on the existing arrangement. You must realise I am incredulous and feel unjustifiably marginalised.'

General Pashman cut across him. 'General Dower, you may feel incredulous and marginalised, but you will be compliant. This plan has been devised by the leadership to give Earth the best possible chance to recover and to expand our horizons, to exploit the myriad resources that the new technology has put within our reach. I repeat, you will comply. That's an order.'

Longthorn looked along the table toward Pashman. 'Thank you, General Pashman. I think that's made things clear for General Dower. Now, general, let's get your group in and spell things out to them. I don't want any misunderstandings, and I will not tolerate any dissent or disobedience. The fate of humanity rests on our plans being implemented.'

Colonel Coral stood and opened the door. He stepped outside. 'We're ready for you now. Please come in and assemble in line with General Dower.' He returned to his place on the panel and watched them form a line.

Longthorn III produced a notepad, rare on Primo, and flicked through several pages before finding what he wanted. After taking a long minute to study the note carefully, he looked up at the standing rank. 'I'm sure General Dower will have taken the opportunity to brief you beforehand, so just a brief recap.

'We three surviving elected politicians, led by Senator Longthorn, are the legitimate voice of American political life and decision-making. The military is represented by General Pashman who is now confirmed as permanent chairman of the Joint Chiefs of Staff. He and all American commissioned officers have sworn to serve and uphold the constitution of the United States, protecting it and the civil political leadership of the country.

'General Pashman is presently the supreme military officer. As such, he's General Dower's direct line commander. You are all under General Dower's command and so also subject to the authority of General Pashman.'

Steph bristled. 'He's not my commander. I'm British, and a civilian.'

'Ah yes, you…' Longthorn III referred to his notes. Everyone knew he knew who Steph was, even as he stretched out a moment of silence, appearing to read tightly packed notes. 'It's Miss Simpson, isn't it?'

'No. It's Professor Simpson.'

Longthorn III looked at her sharply. 'Poetatoe, pataato, toemaeto, tomaato; you are who you are. At present, you work under secondment to this project from your university. That arrangement can continue, provided you continue to accept the refreshed management and command structure.'

'Failing which?' said Steph.

'Failing which, you will be immediately returned to your home and permanent employer, the University of Edinburgh.'

'There's nothing left there, almost everyone's dead. From fourteen thousand staff to probably less than a hundred and fifty.'

'Well, I'm sure you'll want to help in their recovery efforts. I should add, when taken off this project, you will also be obliged to surrender your bio-suit; you'll not need it where you're going. If, as and when you're ever selected for induction as a volunteer in the future, you can be supplied with a new suit. I think that's clear enough,' said Longthorn III, looking along the seated panel to his grandfather who was nodding in support.

'Just a moment,' said Dower, taking a half-step toward Longthorn. 'What you're doing is wrong. I know it, you know it, we all know it. Ditch me if you must, but whatever you do to me, for the love of God, man, Steph is the most useful human alive today. You need her here at the centre, fixing the mess!'

Longthorn III stared furiously at the general. 'Your comment is out of order, general. It will be struck from the record. You will remain silent until invited to speak. Now shall we continue?'

Senator Longthorn nodded in support of his grandson's statement. 'Thank you. And yes, I believe the position is now clear to all. So, before I share the exciting new allocations with you all, Professor Simpson, are you in, being content to serve within the project's revised command structure, or would you like to leave for Earth now? An observer is on standby, ready to transport you away at once, and any others who will not comply.'

Steph was raging inside, struggling to keep it in. She looked across the table to Senator Petraeus, her eyes searching for his support. 'Do you support this?' she asked.

Petraeus remained tight-lipped. His eyes dropped, and he stared intently down at the table before him.

'God!' said Steph in disgust. 'Really? You'd let them do this, after everything we did for you?'

'I'm sure the senator appreciates the work you did for him. But let's be clear, that was science work – you simply did the right science, the routine requirement of your job. Now, this is our work, strategic political work, and right now, the senator, like all of us, is doing the right strategic thing, except not just for one beneficiary, for all humanity. Personal feelings can't be allowed to influence decisions.'

She looked along the standing line toward Jamie. He grimaced, drew the tightest of smiles and mouthed the words *In, please.* She pursed her lips, stared up to the ceiling for a long moment then glared at Longthorn: 'I'm in, but I don't like your style.'

'You don't need to like anything, my dear. You just need to obey the rules,' said Longthorn. 'And this is an appropriate moment to say we have studied all of your actions of the past year. Many good works are acknowledged, but another reading of events could point to significant errors and, in some cases, even culpability for what has befallen Earth and her people.

'However, notwithstanding that, we prefer to consider that you also represent a reservoir of knowledge and experience that will help Earth recover if applied appropriately. Now, before we proceed further, Senator Petraeus, have you anything to add?'

The senator shook his head. Still unable to look Steph in the eye.

'Thank you, Senator Petraeus. General Pashman, your comments?'

'None at present, thank you, senator. Clearly, I will have a lot to say to the serving officers once you have completed your strategic overview.'

'Then we shall begin, and be assured, none of this is up for debate. Your political leadership has thought long and hard over these matters, and you will comply, fulfilling your new roles within the new command structure.' The senator looked along the standing rank before him. He smiled briefly. At last he had achieved his goals: American control, and the current leadership brought to heel. His heel. This was finally his project. America was his. Perhaps, everything was his.

The room was silent throughout the senator's discourse. The three politicians would immediately establish a permanent office at Primo and a permanent Earth base; they would flit between the two as required. Their function, to provide leadership and oversight across all aspects of Primo and human engagement in the galaxy *and* to support and lead the Earth recovery.

Longthorn III to have particular responsibility for creating an environment where fair elections could be held, with a provisional target of a ballot within three to five years.

General Pashman to immediately move his permanent location to Primo from where he would command and direct both Earth and space activity, reporting directly to the political leadership who would act on behalf of the electorate. The general's current duties directing United States recovery to be delegated appropriately.

Colonel Coral, who had to date served as a liaison for the political leadership over the recovery and development of human resources, would continue to fulfil that role and would have a Primo-based role to ensure appropriate continuing support and task allocations for all current crew and future volunteers.

'We considered it sensible,' the senator continued, 'to maintain General Dower's original designation of three sectors of operation: Orion Arm controlled from Primo; Perseus Arm controlled from Secundo; Sagittarius Arm to be controlled from the as yet undeveloped Trosos base. We intend to continue that arrangement, with further development through encouraged colonisation of life planets within each sector.

'Colonel MacMillan will return to Secundo with his Leviathan HA-1, now to be renamed P-4. He will resume command there. That will result in Secundo now being equipped with four Leviathans. Three will support the base and expansion into Perseus as originally conceived. P-4 will be designated to establish a regular transport run between Primo and Secundo.

'Due to the failure of Brigadier Smith-Brown's original expedition to Sagittarius, including the loss of two Leviathans, that sector remains largely unknown to us. We direct that General Dower will lead a fresh expedition to establish Base Trosos. The remaining four Hunter Leviathans are allocated to that command and renamed as S-1 through S-4. One will be detailed to maintain a regular transport service between Primo and Trosos.

'The remaining Leviathans will be allocated to the Orion Squadron, based at Primo under the direct control of General Pashman and designated O-1, O-2 and so on.

'General Dower will be supported by Brigadier Smith-Brown who will, in due course, proceed beyond Base Trosos to identify suitable planets and support their colonisation. A small number of the samplers used in the rescue of Earth will be allocated to that task. With a corresponding allocation to Secundo.

'Steph Simpson and Jamie MacAulay will fit under General Dower's command as he sees fit and travel with him to Sagittarius.

'These are permanent postings that will drive humanity forward into the stars while ensuring the smoothest possible Earth recovery.

Colonel Coral has been exceptionally busy reviewing all the staff who originally transferred to Primo before the disaster. Unfortunately, due to decisions taken during the course of the past year, many good people have been lost to us. But there are still over five thousand spread across the bases and on board the Leviathan fleet. Colonel Coral?'

'Thank you, senator. As you say, I have spent much time considering our staffing disposition. It makes eminent sense that much of the accumulated experience here at Primo and around the fleet should be applied where it is most needed – at the new frontiers.

'The majority of these experienced people will be transferred to Secondo or Trosos, creating space for the introduction of more volunteers from Earth to learn and operate Primo systems, so expanding the depth of humanity's skill base. Clearly a core of Primo's current staff will be held in place for continuity and to support training. Our goal must be more people, more skills.'

'Exactly, that's what we need. More people, more skills, and the colonel's plan is designed to deliver just that,' said Longthorn.

'Thank you, senator. I've taken the liberty of compiling staffing lists for transfer from Primo to join the expeditions. There are more allocated to Trosos, but as you all know, that is being developed from scratch, whereas Secundo is already up, running and populated. I will forward the staffing lists to you all directly after this meeting. Senator?'

'Thank you, colonel. Now, I'm sure you will have questions, and there will be time to answer them all in due course. Our plan is to allow forty-eight hours before the Leviathans depart on their respective missions.'

'We can't be ready in such a short time. Crews need leave, time to recharge, consider whether they accept the postings they are being offered, and to appeal if they want,' said Dower.

'That, general, is the timeline. It will stick,' said General Pashman. 'And to be clear, nobody is being offered posting options – people will be posted as deemed appropriate.'

Dower fell silent for a moment. Then asked, 'What about defence out there? How many warbirds will we take?'

'After the losses of the recent expedition into Perseus, there are only twenty-eight functioning or repairable warbirds. I have judged that Colonel MacMillan will need a compliment of eight. The Trosos expedition will need four, which leaves sixteen here, protecting Primo Main Base, Earth, and supporting exploration of the Orion Arm.

'But that leaves Sagittarius light. Can't we have a more equitable distribution of warbirds?' said Dower.

'There is no evidence of exceptional need in Sagittarius,' said Pashman.

'We've scarcely been in Sagittarius to know what it needs.'

'General Dower, the warbird allocations are based on careful calculation. In the unlikely future event of an evolving threat, I can dispatch reinforcements from here. There will be no change in warbird allocations.'

'Thank you, gentlemen. Gentlemen, please,' said Longthorn, speaking over a light rapping of his knuckle on the desk. 'Enough. I'm sure you will find the opportunity to discuss this further in the coming day or so. Right now, I'd like to congratulate you all for your service to date and thank you for taking on these new, challenging and essential tasks. I suggest, instead of complaining about a time shortage, you all engage at once to make best use of the available time.'

Chapter 50

Base Primo: Departure

When Coral's staff transfer list was disseminated, it became clear very few of the original Primo people were to stay, so the goodbyes had been few and far between; friends, acquaintances, workmates, almost everyone was going. Those with key skills who were not rostered to leave quickly began to feel they were the ones left out. Prime among them was Celine who found herself appointed to the role of Primo's new chief scientist.

Once the first shock at the change of leadership and their new approach to operations had passed, it had triggered a turbulent and emotional forty-eight hours. Everywhere, there had been confusion. Later, that changed to anger. Some had talked of resistance. It was, after all, their Primo. The prospective rebels had been quickly quieted when General Dower went public to make clear that, like it or not, orders were orders. The change affected everyone – everyone had to live with it.

Time flew past in the rush to make ready, and then, in the final hours before departure, an air of despondency settled across all Primo's old hands – leavers and stayers alike. Again, the general spoke with everyone, recognising that it was not going to be easy but that they were teams forged in adversity, teams that did not break. While he and Colonel MacMillan were anticipating challenges at their respective sector commands, every member of Primo had faced challenges before and come through with flying colours. Together, they would do so again and build something new, something exciting and something for the future – their futures.

The seeds of a new mood began to form among many. Almost everyone had lost everything they had known on Earth. They'd done their best to save it, but… perhaps there really was nothing left to cling on to. So, where better to be than at the new frontier?

Once the crews and passengers had all boarded, the greatest manned fleet ever to leave Primo was ready to set off. Five Leviathans and twelve giant samplers – carrying nearly five thousand souls between them were waiting for the order.

Longthorn, accompanied by his grandson and Senator Petraeus, stood at the same viewing port through which they had only recently watched the Hunter squadrons return. In the concourse today there was no cheering crowd to see off the fleet, just the politicians and their security detail and, a little further off, a small gathering of old hands clustered around Celine to wave their goodbyes. There were no cheers, and even from a distance, Longthorn could see there were tears.

'Well, gentlemen, I don't think we can do any more here. I suggest we return to my office and toast a memorable day,' said Longthorn.

The others murmured agreement, and as the hangar doors began to swing open, they turned away from the viewing port. Petraeus was walking unaided, and as the three retreated across the concourse, he cast a brief glance back toward the viewing port.

***

'Come in, take a seat. I think we all deserve something. Something strong,' said Longthorn, pointing his grandson toward a bottle and glasses. 'You do the honours.'

They leaned in and clinked their Bourbons. 'To civilian rule!' said Longthorn, and the others echoed the toast. They refilled their glasses.

'You've kept quiet about your reasons for transferring people the way you did, senator. Now they're gone, can I ask why we didn't just shunt them all back down to Earth? It would have been easier.' said Petraeus.

'It's simple. You know we needed to move Dower and his gang out. As long as they were here, they'd have some vestige of power and influence just from having been at the heart of things. More importantly, people would believe they held some power still. That would certainly be a challenge to our democratic civilian rule. They had to go.' He paused to light a cigar, plumper and longer than his usual. 'This one's to celebrate today's win. A big win.' He drew and puffed before continuing.

'We couldn't send them down to Earth. Nor could we send all their original Primo loyalists. Could you imagine them whispering and whining? There would be a clear risk of undermining the civil administration. This way, those loyal to the general and his team see him still with a job to do within the system. So, no problems, they follow their leader. But now he will be far enough away to ensure he has no influence on our survivors.'

'I see that, sir,' said Longthorn III, 'but we've created power bases at Secundo and Trosos from which they might challenge us one day.'

'No, not at all. You're reading it wrong. Neither Dower nor MacMillan will break military regulations. They've got jobs to do. And by making both Secundo and Trosos military commands subordinated to Primo, it ensures they will always be within the chain of command, must comply with the orders issued from here. Beyond developing their bases, they are to find suitable sites for colony formation and then help in their development. That will keep them busy forever.'

'You can't build a string of colonies from a few thousand people,' said Petraeus, leaning forward to recharge his glass.

'Exactly, and we have the solution in hand for that. Colonel Coral has determined Earth survivors fall into three categories: those who support our approach, those who don't care, and those who are objectors. I intend to ensure it's those objectors who get the first chance to build new lives in the distant colonies. Coral has already begun work on identifying candidates and some schemes to encourage specifically them to travel.'

'That's why you've set up Leviathans on regular runs to Secundo and Trosos. They are going to be migrant carriers,' said Longthorn III.

Longthorn smiled sagely and raised his glass. 'And if there's one thing I've learned about dissenters, they invariably end up grumbling about whatever's in front of them. So, here's to the malcontents. They'll be far away and out of our hair, and eventually, they'll keep

Dower and MacMillan permanently busy with fresh local grumbles. It's two birds with one stone.'

'But still,' said Petraeus, 'they may develop into powerbases. We should be cautious.'

'Yes, always cautious, but we don't want them without any spine. There's one other service Dower and MacMillan will provide. We've already seen there are some bad things out there in the galaxy. Our departing friends will serve as a first line of defence and a shock absorber. To shield Earth and us from whatever might come our way.' Longthorn raised his empty glass toward his grandson who quickly recharged them all.

'To shock absorbers,' said Longthorn.

'To distant shock absorbers,' said Petraeus.

The glasses clinked in celebration.

Chapter 51

Exodus

The fleet was nearing the folding point where, on Dower's orders, it was to pause in normal space before folding. Since leaving Primo, Steph and Jamie had not had a moment to themselves.

Jamie had been poring over the details of the fleet's military strength, trying to pull together some structure of preparedness for any eventualities. It was frustrating – the loading had been done with such haste, troops and equipment were scattered at random. There was a lot of work to be done.

Meanwhile, Steph had been pressing her team to collate every bit of information they could about the Sagittarius Arm. This wasn't a research expedition; it was a permanent move. For every answer they'd found, there were a thousand questions unanswered. They'd already learned the greatest dangers came from the unknown – which was exactly where they were being sent to.

She could see the anxiety building in the science team – they just couldn't answer all the questions in time. In truth, they couldn't answer most questions at all. She called a halt, instructing all the science team to take a break, relax and get ready for the folding. She headed for her quarters and called Jamie's collar-phone.

***

Steph looked across to the opening accommodation door and smiled as Jamie entered their quarters. She handed him a drink as the door slid shut behind him. They raised their glasses and clinked them together. It was less a celebration, more a dry cheer that at least they'd made it this far. And made it together.

They sipped the spirit then, without a word, leaned in and hugged while being careful not to spill the glasses. Holding for a long time, they rocked gently together. Finally drawing apart, Steph finished her drink in one.

'It's a complete mess,' she said; 'my team are simply drained. Too much to do, no time. I've got the wrong people on the wrong craft, nothing's organised.'

'Same with the military,' said Jamie. 'Hopefully, there will be time to get things worked out in the Fold before we reach Sagittarius.'

'I hope so. We just don't know anything about the Sagittarius Arm. It's a blank. A nightmare.'

'What about Weeman? Can't he help?'

'I don't know. When I told him what was happening, he went all cryptic on me. I've not seen him since before we set off. I'm sure he was coming, but he said he had things to do. Since then, radio silence.'

'Well, he's never let us down. I'm sure he'll turn up when he's ready.'

'I don't know if he's even on board. He was able to flit between LPAs on Primo, but I'm not sure about getting on to the Leviathan. I'd thought he would travel over in my bio-suit. What if he's been left behind?'

Tears welled in Steph's eyes; Jamie hugged her. 'Jamie, we need Weeman. We've lost so much. He knows so much. I need him. I need you too. And we're a team now. When we get to the Sagittarius Arm, I'm not planning on letting you go anywhere without me. Okay?'

She felt Jamie's head nod against her own and smiled through her tears. 'Whatever comes next, we're facing it together, right? The two of us.'

Jamie nodded again. 'I think you mean the three of us,' he said as a flurry of lights disrupted what had been a steady display in the LPA. He gently turned her around so she too could see.

'Weeman! He came! He made it!'

Their collar-phones activated simultaneously. General Dower was summoning them.

***

A flurry of observer craft shuttled the senior staff to Dower's flagship, and they assembled in the large workroom he had appropriated for his command base.

There followed a detailed briefing and analysis with a vigorous question-and-answer session. Everyone had a chance to express their worries and their hopes.

Finally, Dower stood in front of the assembly. Ranged before him were those he trusted most. Colonel MacMillan, Jamie, Steph, Ossie, the fleet's Leviathan and sampler captains, their chief scientists, the various military company commanders and, closest to him, his wife and daughters, Fay and Lily – a very full room.

'So, there you have it, people. I know most of you believe we were manoeuvred out by a cynical exploitation of old rules. The colonel and I won't disagree. Rules that I think, in the near future, will be swept away by Earth survivors themselves. But they are the rules today, and we were not in a position to break them. To have done so would have triggered a confrontation that would inevitably have escalated into a civil conflict on Primo and beyond. Regardless of the outcome, it would have resulted in the deaths of many of those people who are travelling with us today, our friends and colleagues. Those are lives both I and the colonel hold too precious to squander. Yes, I know – they're the same lives we have risked in recent conflicts, but risked for the sake and needs of all humanity, not in petty personal power games. A civil conflict would have set back Earth's rescue and recovery by many months, perhaps longer, and likely cost countless more lives of innocents waiting for rescue down on the surface. We could not countenance that, and I know you all well enough to be confident that neither could any of you.

'You should know this is not the end. This is a new beginning, and every one of you must hold on to the central concept that, while we press ahead toward new frontiers for humanity, we will only support that which is good and fair. Our guiding path must be lit only by truth, integrity and equity. While things behind us look dark today, there will be a time when Earth needs us again… and we will be ready.'

The general paused and looked along the table. 'Steph, you wanted to say a parting word.'

As she stood, Steph felt a ripple within the arm of her bio-suit as little light spots circled within. They hurried up and down her arm, making the sleeve display glow more brightly than normal. Weeman was with her. He was with them all.

'Thank you, general. I know your and the colonel's sentiments are shared by me and by Jamie – by all of us. It took courage and strength to put the people ahead of your own positions. We all appreciate that and recognise the many lives you have spared in so doing…' There was murmured agreement, and Steph paused a moment to allow it to subside.

'Thank you everyone, I'm so glad to hear such harmony. If only the same had been present among our political leaders, things may have played out very differently. Meanwhile, I have heard the voices from across the fleet making clear that, if there is a greater worry than being sent into the unknown, it's the fact we are in large part being removed from the technology, capacities and sophistication of Primo. No Goliaths, very limited print manufacture capacity and all the rest. That's true. But you should ensure everyone on every craft knows that I have confidence we will be able to cope. In fact, I can assure you I'm already working on that, so don't lose heart for the longer term – that's a bridge I'm certain we'll cross.'

The captain of one Secundo-bound sampler raised his hand, and Steph reached her arm out, inviting him to speak.

'Great to learn of your confidence, Steph. Like everyone else here, I have faith in you and the whole science team's ability to deliver when needed. It's true we've lost access to the Goliaths and much more, but hopefully, you'll find workarounds sooner rather than later. My concern, and others too, is we're being split up between Secundo and Trosos, with Primo in the middle – there are fears of divide and conquer. Both frontier bases are going to be isolated.'

'Thank you, captain. Our attitude must always be to search and hope for the best in every situation. You're not alone in your concern. I can say, and this is strictly confidential, only for the ears of you all gathered here and no further, we have planned a little workaround to keep us together.

'On this Leviathan, my team has programmed a number of our signal buoys to home in on a Lagrange point in the Opsythia system, not so far from Secundo. Once Base Trosos' location is determined, using one of those signal buoys, we will transfer the location of a Lagrange point near the Trosos base to Sevrine at Secundo. She and her team will program reciprocal signal buoys that will home from Secundo to Trosos. We will then have a private and unmediated line of communication between General Dower at Trosos and Colonel MacMillan at Secundo. And I'm sure others will be able to access it to communicate with their friends too. Nobody will be isolated. What we learn and develop, we will share together.'

Once again, a murmur of approval ran round the table. 'Thank you,' said Steph, and she sat down. Spontaneous applause broke out and her gaze settled on Jamie who beamed an approving smile in return.

As General Dower stood once again, his hand rested lightly on his wife's forearm, triggering a prearranged response. Gail and his daughters slipped from their seats to open a wall panel.

'So, everyone, take heart. You know Steph understands scientific and project information that is beyond the comprehension of most of us. If she thinks there are ways for us to advance, that's more than good enough for me. In the meantime, the colonel and I can assure you all we will not be divided. For the sake of humanity, Secundo and Trosos will work and stand together and share together as one…'

He paused at the sound of Fay releasing a champagne cork. A gentle cheer rose round the room as Gail began pouring the champagne into glasses. Fay popped open another bottle, and Lily quickly began to distribute full glasses.

Dower grinned. 'Thank you, Fay. I'll take that as a signal that I should stop talking! Now, has everyone got a glass? Good. Gail, girls, come back here.' The general raised a hand, inviting the party to stand.

'It's been a hard road to get here, and there are still hard miles to tread, but this is a celebration of better tomorrows. Now, return to your craft, and as one, we will all take the next step on our journey.

'We made it through the dark times, together. Together, we'll walk the road ahead.' He raised his glass. 'Humanity, together!'

The whole room responded as one, 'Humanity, together!'

Glasses drained, the tension within the room seemed released. Friends hugged and said their au revoirs. No goodbyes – they would be together again, wherever the challenge took them.

Books by D. C. Macey

THE POST CONTACT SERIES

Set tomorrow. Post Contact is a near future action series that carries humanity to the heights of new opportunity and down to the brink of extermination.

- Post Contact: First Days
- Post Contact: Holding On
- Post Contact: Breaking Back

THE TEMPLE SERIES

Contemporary archaeological action thrillers unfolding through a weave of historical facts, mystery, secrets and contemporary action.

- The Temple Legacy
- The Temple Scroll
- The Temple Covenant
- The Temple Deliverance

About the Author

D. C. Macey is an author based in the United Kingdom. For more information:

contact@dcmacey.com and visit: **www.dcmacey.com**

Post Contact: First Days

(Post Contact - Book 1)

Today a new order is forming across the galaxy. Will humanity be at its centre or lost as victims of change?
A chance encounter offers humanity the opportunity to instantly progress from moon shots to galactic travel. But the exciting opportunity comes with a heavy responsibility that humanity may not be able to bear. As Earth balances on the cusp of a brilliant and unexpected future, age-old human failings assert themselves when greed, betrayal and violence undermine everything.

Even as Earth's leaders fumble humanity's greatest opportunity, first contactors Steph Simpson and Jamie MacAulay rally a few good people to join with the last remnant of an ancient species and face out to the galaxy with its unknown challenges.

Embark on a new enthralling and sometimes frightening adventure, read this first in series book, ***Post Contact: First Days***.

Post Contact: Holding On

(Post Contact - Book 2)

Outnumbered, unprepared, inexperienced: redemption or extinction?

Fierce adversity can bring out the best of human traits. Today it must. Through sweeping space battles to vicious hand to hand combat with cruel alien species, everywhere mankind is beset. Everywhere humanity's remnant is desperately holding on.

Stunned by Earth's calamitous collapse, the few survivors are kept going only by a grim determination that humanity must continue. With resources stretched paper thin, they face daunting tasks. Against the clock, Professor Steph Simpson and her team struggle to unravel the puzzles of the new technology in a desperate race to rescue any who may survive on Earth.

That same technology is needed elsewhere to fend off terrifying alien attacks and fulfil the responsibilities that accompany the new technology. Meanwhile Jamie MacAulay is marooned, lost in the furthest reaches of the Orion Arm. He and his crew struggle amidst an alien nature and environment. Everywhere the threats grow, and everywhere the price of resistance rises.

Follow humanity's journey to the edge in this second in series book, ***Post Contact: Holding On.***

Post Contact: Breaking Back

(Post Contact - Book 3)

Success, Failure, Betrayal. Humanity must stand against the odds.

The survivors at Base Primo continue their struggle to save humanity, desperately striving to turn the tide of adversity that threatens them all. Backs against the wall, they grapple with the turmoil of old foes resurging, the appearance of new enemies, space conflict, and the gritty cruelty of close quarters combat.

Amidst all the conflict, efforts to unpick the new technology continue. But danger lies in the least expected places, and as humanity's old failings resurface, emerging betrayal is the bitter reward. For Steph, Jamie and General Dower, overcoming alien foes may ultimately prove the least of their problems.

Humanity's struggle for survival continues.

Temple Legacy

(The Temple - Book 1)

Seven hundred years ago, in a time of war and betrayal, Europe's greatest treasure disappeared amidst a frenzied and brutal grab for power. The men who guarded it vanished into history.

In Edinburgh today, former élite British Military Intelligence officer Sam Cameron has turned to the quieter world of archaeology. Together with young church minister Helen Johnson, he leads his students on a field trip. What they unearth raises exciting questions. What are the mystery objects? What is their connection to the Knights Templar?

But others are asking the same questions and the thrill of discovery is quickly clouded by the brutal killing of a retired church minister and a spreading rage of violence and death.

Now Helen and Sam must race to unravel an ancient mystery, find how it links to the murdered minister, and fend off a very modern threat. Failure will cost their lives and the lives of many more. Success will answer the greatest unresolved mystery of the medieval world.

The Temple Scroll

(The Temple - Book 2)

A lost treasure, an impenetrable puzzle and a psychopathic killer: a deadly combination.

The Temple Scroll is a rollercoaster ride of danger, mystery and murder. From New England to the islands of the Mediterranean, it follows the deadly hunt for the Templars' lost treasure.

Archaeology lecturer Sam Cameron and church minister Helen Johnson thought their old problems were done. They were wrong. Killers are set on finding the Templars' treasure and they believe Sam and Helen hold the key.

As the psychopathic Cassiter directs his team of killers towards their goal, the calm of summer vanishes in an explosive bout of blood and suffering.

Under pressure from every side, Sam and Helen must draw on all their instincts and professional skills to stay alive as they attempt to crack the puzzle that protects the Templars' treasure.

As the search for the Templar hoard moves inexorably to a conclusion, Sam and Helen must risk all in a frantic bid to save their friends, the treasure, and the priceless holy relics of the early Church. Now there is no mercy and no escape - there is only win or die.

The Temple Covenant

(The Temple - Book 3)

A quiet sabbatical spent visiting archaeological sites in the Great Rift Valley offers Helen Johnson and Sam Cameron the perfect opportunity to unwind and put the violent climax to their recent adventures behind them. But where they go trouble isn't far away.

Disturbing alarm bells start to ring when Helen attracts the attentions of the mysterious Bishop Ignatius of the Ethiopian Orthodox Tewahedo Church. He is desperate to meet with her and will not take no for an answer.

Elsewhere, news breaks that senior British Intelligence Corps Colonel Bob Prentice is missing in Nairobi and security chiefs have cause for concern. Concern turns to panic when it's realised an operational prototype of the British Army's latest super-weapon has vanished too.

In a last gasp attempt to retrieve the situation the British Government turns to former Intelligence Corps officer Sam, hoping that his civilian status can keep him under the radar and his old skills might just be enough to turn the problem round.

Meanwhile, Helen is co-opted into a role that goes against her every belief - a role that her patriotism demands she fulfil even as she struggles to evade the determined attentions of Bishop Ignatius and his men.

Far from the cloudy skies of Edinburgh, a frightening and bloody hunt plays out beneath the burning sun of the East African bush. Racing against the clock, and with scant support, Sam and Helen must risk everything to resolve the challenge of the enigmatic Bishop Ignatius while fighting to preserve the West's place in a dangerous world.

The Temple Deliverance

(The Temple - Book 4)

Jolted out of their holiday season calm, Helen Johnson and Sam Cameron find they must play one last hand in a deadly game.

The final hunt is on to unpick an ancient code that hides the incredible nature of the Templars' greatest secret. From the depths of northern winter to the sun-kissed beaches of North Africa, Helen and Sam must hurry to piece together the final clues in a race against time to save themselves, their loyal friends and Christianity's greatest heritage.

Beset by danger, they must contend with the return of old foes who are hell bent on vengeance and determined to snatch the ultimate prize they have coveted for so long. As violence and death sweep across the continents, innocence is no protection; knowledge and grit are the only currencies of survival. Calling on trusted allies, Helen and Sam struggle against the odds, knowing that this time only one side can walk away.

Printed in Great Britain
by Amazon

56321566R00153